OLDHAM
Education & Culture

SURPLUS		
STOCK		

About the author

Patrick Sheane Duncan is the author of numerous screenplays, including *Mr Holland's Opus*, *Courage Under Fire* and *Nick of Time*, for which he was nominated for a Golden Globe award. He lives in Los Angeles.

Courage Under Fire

Patrick Sheane Duncan

CORONET BOOKS
Hodder and Stoughton

First published in the United States of America in 1996
by G.P. Putnam's Sons
First published in Great Britain in 1996
by Hodder and Stoughton
a division of Hodder Headline PLC
A Coronet paperback original

10 9 8 7 6 5 4 3 2 1

A C.I.P. catalogue record is available from the British Library

ISBN 0 340 67462 8

Printed and bound in Great Britain by
Cox & Wyman Ltd, Reading, Berkshire

Hodder and Stoughton
A division of Hodder Headline PLC
338 Euston Road
London NW1 3BH

This book is dedicated to
LESA MEREDITH DUNCAN.
*It would take another whole book
to list the reasons why.*

Acknowledgments

The author would like to thank the following individuals for their professionalism, knowledgeability, and the cooperation they gave me in researching this project. They gave me an admiring respect for the "New Army."

Thank you, gentlemen, one and all:

MAJOR ROBERT E. MILANI
Public Affairs Officer
First Cavalry Division

SERGEANT MAJOR RODNEY CAESAR
HQ, First BDE
First Cavalry Division

Colonel John Brown
HQ , Second BDE
First Cavalry Division

Captain Lee Roupe
Flight Operations Officer
507th Medical Company (Air Ambulance)

Captain Jeff Foe
S3 (Air)
36th Medical Evacuation Battalion

Major Ulmont Nanton, Jr.
Commander
507th Medical Company (Air Ambulance)

All at Fort Hood, Texas.

Thanks also to Shawn Toss of the Troy Fire Department Paramedics, Troy, Illinois, for some last-minute medical expertise.

And a huge shout of "Hoo-yah!" to Russ Thurman (U.S.M.C., Retired), technical adviser, friend, co-conspirator, and the man who put the topspin on the idea.

COURAGE

UNDER

FIRE

1

Boylar was on fire. His whole body was aflame, his head and hair a burning torch. Through the flickering flames Serling could see his eyes. The eyelashes were curling under the heat, shriveling and falling away. The eyebrows went the same way. Boylar's face blistered and peeled. The curling skin blackened, but he didn't scream or exhibit any pain. He just stared at Serling.

Then Boylar raised a hand and pointed a finger at Serling. The flames danced along his arm to the tip of the accusing finger. There was a ring on the third finger of his hand. "You did this." The blistering lips moved, the voice was from hell.

Serling backed away more from the accusation than the fire. He wasn't afraid of the fire. He even watched with mild interest as the flame suddenly left Boylar and began to trace a lazy path across the instrument panel.

They were in a tank, Serling's tank—Firebringer. Serling recognized the interior, the trinkets, the little stamps of personality on the olive drab steel hull. Patella's "What, Me Worry?" Alfred E. Neuman decal was peeling, turning brown at the edges as the fire pried it away from the bulkhead.

Boylar screamed.

"YOU KILLED ME!"

Serling didn't want to look anymore. Boylar's hair was burned to a frizzed stubble and his eyes were gone; now only black holes in the cracked skin of his blazing face remained.

Boylar's burning claws grabbed Serling by the shoulders and dragged him close.

They were face-to-face, eye-to-eye. Serling stared into those black sockets.

And all he could see was fire. Fathomless fire, red flame, then orange and yellow, going on forever.

Boylar opened his mouth and screamed again.

"I DON'T WANT TO DIE!"

Then the fire overtook Serling.

✳

Serling's hand trembled, the glass halfway to his mouth, and the rattle of the ice cubes pulled him back to the tavern. He looked into the glass, the amber fluid too much a reminder of the fire he had just shaken off, and he drank the memory away in one swallow. The liquor burned, but it was a familiar burn, a comforting sting in his throat.

Setting the glass down, he wiped his face vigorously, the sheer physical sensation pulling him out of The Dream. He looked at his watch: 10:54. Time to go. Taking one last sip of the drink, with little left in his glass now but ice water, and leaving the change on the bar, he walked out.

It was bright outside. He blinked in the light, put on his sunglasses, and reached for the Tic Tacs. A half dozen of the mints ought to do it. He really didn't need that second drink, but . . . When he had the first drink this morning he had promised himself that he wouldn't have another until lunch. It was a personal pact. Now broken. Along with a long list of other promises and oaths that he had reneged on lately.

He was in so-called Suitland, Maryland. A place he hated. It was another suburb of D.C.—the natural habitat of the bureaucrats, their haven. Big, anonymous buildings full of people shuffling paper to other people in other anonymous buildings.

Bureaucratic heaven—a certain level of hell for a combat officer. Which Serling wasn't anymore, he reminded himself.

He looked at his reflection in the window of the entrance. No, he was just another Army Lieutenant Colonel. Looking tired, weary. At least that's what he told himself. Not a drunk. Not yet. A combat officer who had spent too much time working under fluorescent lights rather than in the sun. He was tall, thin, with a command presence that made other men look weak and women look twice. But the face looked a bit haggard, and the eyes . . . Serling quickly looked away. His eyes looked dead, dull, and weary. Eyes that had always communicated enthusiasm, intelligence, a contagious excitement at the very prospects of the next moment, eyes that had demanded respect and gave it back, were now flat and empty. He couldn't bear to look at himself anymore.

He hated Suitland. It represented everything he despised about

3

D.C. and the side of the military that gnawed at him like a bad toothache. Endless, nondescript buildings of glass and stone full of nondescript clerks who sorted through an endless stream of paperwork, waiting to mark it with their own spoor and pass it on to the next desk. If you wanted to know how many rounds were fired from what boat during what battle, there were people here who could not only list the rounds, but the caliber, target, and range–by the minute. But they couldn't tell you why anyone fired in the first place or what was in the heart of the man behind the gun.

Serling went inside, swallowing the mouthful of Tic Tacs–and felt them turning his stomach sour as he walked up the stairs to the second floor.

There was a sign on every door. Naturally. This was the Army, everything was labeled neatly.

U.S. ARMY–AWARDS AND DECORATIONS.

Serling entered. There was a Specialist Fourth Class behind the desk. A woman, Carter, by her name tag. Serling announced himself. She slipped into the rear office and came back to ask if he wanted coffee. He declined. He could see the Mr. Coffee sitting on top of the tiny refrigerator. The half pot of coffee looked like roofing tar.

She led Serling into Colonel Levine's office.

Levine was a little man who wore his uniform as if it were a Brooks Brothers suit. He gave Serling a little smile.

"Have a seat, Serling. The General isn't here yet."

Serling could see it in Levine's eyes.

He knows.

Serling swallowed that knowledge like he had swallowed the TicTacs. All right. So he knows. Remember you asked for this. You asked for it.

And Levine's little smile meant that this pipsqueak Colonel was going to give it to him.

THE first thing that morning after his three-mile jog and his shit, shower, and shave Serling had stopped at the Blue Light Lounge, one of the safe little harbors within coasting distance of the Beltway. It was located conveniently between Serling's Bachelor Officers' Quarters and the Pentagon. He often stopped in for a quick one on the way to work—and a few slower ones on the way back to the BOQ.

Actually it wasn't always just one in the morning these days. One drink didn't banish the burning man. So Serling didn't count anymore. He just drank until he felt a comfortable numbness. The fact that it was taking more and more alcohol to get there wasn't lost on Serling. He just didn't care.

This morning the fire took a long time to put out, and when Serling got up to leave he was alone with the owner/bartender, Kwong.

The back wall was lined with autographed photographs of every Marine Corps Commandant and Sergeant Major from the last thirty years. One of the pictures behind the bar was of Kwong, a lean, mean Marine twenty years young in his dress blues.

Serling wasn't friendly with the man, but he had heard his name in passing from the regulars, old men with big guts, retired Marine gunnies, and Navy enlisted men sipping a little liquid decompressant after a day in the trenches. The regulars had looked at Serling's Army uniform, eyed the patches and the ribbons, made a few stabs at conversation, which Serling deflected, and then, out of respect for the solitary drinker, moved on. That's why Serling continued to come here. As well as the fact that he wouldn't meet any of the Army personnel he worked with in a "jarhead" hangout.

Serling slid a twenty across the bar and stood up, reaching for his Tic Tacs out of reflex.

"On the house." Kwong slid the money back. "A courtesy to the professional."

"Military discount?" Serling was surprised.

"No. Anyone who drinks hard liquor before nine in the morning is a pro to me. You guys are my profit margin. I like to keep you happy."

Serling took his twenty back and walked out to his car, the Buick. Meredith had the Jeep. Meredith . . .

During the drive in to the Pentagon his stomach roiled—not from the booze, not from the damned breath mints. From self-loathing. Kwong's words had dissolved the comfortable layer of padding he had built up with the liquor. Now he was naked, unarmored against any emotions that came his way. And they came.

I'm not this person. I don't have to be this person. I can fix this. I just have to find a way out.

When he reached his destination, the River Entrance parking lot, he parked and walked toward the Pentagon with purposeful strides, counting the half mile he had to walk as part of his morning workout.

Getting inside the Pentagon only renewed his determination. The tacky, worn-out corridors. The ugly, worn linoleum floors. The dull paint on the walls; the discarded, broken furniture; and the file cabinets stacked in the halls. It was a depressing environment, chock full of Colonels, the worker ants of the Pentagon. Brass everywhere, scurrying about doing God knows what.

Serling had once seen a gruesome documentary on PBS, watching with his daughter Cheryl, a documentary about a nasty little creature called a mole rat. A hairless, bucktoothed, and blind rodent that spent its entire life span burrowing underground like an insect. It never foraged above the ground; it never saw the sun. The soldier mole rats ate roots and the rest of the colony fed on the feces of the soldier rats. Every time Serling walked the hallways of the Pentagon his mind flashed back to that documentary.

Now more than ever he felt part of the colony. Just another mole rat. The only question left was, did he do the crapping or the eating? He wanted out before he had an answer.

Avoiding his office, Serling went straight down the hall toward Hershberg's section, uncomfortable with the ease he had in finding his way through the legendary labyrinth that was the Pentagon.

He didn't have to go all the way to Hershberg's office. Hershberg's adjutant, Captain Banacek, was standing in the hallway chatting up a pretty secretary from Logistics and Supply. Serling waited for them to finish the casual flirtation that had most likely been initiated by the secretary.

Banacek was Sears-catalog handsome and the focus of a lot of coffee-room speculation and the target of a good many single and not a few married female Pentagon staffers. All of whom he resisted, sending his attractiveness quotient up a few more notches—a fact of which Banacek was fully aware.

"Ban, I need to talk to the General."

"Sure, Colonel." Banacek looked Serling up and down—enough for Serling to check his gig line to see if it was out of whack. "Later in the week. Come by later and we'll check his calendar."

"Now. ASAP." Serling tried to keep the pleading tone out of his voice as he followed Banacek to his desk. "C'mon, Ban."

"I don't think so, Nat. We're up to our ass in legislative alligators right now, and the Chief just dropped a ticking bomb into our collective lap."

"I *need* to see him, Ban."

Banacek caught the tone, looked at the calendar while opening his desk drawer.

"How about tomorrow?" Banacek pulled a roll of Pepomint Lifesavers from his drawer and tossed it to Serling. "We could do a quick and dirty before the—"

Banacek was interrupted as General Hershberg came out of his office, at the usual half-trot. Banacek had to grab his files and run to catch up. Serling joined the parade down the hall.

"Hey, Nat"—Hershberg thrust a file at Banacek—"how are we holding, Ban?"

"Running late, sir," Banacek replied, handing the General a different file.

"That's S.O.P." Hershberg smiled. "Time to reevaluate our calendar allotment. That sound Pentagonesque enough for you, Nat?"

Serling and the General had a three-year dialogue going about the ever-changing, always slippery world of Pentagon doublespeak, sending each other memos of their favorite new linguistic creations.

"Sir, permission to speak while you walk?" Serling knew that the formal request would get Hershberg's attention. Hershberg looked Serling over.

Hershberg was short, especially for an Army General, but he made up for the deficiency in height with a pugnacious attitude and a face that bore the scars of four years as the All-Army Bantamweight title holder. There was scar tissue across his brow ridge and an ear that looked like a large wad of chewed bubble gum. But under that scar tissue were blue eyes that could charm, wink, or cut into you with the precision of a diamond cutter.

"Proceed, Nat."

"Sir, I need to get out of here."

"Need? Did this man's Army inquire about your needs,

Colonel?" If Serling was going to put things on a formal basis, the General knew how to reply in kind.

"No, sir. Let me rephrase, sir. I am not being utilized properly and to my fullest ability and qualifications in this current assignment, sir. I have repeatedly requested reassignment, but so far no transfer has been given."

"Noted." This was old ground. Serling was going to have to do better.

"I sit in a little closet and rubber-stamp other people's rubber stamps, sir. I *need* . . ." Serling knew he was bailing old water.

"Take a breath, Colonel." Hershberg stopped in his tracks. Serling faced him, like a kid caught running in the school hallway by the principal. He tried to slow his heaving chest so that he wouldn't breathe on the General.

"I'm a field officer, General," Serling said, starting over, "a damn good one. You've seen my file, my fitness reports—"

"I wrote one of them, Nat." The General's voice betrayed none of the hurry he had before. He made Serling feel like he would take all the time in the world to hear the junior officer out. That was one reason that Hershberg was so well liked by his men.

"Yes, sir. I'm . . ." Serling tried to think of a new tactic, something that hadn't been said before about this same subject. "Look, sir, I don't know what's holding back my transfer request . . ."

"Yes, you do, Nat." The other side of Hershberg's strength, cutting to the heart of the matter, through all the bullshit. The other reason Serling admired the General so much, even though that sword cut both ways—like now.

"Yes, sir, I do. But I was cleared of any responsibility for Al Bathra. Totally cleared, sir. Now, higher-on-higher may think otherwise, but I was, for the record, cleared."

9

"We all know that, Nat. And this record is getting scratchy. Do we have another song to play? If not . . ."

Serling knew he had to come up with something. C'mon, Nat. This is what you've trained for. Quick thinking under pressure. Now show a little of it.

"I have a plan, sir." Just in time. The General was two steps into his trot again. He stopped.

"Proceed, Colonel." Serling closed the distance between them again. C'mon, Nat, what's your fucking plan!

"Give me an apple for the teacher, sir."

"An apple?" Serling could see the General was getting impatient.

"Give me an assignment so I can shine for higher-on-higher. So they can justify some kind of field reassignment." Not bad, Nat. But was it good enough to fly?

"An apple," Hershberg repeated. "So you can shine."

"Yes, sir." Serling's hopes soared. He knew he had Hershberg. "Yes, sir." Serling looked Hershberg in the eye. "Please." Serling hid nothing behind that "please," letting Hershberg see the naked desperation in his eyes, counting on honesty.

"I have something that just might fit what we need to do here." Hershberg turned to Banacek. Serling's chest filled with hope.

"But you're not going to like it, Nat."

"I don't have to like it, sir. If it can get me that field assignment . . ."

Hershberg looked up from the appointment book Banacek was holding out.

"Meet me at Awards and Decorations—Suitland, I think. Ban here will give you all the details. Tomorrow at eleven hundred hours."

And Hershberg was off at his trot again. Banacek hung back.

"He's right, Colonel, you're not going to like this."

Banacek wrote down the address and time for Serling, and then tried to catch up with the General, who was already quite a few meters down the hall.

Serling just stood there smiling, feeling a bit foolish but not giving a damn. The river of Colonels flowed around him, and for the first time in four years Serling didn't feel like one of them.

WHETHER he would like the assignment or not, Serling didn't know, but he did know he didn't like Levine. He was short and balding with a thin, oiled comb-over of graying hair and a pursed little mouth that was turned down in permanent disapproval of Serling and of the world. He had a narrow strip of mustache that he dyed jet black. It didn't help his appearance.

The man's office was immaculate, the items on the desk looked as if they had been laid out with a ruler and a T square. The usual nameplate with flanking gold pens was in front for all to see and admire. COLONEL S. CLARKE LEVINE. Serling was ready to take bets that there was a shining new nameplate engraved just as handsomely with GENERAL S. CLARKE LEVINE waiting in a desk drawer. Probably next to the bottle of Windex, ready to clean the glass desktop. It sparkled, not a mark or smudge on it.

Levine fidgeted with a file on the desk in front of him and looked at Serling's ribbons. Serling let him squirm. Make the bastard have to say it.

"I was in Desert Storm, too." Levine tried to smile. "Twenty-fourth Mech."

Serling let it hang, waiting for the other shoe to drop. Little men with a little power. They flex it any way they can. In this instance I know something you may not know I know.

Levine let the attempt at a smile drop.

"Frankly I'm surprised you're still in the service."

"So am I," Serling replied, stopping Levine cold.

Serling busied his mind by examining the hierarchy of Army awards, starting with the rather mundane Good Conduct Medal and on up the familiar pyramid of Army Commendation, Bronze Star, Silver Star to the rather beautiful and frankly still impressive Medal of Honor. That soft, pale sky blue ribbon with the thirteen white stars, the gold eagle and green wreath, the helmeted warrior, and the little gold rectangle with one word inscribed in bold relief: VALOR.

Levine fiddled with the file, a millimeter adjustment on the desktop. He'd try again.

"I don't agree with this assignment," Levine pronounced, as if it were even in his province to make the decision. "I'm sure the General has his own reasons."

"I'm sure." Serling's reply was as noncommittal as he could make it. But he was curious. What was he doing here? What was Hershberg up to? Serling tried to sound casual, not wanting to give Levine the slightest edge. "Could I see the file?"

Levine smirked and Serling knew he had made a mistake. He had snapped at the bait and now he had to sit there with the hook in his mouth.

Levine looked at the file on the splendidly neat desk.

"I'm not required to release the documentation until I am in possession of all of the proper forms and orders." The words dripped from Levine's ripe little mouth.

Serling smiled. The paper-pushing asshole.

"Something funny, Colonel?"

Just little men like you who don't have any real power but pounce on any semblance of it like a crow on a roadkill, Serling thought. But he kept his mouth clamped down on his smile. He needed this gig, whatever it was. Don't fuck it up just to scare a rat back into its hole.

Serling thought of just admitting his ignorance of the assignment, but Levine probably wouldn't tell him anyway. As it was, the little man had a hard-on, his hands possessively resting on the file and harboring his power for as long as possible.

So Serling let his mind drift again. Awards and Decorations. What could Serling be used for here? Not any Public Information duty—his past put the kibosh on that. Some scut work, paperwork to give a few Generals their Commendation Medals for desk jockeying before their retirement?

But Levine couldn't stand the silence.

"Tell me, Colonel, how does it feel to kill some of your own men?"

Serling almost gasped for air. *Fire, flame, Boylar screaming. I don't want to die! A hand with a ring.*

A ring just like Levine's. Annapolis–West Point. Serling couldn't see the year, but he focused on the ring. He couldn't believe Levine had just blurted the question out like that. How does it feel? Did Levine really want to know?

No. It was a dig. Just some of the Washington thrust and parry of the usual D.C. infighting. In this case, a hard, brutal stab—and Levine had drawn blood.

Serling felt his face heat up. He was about to spit out a reply when the door opened and Hershberg strode into the office. Serling and Levine stood and saluted. The General nodded them back into their seats. Serling could see Banacek through the doorway going to the coffee machines. *Poor bastard, but he probably needs all the caffeine he can get to keep up with Hershberg.*

The General slid his butt onto Levine's desk, sweeping the nameplate to one side. It was Levine's turn to swallow bile, and Serling enjoyed the other man's discomfort.

Then Hershberg committed the ultimate offense. He grabbed the file off the desk and tossed it to Serling. Levine made a little noise in his throat.

But the General had his back to the little man, dismissing him completely.

"Nat, this here is a little hot potato and in that weird form of Washington alchemy it could turn into a real political football." Hershberg gestured at the file. "Captain Karen Emma Walden, the first woman to be eligible for the Medal of Honor."

"In combat," Levine piped up.

Hershberg went on without a hitch.

"In combat. So we have some speed bumps ahead. One, this whole stink about women in combat. There's a whole slew of political sharpshooters who will gladly take aim at that target. Then there's going to be a whole 'nother group on our hairy ass saying we're only doing this to overcompensate or distract the public from the charges of sexism and sexual harassment in the armed services."

"Bullshit." Levine tried to wedge into the conversation again.

The General looked at Levine as if he were a cockroach on a birthday cake, then turned back to Serling.

"None of that is your problem, Nat. Leave that to the boys who get paid to fret. There are only two things you have to remember: I want this. And the President wants this. His reasons . . . ? As usual, I haven't a clue.

"I want it because I think she deserves it. Put it under a microscope—with your usual thoroughness, Nat. Any problems, call Banacek. Or me. No slacking. Not that I expect any."

He leaned over and looked Serling in the eyes.

"This is important, Nat. To the nation. To the Army. To me." The General stood up. "Let's go."

Serling and Levine rose with the General.

"Sir"—Levine got the General's attention—"I can't let that file leave this office. I haven't received my Twenty-nine-thirty or the Two-sixty-four."

The General turned and faced Levine. Serling almost felt sorry for the little Colonel.

"Colonel, there's nothing I detest more than little D.C. hamsters that can't see beyond the paper at the bottom of their cages."

The General led Serling out. All Levine could do was return his nameplate to its original place.

Serling and Banacek followed Hershberg out of the building, the General mumbling under his breath all the way. Both men knew better than to interrupt.

Once outside, the fresh air seemed to calm the General. He jabbed a thumb at the building.

"That's what's killing this country. Not crime or pollution or . . . My daddy used to tell me, 'Look close at the word *bureaucrat*. There's always a rat in it.' "

They reached the General's car, and Hershberg turned to Serling.

"Do this right, Nat, and you can pick your assignment."

"Yes, sir."

"Banacek has a list of eyewitnesses and their current postings. Coordinate everything with him. I want you on this immediately. Need a ride?"

"No, sir. I drove my own car."

The General nodded. "Well, don't blow through a stop sign. That breath will lose you your license."

And he got into his car. Banacek, to his credit, didn't smile.

The General's car pulled away, leaving Serling standing on the curb, totally embarrassed. Suddenly the car stopped, backed up. The General unrolled his window.

"Do this right, Nat. Captain Karen Walden deserves it. And you need it."

Then he was gone again.

Serling walked across the immense parking lot toward his car, fighting himself every step of the way, trying so hard not to veer off into the dark sanctuary of the tavern beckoning from across the street.

He got into the Buick and sat behind the wheel for a second. He was sweating. He needed a drink. He looked at the bar.

Serling considered it a point of pride that he drove away.

IT was a big house with a big green yard surrounding it. School was out by the time Serling got there and a half dozen kids were playing outside with what looked like a refrigerator box. From where Serling sat in his car, he could hear them arguing whether to convert the box to a house or a fort. The youngsters seemed to be divided evenly, then one of them decided a McDonald's was an even better idea—if they could get Mom to go to the real McDonald's for a supply of burgers, fries, and Cokes. And pie, another chimed in. The more practical of the bunch listed a few concrete reasons why Mom would never cooperate.

Serling agreed. Meredith was death on McDonald's ever since his last cholesterol count was taken and she had put out a ban on burgers, fries, and pizza. "Fat is not a reward," was her latest answer to all pleadings from the children.

Serling surveyed his house, his land. It was only a double lot, but it seemed like a veritable forty acres for a former city kid like him. He and Meredith bought the house because of the vacant cottage next to it, an unkempt one-bedroom bungalow that an old woman had died in, childless and heirless. They had purchased both houses and torn down the ramshackle little place and planted a few trees and a lot of grass. The sandbox and swing set came later, and were followed by an inflatable pool for the dog days of August.

The theory was that the kids wouldn't wander as much and that the yard, like any vacant lot, would become a lure for the rest of the neighborhood kids. That way Serling and Meredith would have the security of watching their children break their necks in their own yard. It had worked. It was more than a bit noisy at times, especially hard when he brought work home, but it was a good plan and it had worked. He took a lot of satisfaction in that alone.

One of his few plans that had come out right.

The house was big, with four bedrooms and a study that had started out as Serling's but was soon taken over by Meredith for her own business use. She had a small personal accounting service, income taxes and such, and she was working toward becoming a CPA. Most of her work in the home office was done through her computer and modem. It was all Greek to Serling, but the added income was welcome and it was just damned pleasant to hear her talk about her work with such contagious enthusiasm. And the woman could manage money like nobody's business.

It had taken both their incomes to purchase the house. An old Victorian on a tree-lined block that was just shy of the Virginia countryside. The whole family had painted it together during the last Summer Olympics—cream siding with forest green trim. They brought the radio outside and listened to the Olympics while they worked, but would hop down the ladders and run into the house over a path of drop cloths to preserve the carpet and watch the playback on television, all five of them.

Serling had taken a two-week leave and went back on duty tired and sore, but it was still a cherished memory for him. There was a photograph in his wallet of the whole family, except for Louie, who hadn't been born yet, in front of the finished house. Their clothes were paint-splattered, their hands and faces smeared with paint, with more old paint chippings in their hair—happy.

And then The Dream had begun.

He looked over at the house. A few posts on the big porch railing needed replacing. And it was time to paint again. Get out the scrapers, brushes, pans, and roller.

Occasionally one of the kids would glance over at the Buick and at Serling. Lynn, the second oldest. She was a little clingy with her father. It worried Serling as much as it pleased him. It was the girls he fretted over. He thought he knew how to raise a boy, but the ways of females—big or little—were never his strong suit. But he had more than managed so far—with Meredith's help every step of the way.

Cheryl and Roger ran into the house and came back with a big pair of scissors, fat felt pens, and a hacksaw blade. The kids all attacked the box, although, as far as Serling could tell, the decision to build a fort or house had not yet been agreed to. He hoped the felt pens weren't the ones from his desk. Louie, the youngest, was using one like a dagger, punching holes, for what purpose Serling had no clue.

Lynn looked over at him again and their eyes met. It cut into his heart like an ice pick. He had to look away.

When Serling looked back across the street, Meredith was walking toward him, carrying a cup of coffee. He had a momentary flash of objectivity, as if seeing her for the first time. She was beautiful. His eyes flicked from one favorite spot to another. The curve of her eyebrow, the little scar on her upper lip (a cat claw at the age of six), the hollow of her neck, the sway of her hips as she walked. She walked like a man, but sexy. He told her that once and she didn't get it. He never said it again, but he knew what he meant. Strong, purposeful, proud, and somehow knowing. You knew she was in touch with every muscle in her body—and maybe yours.

Meredith reached the Buick and handed him the steaming cup. He recognized it, the one Roger insisted on drinking his soup out of when he had the flu.

"I just made a fresh pot." She was looking at his face. For signs of what? He didn't want to know.

He hid by bending his head to sip. Cocoa. She had put a touch of Nestlé's in the coffee for him. Another stab in his heart.

"Thanks." He sipped again, avoiding her eyes. "You get a new fridge?"

"Yes. The noise it used to make at three in the morning? That horrible rattle and moan? Didn't make it night before last."

She leaned into the window. No escape for Serling. She could do that to him. She never let him get away with anything.

"Got up the next morning and found a big puddle on the kitchen floor. Warped the linoleum. We'll see if it flattens back out. Had to throw away a whole chicken. Lost that slice of Louie's birthday cake. The new one's more efficient and has an ice dispenser in the door."

She waited until he finally looked at her.

"You can't do this anymore, Nat. It scares the kids."

Serling looked across the street. All four of his kids were watching their parents now, glancing at them furtively while reconstructing the refrigerator box. Even the two neighborhood kids were curious.

Meredith wasn't going to let up.

"They don't understand why their daddy chose to move out and leave them." She sighed. "Neither do I."

"I explained it to you, Mer. I have to work out this . . . thing."

"I hear what you say, Nat. That doesn't mean I understand it. But the kids . . . they think it's their fault. Don't do this to them anymore, Nat."

"I . . ." He realized he had no way of defending himself. "I'm leaving town for a few days. Hershberg has me taking a Medal of Honor and wrapping it up in shiny paper and ribbon."

"Medal of Honor?" She wasn't really curious, he saw, just treading conversational water.

"A woman." That got her attention.

"Good for her."

"Posthumous."

"Too bad. But still good for her. It's about time." She looked at him again. "How long will you be gone?"

"A week. Ten days."

"When you get back we have to deal with this. One way or the other."

Her tone sounded so ominous that for a moment Serling felt his heart stop. He tried to take the pressure off with a light smile.

"Sounds like an ultimatum."

Meredith didn't smile at all. Suddenly the taste of the coffee turned bitter, cocoa or not. He swallowed.

"It is. I don't want you haunting us like this, Nat. Either you come through that front door—to stay—or you don't come back here at all." She took a deep breath. "That was hard to say."

And she turned away and walked back to the house. Her walk was different, the purpose gone, just trying to maintain some composure in front of the kids.

She had tears in her eyes. Serling knew. He didn't have to see her face.

The coffee cup was empty.

Serling held it out the Buick window, ready to call out to her, any excuse to call her back.

But the screen door slammed shut and she was gone.

Serling started his car and put it in gear. The cup was dropped to the floor.

He drove away. The kids watched his car disappear down the street, ceasing their play for the moment.

SERLING'S room at the BOQ, an old converted World War II barracks, didn't have a bathroom. All the officers used a communal latrine at the end of the hall, reminiscent of Basic Training facilities. Serling was washing the coffee cup at a sink when Banacek walked in and slapped him on the back.

"Serling, you unlucky sonofabitch! What are you missing this weekend? Well, maybe you'll be back by then, but I doubt it. ZZ Top! Four tickets! Beakey from Naval Intell., Rogan, the Marine PIO, and not you!"

Serling marveled at Banacek's transformation. The General's adjutant insisted on absolutely formal military decorum during duty hours. But as soon as the flag left the Post he fell into his possibly true persona of a raucous frat boy. Serling, after three years of working around Banacek and occasionally fraternizing with him, still couldn't figure out which one was the real Banacek.

"Barbecue at The Rib Joint, then a joyful noise louder than God! Fourth row, left center. Hear 'La Grange'! Billy Gibbons turning the air to cottage cheese! We'll be deaf for a week!"

Serling walked back to his room, where his suitcase was spread open on the bed, and continued to pack. Banacek followed.

"I'm missing it already, Ban. Why don't you ask that blonde at the golf shop you've been rhapsodizing about?"

"Boys' night out. Women don't get the 'Z' men. Too much of a testosterone- and jism-driven twelve-bar thang. Women are out of the wavelength. 'Cept maybe Bonnie Raitt. No, I'll find some other hard-on to do the 'Z' with. Oh, here's your itinerary and tickets."

It was odd how Banacek's voice dropped back into the military tone and cadence just for that one official sentence. Serling smiled at him, looked at the papers, put them in his briefcase.

"Thanks, Ban. Sorry I'll miss the show, but when I get back maybe we can do something else. Barry Manilow or *Cats* or something. So, what do you think? Did the General toss me a crumb to shut me up or is this the lever I need to pry out a transfer?" Serling looked at Banacek. This was dangerous territory, duty conversation on off-duty hours. The younger officer often clammed up at times like this.

"The General likes you, Nat." Banacek reverted to his adjutant-speak again. "The assignment was given in good faith, I'm sure. He was . . . very pointed that you be given all the cooperation you need to do a proper job. Did you read the Walden file?"

"Not yet. I thought I'd read it on the plane to Bragg." Serling didn't want to admit that he was somehow reluctant, a bit afraid to read the citation or the eyewitness accounts.

"The General gave you this one for a reason."

"I know. If I didn't know him better I'd say it was a sick joke on his part. Or maybe punishment."

"How's that?"

"Think about it. Who do you send to investigate a hero? Someone who isn't one. Someone who is just the opposite. Someone who is as far from a hero as you can get."

"That's not true, Nat. You know that. Don't even talk that way. It pisses me off."

Serling let it go without a further response.

"Besides, you know the General better than that. He likes you, Nat. He's commented more than once that he thinks you're one of the finest tankers he's ever come across. Hell, he brings you into every armored discussion he has. He's got you writing reports that he sends right to the top—without a note or comment."

"Then why . . . ?"

"Don't press it, Nat. Any more than that and I violate my privileges. Just think of this assignment as . . . as a Lessons Learned."

"Lessons Learned. Got it. Thanks, Ban."

"No problemo, less-than-radical boogie-deprived dude."

And Banacek left. Serling could hear him growling an air-guitar version of what sounded like "Pearl Necklace" all the way down the hall.

Serling wondered about Hershberg's intentions. The General had handpicked Serling out of the Army War College at Fort McNair to be on his Weapon and Planning Staff at the Pentagon in the spring of '89. He was a Scout Platoon Commander at Fort Riley, Kansas, at the time and he really didn't want to leave his unit, but he knew a career opportunity when he saw one and he took the job.

He worked hard and Hershberg rewarded him with a promotion to Major. He and Meredith bought the Victorian on Atlanta Avenue that year and they went about having another kid—Louie.

Then Iraq invaded Kuwait and Serling saw what was coming—combat. Real combat. He begged Hershberg for the field assignment. The General pulled a few strings, called a few friends, and that, with Serling's record as a field officer, put him at Fort Hood, Texas, with the First Armored Cavalry.

He shipped out with them, commanding an Armored Company of his own. He was never so happy, never so proud.

Then Al Bathra.

After the incident and during the investigation, Serling was sent back to D.C., where Hershberg, now an Army Liaison Special Assistant to the Joint Chiefs of Staff, once again took him under his three-star wing.

Serling was eventually cleared and even commended and promoted, but Hershberg wouldn't let him loose in spite of a steady onslaught of transfer submissions and personal requests.

That told Serling one thing—that the General didn't trust him. The General knew Serling wasn't fit to command anymore, that all he would ever be capable of wielding was a rubber stamp.

Serling would rather die than continue to live this way.

He was finished packing. He put the cup on the dresser next to the picture of Meredith and the kids. The picture went into the suitcase. It was the only item in the room that gave any indication of the person who lived there. Without the picture, anyone could live there—or no one.

ON the plane Serling ruminated over the phrase "Lessons Learned" that Banacek had used. Lessons Learned was pretty plain for military speak, and every field exercise or combat incident had an aftermath report and the Lessons Learned at the tail of it.

The battle at Al Bathra had generated quite a few reams of aftermath reports. Serling had read them all. And all the Lessons Learned. He knew them all by heart.

Serling shoved Al Bathra out of his thoughts, ordered another drink from the steward, and took out the Walden file. It was getting dark in the cabin and he turned on the overhead light before beginning to read.

He didn't know how long it took to read the whole file. Twice through the official recommendation, a few pages of second-party accounts, and then the three eyewitness transcripts—Altameyer, Monfriez, and Ilario.

By the time Serling finished with the file, the cabin was totally dark, most of the overhead lights out, most of the other passengers sleeping.

Serling closed the file and turned to the window. Outside it was deep black. There was nothing to see but his own reflection. There were tears in his eyes. It surprised him.

The flight attendant, a kind-looking woman in her fifties, came down the aisle and stopped at Serling's seat, looking at him in concern. Serling wiped his face with the damp napkin from under his glass and turned off the overhead light, embarrassed.

The flight attendant walked on, a little embarrassed herself.

Serling turned back to the window.

And looked at the face reflected in front of him. He looked tired—and in pain, a lot of pain.

He pulled down the plastic shade.

And signaled for the flight attendant. When she came he ordered coffee and bourbon, figuring that he needed both the caffeine and the alcohol. The airy drone of the jet engines made him sleepy. He didn't want to sleep—he didn't want to see any fire.

2

Serling awoke in a sweat. He
didn't know if it was from The
Dream or the booze. He couldn't
remember any nightmares, and
for that he counted himself lucky.
For one night. He wasn't counting
on anything more.

He got up; dressed in a T-shirt,
shorts, and Reeboks; and went
outside to run off the remains of
the alcohol.

He stepped out of the Fort
Bragg BOQ and chose a route

along Ardennes Road, through the heart of the Eighty-second Airborne Division quarters.

Serling liked Fort Bragg. He had been here before for special tactical courses, and after spending years in the dry Texas plains of Fort Hood the pleasant green of Fort Bragg's North Carolina pine forests was a welcome respite. Of course the humidity was a little hard to take, but he had gotten used to that in D.C. It was going to be one of those kinds of days; he could feel the heaviness of the damp air as he sucked in wind. He tired early. Age or alcohol, he didn't know. Maybe both. It was odd how everything now became factored with his alcohol intake. He swore not to have a drink until dinner today.

He passed an Airborne company, Artillery by their guidon, running in formation and calling cadence. Tanned young soldiers, perfect human specimens in the prime of their life. Recruitment-poster soldiers. The Post was clean, spotless, with grass on the parade grounds and modern buildings of beige concrete block but with plenty of space between them. A nice-looking Post. Large, active, it made you feel good about being a soldier, proud to be in the same military.

For a brief moment Serling felt as though he belonged, but then he jogged past a tank, an old Patton M-48. Nothing like the M-1 he had commanded, but it was enough to take him out of his runner's reverie. He stopped dead in his tracks, sweat running off his body in streams, suddenly exhausted.

It was a long walk back to the BOQ. He shaved and showered and dressed in his khakis and was outside to find his driver and car waiting fifteen minutes early.

Serling read the PFC's name tag as she saluted.

"Quigley, can I get a decent cup of coffee, or an even not-so-decent coffee, on our way to wherever we're going?" He returned the salute and got in the front seat. He knew the backseat was de rigueur, but he had found out a long time ago that when riding in a military sedan it was wise to always sit as close to the air-conditioning vents as possible. They were often feeble at moving the air, if they worked at all.

Quigley got behind the wheel. "Well, sir, Second Bat, 505 S-3 has its own private espresso machine, but you have to drop a buck in the kitty."

"Here's two. Get yourself one." Serling handed her the money. "If we have time."

"It's a little detour, but we can make it, no sweat."

She drove and Serling opened the Walden file, prepping for the upcoming interview and making notes on his legal pad.

Quigley parked in front of one of the headquarters buildings and left the car running. Serling was grateful for the thought, but the air-conditioning started to falter as the engine idled. Soon it was blowing hot air into his face, so he turned the ignition key off.

Quigley returned with two cups. Hers went into a plastic cup holder. As Serling sipped his she looked at him expectantly.

"That's good stuff. More than worth the money. Thanks."

"No, thank you, sir."

She drove and he did the elbow-as-shock-absorber routine, sipping during the smoother portions of the ride. The espresso was good.

The interview would take place at an empty medical company training classroom. When Serling entered, he set his coffee and briefcase on the empty desk. The room was already filling with young soldiers.

Someone called, "Attention."

"At ease. Is there a . . ." Serling looked at his pad. ". . . Lieutenant Chelli present?"

"Here, sir!" First Lieutenant Chelli entered, wearing crisp fatigues. A young face, heavily pockmarked, with dark, serious eyes.

"Let me know when everyone is here. Until then, tell your men to relax."

"Yes, sir." Chelli went to his men.

Serling looked around the room. Evidence of the last use for the classroom was hanging from the blackboard. Large photographs of infected mouths, with each oral grotesquery labeled. "Pyorrhea, Trench Mouth," and so on. Every photograph was blown up to three feet by six, in lurid color and nauseatingly graphic. It made Serling run his tongue across his teeth just to reassure himself of their healthy presence. He made a mental note to floss more and turned the posters to the wall.

Typical Army teaching methods, good dental hygiene by scare tactics. Killing an ant with a hammer, as Serling's old First Sergeant used to say. Serling wondered briefly when the last case of trench mouth had occurred.

Serling sat at the desk and opened the file, then looked at the men gathering in the room.

It was a reunion of sorts. Hugs, backslapping, high fives, and handshakes. A few unashamed tears. "Strain!" "Thompson!" "Kopola!" "Casey, dude!" "Feidler, my man!" "What have you been doing?" "Jenkins!" "Going to meet with us after?" "You're getting fat, man."

A man in civilian clothes entered and was surrounded instantly by the others. "Egan! Where you been?" "How's civilian life?" "How's the legs?"

Egan pulled up his pants legs to reveal two artificial limbs. That brought about a round of scar comparisons as clothing was peeled away and even dropped to expose the shiny tissue.

War wounds.

Serling let it go on, a little envious of the obvious camaraderie, knowing the bond these men shared.

First Lieutenant Chelli counted heads, checked his roster, and walked over to the desk.

"All present and accounted for, sir."

The men didn't need an order to take their seats. As Chelli took his seat so did the others. Serling stood and faced them from the front of the room. Eight men—eight survivors.

They seemed incredibly young, almost boys, mostly because of their close-cropped whitewall haircuts and kids' faces. The file in front of Serling on the desktop said they had grown up quickly one night in a foreign desert. They were men.

"I'm Lieutenant Colonel Serling and I'm trying to confirm the sequence of events that occurred on or around Al Kufan on twenty-six February 1991. How did you men come to be on the Blackhawk, designated Dust-Off Two, piloted by Warrant Officer Fowler? Was it a combat Medevac?"

"No, sir," Lieutenant Chelli started, a little embarrassed. "A traffic accident."

"Damn Saudi drivers, sir." Serling read the man's name on his visitor's pass; Egan. "Thought they were driving cabs in New York or something."

"Most of them are," Thompson threw in.

There was laughter.

"We'd have a convoy of thirty vehicles or more and they'd decide to pass," Chelli clarified.

"And another kamikaze Saudi would be coming the other way," Egan added.

"They couldn't go to the shoulder," Thompson explained. "Minefields. They'd . . ."

Serling held up a hand to stop them.

"If we could start from scratch. Where were you? What was your mission?"

Lieutenant Chelli brought the narrative back on track.

"We were heading along the north end of Iraq to set up a fueling depot for the Twenty-fourth, part of Schwarzkopf's Hail Mary." Chelli took a breath. "Some mad Saudi in a deuce-and-a-half goes to pass the convoy and suddenly there's another convoy coming the other way."

✻

The long column of military trucks rolled down the narrow road, their exhaust stacks spewing black smoke that quickly mingled with the black, hazy pall wafting in from Kuwait, far out of sight across the endless horizon of sand.

In the back of the sixth truck from the tail of the convoy sat twenty-four men, including Second Lieutenant Chelli, Egan, Thompson, and the others. As they swayed and were jostled in unison the men smoked and joked. In one corner the men were competing to tell the grossest joke. The gross index was going up and the initial laughter had turned to groaning and wincing. They were all bored.

What they didn't know about and couldn't see was the Saudi driver in the baby blue piece-of-crap Mercedes truck that was thundering up to the rear of the convoy. It passed the last vehicle and, despite the waving and shouting of the soldiers, kept on passing trucks and fuel tankers. The driver seemed oblivious, bouncing his head to whatever was being pumped into his ears from his Walkman headphones.

Then he saw the other convoy approaching him—head-on. He leaned on his horn. Maybe he thought the oncoming trucks were all just going to stop and back up.

They didn't.

He looked for a gap in the convoy he was passing. But there was none. There would usually be an interval large enough for his truck to fit into, but

one of the trucks ahead had slammed on the brakes and the convoy had ac-
cordioned into bumper-to-bumper traffic.

The Saudi driver looked to his left. Nothing but sand. No problem there,
but every twenty meters was a sign—MINEFIELD—with the accompanying
symbol that every Middle Eastern citizen had become sadly familiar with.

He panicked.

And slammed on the brakes. The truck went into a four-wheel skid, then
fishtailed.

Chelli and some of his men saw it coming. But it happened too quickly
to do anything.

The two trucks collided! They hurtled off the road and hit the shoulder.
Now, welded together, they slid across the sand. A mine was hit!

The Saudi truck exploded with fire and smoke! The big five-ton full of
American soldiers flipped on its side and skidded back across the road. The
Sergeant riding shotgun was thrown half out of the cab and crushed, dead
instantly.

The five-ton plowed up the sand for fifty more meters.

Another mine went off.

The truck stopped.

The passengers littered the sand in its wake.

Wounded men, some crying out, some screaming, a few very still and
quiet as they looked up at the smoke-filled sky, stunned.

A few were dead.

Scattered around their bodies were boxes of Pampers, bright bundles on
the sand, incongruous tokens of civilization sprouting from the scorched dunes.

And flip-flops. Shower shoes in a variety of bright colors tied neatly to-
gether in pairs. Plastic sandals on the endless beach.

✻

"His cargo was all over the road." Egan tried to smile but it faded
quickly.

"The Saudi truck burned," Thompson said. "The driver was a crispy critter."

"We had twelve injured," Chelli added. "Mostly broken bones, contusions, two shrapnel, and a burn—Casey." Chelli looked for Casey, who nodded grimly.

One of the men, Jenkins, snorted and shook his head in disbelief.

"Here we are running around the desert scared shitless of poison gas and Scuds and the damn Republican Guard, and we get taken out by some Saudi speed merchant with a truckload of flip-flops."

"The Medevac, Warrant Officer Fowler's bird, picked us up and headed south to some MASH unit." Lieutenant Chelli pulled the conversation back to the incident. Serling was beginning to like the young Lieutenant. "Nothing happened on the trip. It was pretty routine."

"Until we got shot down."

Egan's simple statement took the wind out of everyone. It was suddenly very quiet in the room.

Serling prompted. "Altitude?"

"Low," Chelli answered. "Fifty to a hundred feet off the floor."

✳

The Blackhawk Medevac helicopter seemed to skim across the hills and valleys alongside the Euphrates River. The river bottom slid up into rugged mountains on both sides of the shallow water.

Inside the helicopter, Lieutenant Chelli and his men lay on litters or sat next to their friends, bandaged and still bloody. They were quiet, each man withdrawn into his own pain and suffering.

Suddenly the chopper shuddered with a big impact that reverberated through the metallic skin. Each man felt it. The crew shouted at each other. Fowler, the pilot, fought the controls.

The helicopter began to fall. Wounded men were thrown around and bounced off the walls and each other. A wounded man howled as his buddy fell elbow first into his ruptured stomach. Another soldier's broken arm was snapped the other way.

The pilot tried to auto-rotate, let the chopper's big rotors try to slow the fall. But the bird was too low.

It hit the ground. The impact was huge. The skids were splayed, the fuselage split, the door blown open. Men were thrown out.

✳

Serling looked at the men. He could see them now, grimly reliving the crash.

They were quiet for a moment, each man remembering his own private agony, his own personal encounter with the big fear—facing the possibility, the certainty—of his own death.

Serling understood. He let them have that moment. Then he prompted them again.

"Do any of you know what brought you down?"

They looked at each other, some shrugged. Chelli responded first.

"No. Triple-A, a missile-TOW . . . One minute we were up, the next minute we were eating sand."

"When did you see the enemy?" Serling asked.

Chelli was first again. The other men let him respond for them—years later, the Lieutenant was still their leader. Serling wondered how he had earned that privilege.

"Egan thought he saw some enemy movement before we hit."

Serling looked for Egan, found him.

"I was by the window, looking out. Saw some figures below. Could have been Bedouins, hard to tell."

"I thought I saw a flash." That was Jenkins.

"Firearms?" Serling asked him.

34

"Small arms. Maybe."

Serling wrote that down and looked back at Chelli.

"I didn't see anything."

Serling looked at his notes again.

"The pilot and the co-pilot were killed on impact?"

"Yes." Chelli nodded and took a deep breath. "The medic . . . Balkum? Balkum confirmed this. The Blackhawk nosed into the dirt. The medic and Crew Chief . . . I don't remember his name."

"Halligan!" someone at the back provided. Serling didn't see who spoke.

"Yeah, Halligan." Egan took up the thread of the story. "He and the medic started giving first aid to the new injuries. We lost one immediately, Feretic. Another, Rizza, died a few minutes later. He was our . . . Platoon Sergeant."

There was a moment of silence for Sergeant Rizza, then Egan continued.

"The Crew Chief tried to get out an SOS. The pilot didn't have time. . . . But the radio was wasted and he couldn't raise anyone."

"How long before you saw the enemy?" Serling directed the question to Chelli this time.

"About an hour, a little more. Ground troops. They came over the ridge to the northwest of us. They fired on us, then we saw them."

"All we had was the Crew Chief's M-16 and four nine-mils—the chopper crew's side arms," Egan said.

"They stripped us of our weapons when they medevaced us. Procedure," Chelli explained. "The Crew Chief returned fire with his sixteen. We were downslope from the enemy."

"They had the high ground. We were . . ." Kopola didn't finish his thought. Feidler did it for him.

"Fucked."

"Sitting ducks." Egan's tone was bitter.

"But the Crew Chief kept the enemy to the ridge," Jenkins continued the narrative. "The Iraqis didn't seem to be in any hurry. Until sixteen hundred hours . . . around there."

The men were starting to peter out, so Serling took the initiative.

"When he was hit . . . ?"

"Yes, sir." Chelli picked up the baton. "He was on his last magazine. The nine-mils didn't have the range. Rounds fell short."

"Did any of the enemy fire prove to be effective?" Serling asked him.

"Strain took one in the chest. Egan, Casey, they were wounded . . . Jenkins, no, he was later."

"And you, sir," Egan reminded him.

"Yes, sir." Chelli nodded gravely. "I took a round in the leg. And the medic had a bullet part his hair. A lot of blood, but he was still working."

"The chopper provided us no cover at all," Jenkins said. "Bullets went through it like cardboard."

There were nods and murmurs of agreement in the room. Chelli looked at his men, then back at Serling.

"We were in a world of hurt, sir."

Serling nodded sympathetically.

"Did you discuss surrender?" Serling saw immediately that the question cut deeply. Chelli looked at the others again before answering.

"Yes, sir. We were all wounded in one way or another. Surrender was discussed. But we figured we'd hold 'em off as long as possible in case a rescue came. It was a . . . difficult and protracted debate, sir."

"I suspect so." Serling gave a bit of a smile to ease the men. What a genteel way to describe the argument that must have occurred in the downed chopper.

"We weren't trained for that kind of shit, sir." Egan offered this as an excuse.

"Then the tank appeared." That simple statement from Thompson dropped into the room like a stone sending ripples of murmurs throughout the men. Serling heard "the tank" repeated four or five times, each time whispered like a curse.

The men were huddled inside the wreck of the chopper. Ponchos covered the dead. A few men were in shock, just staring out at nothing.

SWOCK! The fuselage took a hit. The sound of the gunshot echoed against the mountains. The men took no notice anymore. The olive drab body of the Blackhawk was already perforated with holes. A few more gunshots cracked through the air.

More swocks. More holes.

Balkum, the medic, his head bandaged, looked up at the ridgeline and saw a few heads bob up and down among the rocks.

Halligan, the Crew Chief, aimed the M-16 and fired sparingly, one round at a time, not wanting to waste any ammo. He had taken cover a couple of meters from the chopper behind a pile of river-worn boulders.

The enemy concentrated their fire on the Crew Chief's position—machine gun and other small arms. Chips flew from the rocks in front of him.

The Crew Chief smiled. His ruse was working. As long as the bastards were firing at him, they ignored the chopper and the men huddled inside. They were pretty well protected from the direct fire by an outcropping of rock, but ricochets and pieces of the aluminum hull flying through the air had taken a toll of casualties. Most of the wounds were little ones, cuts and scratches, but they all bled and they all hurt.

The Crew Chief kept his head down for a few seconds and counted his ammo and wondered how long it would be before the enemy got the motivation or strength to attack in full force.

What the hell were they waiting for? Every man in the ruins of the Blackhawk had the same thought.

Then he heard it. A noise. It was familiar but he couldn't identify it right off.

He peered over his cover of boulders and looked across the river and up the rocky slope to the ridge, but saw nothing. The noise became louder. The conscious survivors of the crash raised their heads to look.

Nothing to see . . . yet.

Then, over the crest of the ridge, nosed a long tube, followed by the clanking hulk of a tank. A Russian T-55. The soldiers had been subjected to hours of enemy weapons familiarization. The silhouette was too damn familiar.

The tank paused on the ridge.

Every man in the Blackhawk knew what that cannon could do. They knew it was over now. It was just a question of how long it would take the tank to get into position to fire and whether they would be alive afterward.

With a clatter and the roar of its huge diesels the tank flopped over the ridge and crawled down the slope. The military crest, they call it. No longer a silhouette against the sky, it was an easy target for an antitank rocket—as if anyone in the Blackhawk had one.

They didn't.

The tank stopped.

The Crew Chief aimed the M-16 at the tank, then lowered the muzzle. Why bother? The .223 rounds would bounce off the tank armor like piss off a hot rock. He could fire now just to announce his presence, but why make himself a target for the big gun without any positive results? Better to see if anyone popped out of the hatch, try to dust one of them. Take somebody with him at least.

The turret began to swivel. The noise traveled up and down the Crew Chief's spine like cold water.

The turret stopped and the big gun made some final adjustments—up, up, left, left, left . . .

The huge barrel was pointed directly at the Blackhawk. From the Crew Chief's point of view it looked as if it were aimed directly at him.

It was an odd feeling, sitting there and watching the huge cannon make adjustments as it prepared to blow them away.

A few more whirs and cranks. A little more elevation, a touch of windage. The Crew Chief could imagine the gunner peering though his sights. What was his aim point? The United States marking on the side of the Blackhawk? The pile of rocks where that pesky M-16 fire was coming from?

BOOM! The gun fired! The tank jerked back from the recoil.

The tail section of the helicopter disintegrated! Just like that. The concussion wave pounded everyone with a big fist.

The medic scurried among the men and checked for new injuries.

The Crew Chief glanced back at the tank and saw it had been enveloped by a huge cloud of dust that had been thrown up by the muzzle blast. With no wind the dust just hung there, then dissipated slowly.

Everyone knew that when the dust settled enough the tank gun would begin to make adjustments.

And fire again.

Second Lieutenant Chelli began to yank on a loose strut, bending it back and forth until it snapped. He tied a white handkerchief to the end. Everyone was watching him.

He rose slowly and stepped out of the cover and took a couple of tentative steps toward the tank, his back erect, his jaw set.

✳

"I figured we'd held out as long as we could and that the lives of the men . . . we had injured who needed immediate medical attention . . ." Chelli suddenly looked like he was younger than his twenty-five years, a boy with a man's responsibilities.

Serling interrupted him.

"You don't have to make excuses for your actions to me, Lieutenant."

"I know, sir, I know. It's just . . ." He petered out.

One of the other men laid a hand on Chelli's shoulder to comfort him.

Serling looked at him and the rest of the survivors, scanning their faces, seeing an echo of something he knew himself, something he had shared with them.

Fear. He felt a touch of it now, a reminder. This time Serling put the Lieutenant back on track for his own sake. Something to get Serling away from the precipice that had opened before him.

"So you approached the enemy. And their response?"

✳

Chelli limped a few feet out in front of the downed Blackhawk and stopped for a moment to rest, grimacing in pain.

It was quiet. The tank turret stopped its grinding and whirring, the diesel engine was just a guttural bubbling that came and went.

The dust settled completely around the tank. Chelli could see the enemy commander sitting up in the turret, the driver's head and shoulders poking out of the bow. They looked at the flag, at Chelli, and spoke to each other.

Chelli saw the muzzle flashes of the tank machine gun, saw the bullets kick up dirt in front of him like a rock skipping across the water. But this time the skips were coming at him and he didn't panic and he didn't yell, he just made the interpolation between rocks skipping water into bullets hitting earth and was going to turn and run. That was his plan, simple as that, turn and run, but his good leg was yanked out from under him and suddenly he was just lying there as the sounds of the machine gun became very audible. Then the pain came in a giant wave that took him under.

Two other men, Egan and Thompson, came running out. They were wounded themselves, but they came after their officer and dragged him back to the chopper. Chelli didn't know he was screaming all the way, his new wound thumping against the rocks, but a few minutes later his throat was raw.

The tank's big gun began moving again. A short additional adjustment, and then it fired.

BOOM! The concussion rattled the chopper's now-frail skin. The round exploded a few meters off the nose of the aircraft, hurling rocks into the cabin, but no one was hurt.

The men suddenly became animated.

"We're nothing but target practice!"

"A turkey shoot!"

"They got us bracketed! All they have to do now is send one down the middle and we're meat!"

"Dead meat."

The Crew Chief, knowing full well the futility of his action, aimed the M-16 and fired off a couple of three-round bursts. The rounds bounced off the side of the tank. The only satisfaction he had was seeing the driver duck.

He was about to fire off another set, maybe get the officer down, when the medic grabbed the weapon and stopped him.

The medic looked at the sky and cocked an ear.

The Crew Chief also looked skyward. He didn't see anything.

But he heard it.

A chopper.

The rhythmic thumping of a helicopter.

He tried to think fast, back to the briefings. Did Hussein have any helicopters?

❋

"There's something about an inbound Huey. You hear that sound, you see that big Medevac cross on the side . . ." Thompson was grinning.

"It buzzed right over us." Chelli was also smiling at the memory. "Then over the tank and it kept going for a bit."

"I was scared for a second that it hadn't seen us and it was going away," Thompson added.

Serling looked at his file again.

"Did it take any ground fire?"

"Right off the bat," Egan said.

"Instantly." Jenkins confirmed Egan's words. "Every raghead ground-pounder wanted a piece of that bird."

"When the Huey came back, someone on board returned fire," Chelli said. "Someone with an M-60."

"That Altameyer guy," Egan volunteered.

"We didn't know it at the time, but yes, his name was Altameyer." Chelli provided the confirmation. "The ground troops went for cover. Just *that* made us feel a whole lot better."

✳

The men in the crashed Blackhawk cheered. Pain and wounds were forgotten for a few seconds as the elation washed over them.

BOOM!

The tank fired again.

For a moment Lieutenant Chelli didn't know what had happened. He was trying to stand, waving at the Huey, and the next thing he was aware of was the medic lying on top of him.

Whether the medic had thrown himself on top of him or was sent flying there by the concussion—either way, the medic was dead.

Chelli rolled the dead weight off to the side. The medic's eyes were open, the rest of his head a mess—just a grisly mass of red and pink meat and white mush.

There was a smell of burning flesh. A stomach-churning sweetness.

The Blackhawk had taken a direct hit.

Men were bleeding, moaning, one was screaming. Someone was reciting the Lord's Prayer over and over and over.

✳

Chelli took a deep breath. Serling waited for him to gather the emotional strength to continue.

"We tended the wounded the best that we could. Besides the medic, Ralone was killed." Chelli looked around the room. "Egan lost his legs."

Egan nodded once, curtly.

"We were waiting for the next round to hit," Thompson said. "Now that he had us bracketed."

"What was the Huey doing at that time?" Serling asked.

"It circled back to go over the tank again," Egan answered.

"Then they threw something overboard," Jenkins continued. "At the tank."

Serling looked at Jenkins for a moment.

"Threw it overboard or it fell off?"

"Couldn't tell the first time," Chelli clarified. "But the Huey banked and we could see the Crew Chief unstrapping something."

"The fuel pod," Egan contributed. "The auxiliary. He was unhooking it. I could tell. I used to work choppers at Fort Campbell."

"And the enemy response?" Serling prodded.

"They were still taking ground fire," Chelli began. "We could see the tracers. The Huey was taking hits, no doubt about it, but it banked again and made another run. This time the fuel pod hit."

"Dead hit," Egan confirmed. "It burst like a water balloon."

"JP8—air fuel—all over the tank." Thompson smiled.

"Then someone in the Huey," Chelli continued, "I don't know who, fired a flare at the tank. And it blew."

The men all smiled at that.

✳

The tank commander, still sitting half in and half out of the turret, was drenched in jet fuel. He was in the midst of yelling commands in Arabic, then he stopped himself.

And began to scramble out of the tank.

It was too late.

The flare made a beeline from the Huey to the tank. And instantly the vehicle was engulfed in flames.

Most of the ground troops began to run from the tank. Two men, braver than the others, or perhaps not realizing the danger, ran toward the tank.

Another figure, a man on fire, began to emerge from the bow of the tank, with a flaming arm, a howling face.

Then the tank ammunition magazine blew. Not with one big explosion, but with a chain of explosions, until the tank finally flew apart. The turret spun into the air, landing on one of the Iraqi onlookers.

The tank blew again. This time it was a big explosion that lifted the back of the vehicle off the ground.

The survivors in the shelter of the crashed Blackhawk began to shout and scream in joy.

✳

The men's smiles lit up the room, and Serling felt himself beginning to grin, too. He let them relish the memory for a moment before he asked his next question.

"Did you see what knocked the Huey down?"

The mood of the men darkened.

"No," Chelli answered. "We were yelling and screaming so much, we didn't even notice the Huey was hit."

"We just saw it spiral down and crash," Jenkins said.

"It landed between the tank and us," Egan continued. "On a little piece of higher ground. Across the river from us."

"How far away?"

"Five hundred meters, give or take fifty," Chelli answered.

"She hit hard," Thompson added.

"Real hard." Jenkins nodded gravely. "Surprised anyone survived."

The mood in the room remained quiet. Serling looked at his file notes.

"Did the Huey at any time climb to an altitude to radio in their position?" Serling directed the question to the room in general. "Did anyone witness any such action?"

"They didn't that I observed, sir." Chelli's response was a bit stiff. "They were taking fire at all times."

"I'm not criticizing the actions of the Huey crew, Lieutenant." Serling tried hard not to sound like a Colonel. "They could have climbed to escape the enemy fire."

"Roger that, sir." Thompson also had his back up. "And left us to take the flak. As long as the ragheads were firing at the Huey they weren't firing at us."

Serling let that response die out before he asked his next question.

"The sun set shortly after the Huey crashed. Was there any more ground fire?"

Lieutenant Chelli as usual responded first.

"The tank was incapacitated—but we caught sporadic ground fire throughout the night. The Huey took most of it. It was between us and the enemy, so—"

"You had no communications with the Huey?"

"No. As I said, our radio was wasted," Chelli clarified. "We tried shouting to them, but that just drew enemy fire, so we . . . stopped."

"Then you spent the night waiting?"

"Longest night I ever spent . . ." Jenkins's words were almost whispered.

"Brady died during the night." Chelli's words were spoken somberly. "It was cold. But . . . we heard voices from the Huey a couple of times, small-arms fire between it and the ridge. What sounded like a brief firefight once. Around three hundred, three hundred thirty hours."

"Could you see into the Huey?" Serling asked Chelli. "Were you able to discern what was happening there?"

"No. There was a spit of land in the middle of the river, a pile of rocks there hid the interior from us. We couldn't see anything in daylight and most of the time the Huey was there it was dark."

"And at dawn came a new attack?" Serling addressed the room in general, but once more Chelli responded first.

"Not quite. The sun came up. We were pretty ragged by then."

There were nods of assent all around the room. Chelli continued.

"On the ridge we saw forty, maybe fifty enemy. They commenced firing at the Huey and moving toward it under the covering fire. The Huey returned fire."

"M-60 and M-16 . . . I could hear some Beretta," Thompson put in.

"The enemy had slipped between us and the Huey along that rocky finger in the middle of the river during the night," Chelli explained. "And there were a few more behind our position. They fired on us but only chewed up the Blackhawk some more."

"Then we heard the rescue team coming in." There was a lift in Egan's voice.

"Another Huey, a Blackhawk, and a pair of Cobras." Jenkins joined in the elation of that part of the story.

"And a big-ass F-14 Tomcat." Thompson was grinning. "You never heard such a beautiful noise."

✳

The sun was just slipping free of the horizon. On the ridge the enemy soldiers who before were just silhouettes now became distinct individuals. Too distinct.

The Crew Chief, weary to the bone, clutched the M-16. The plastic stock was cracked, but he thought it would still fire. Eight times—he hoped. That was how many bullets he had left in the magazine. He had counted them and reloaded more than once during the night.

There had been a yell somewhere up on the ridgeline and the enemy had begun to fire at the Huey.

Lieutenant Chelli had not been aware of the enemy encroachment behind the Blackhawk until he heard the gunfire. He wanted to observe their position but he couldn't walk.

He was trying to figure out who among his men was physically able to carry him over to the side of the wreck when they all heard it.

Incoming choppers!

They all looked up.

Two Cobras zipped overhead first. Sleek, evil-looking monsters, their miniguns belching fire at the enemy, tracers flowing like water from a hose.

Then the F-14 Tomcat blasted overhead.

The fragile skin of the downed Blackhawk trembled with the sonic blast.

The Cobras strafed the ridgeline behind the Blackhawk, 2.75-inch rockets and Gatling guns tearing up rock, sand, and men.

The Tomcat took out the enemy tank once more, for luck or revenge. A TOW rocket. The whole ridge vibrated from the explosion. Then he came in for another run, this time strafing the foot soldiers with his nose cannon.

The noise was incredible, a giant din of helicopter rotors and the alternating low roar and high scream of the jet. The only sounds that cut through the deafening aircraft thunder were the small-arms fire and the occasional human scream.

The rescue choppers landed between the downed Huey and the downed Blackhawk. Medics came running to assist the Blackhawk wounded. Those injured who could still walk needed no encouragement to run or hobble on their own way toward the rescuing Blackhawk.

A second Huey landed next to the rescue Blackhawk and took on three men who rushed out of the downed Medevac Huey. The evacuation took only seconds and the rescue helicopters were loaded and rose off the ground.

✳

"All the wounded were loaded aboard. The dead were left behind." Chelli's voice was just above a whisper now. "We were taking fire at the time. A very hot LZ. One of the Blackhawk medics was hit, I think."

"Again, I'm not criticizing, Lieutenant," Serling said, treading softly. "But why were the dead left behind?"

"It was a major firefight, sir," Chelli stated simply.

"Yeah, this huge noise," Egan said. "It sounded like every gun in the world."

"The enemy was letting loose with everything they had," Thompson contributed. "And the crew of the crashed Huey was still banging away."

"The enemy wanted us, sir. They had encircled us during the night, in strength. They were crawling all over the place." Chelli sighed. "The decision was made to leave the dead. By the commander of the rescue, I think." He took a deep breath.

"I guess we could have taken on the enemy. We had firepower, but it *was* a rescue mission, and I suppose . . . It's not my place to question the orders of a superior officer, sir, and it's not my field, so . . . If it's okay, sir, I'd–"

"No, no." Serling smiled. "It was just a casual question. Did anything else happen on the rescue that you want to add?"

"No, sir." Chelli shook his head. "The last thing we saw was the Tomcat drop white phosphorus on the two crashed helicopters."

There was a moment of silence. For the dead, thought Serling.

"Then we were out of there."

✳

The F-14 Tomcat flew low, hugging the terrain. The bombs fell off the jet, making a lazy path to the ground.

The explosion was brilliant white, difficult to look at in its center. The white smoke that billowed upward was pretty. But the fire below it wasn't.

The white cloud roiled into the sky.

The injured men in the helicopters could see the smoke for a long time after the river, and then the ridgeline and finally the mountains were gone from their sight. It hung in the air, a transitory marker of white smoke for the dead.

✳

"Soldier." Serling looked at Thompson. "You stated that you heard the crew of the crashed Huey 'banging away.' They were returning fire?"

"Yes, sir," Thompson affirmed.

"You saw this?"

"Heard it, sir," Thompson continued. "I know the sound of M-16s. Nothing else like it, not no AK or M-60."

"Anyone else hear the M-16 return fire *after* the rescue choppers touched ground?"

Three hands went up, then a tentative fourth.

"It couldn't have been one of you using your own M-16?" Serling asked.

"That was in the Crew Chief's hands, sir. He was right next to me," Chelli reminded Serling. "He fired off a couple of bursts as the rescue came in, and that was it. Out of ammo."

"An M-16, Thompson?" Serling questioned.

"Yes, sir. No doubt about it. I trained as Infantry, sir. And I saw red tracers from the Huey."

Serling made a note.

"Anyone else see this?"

No raised hands this time.

3

Serling had dismissed the men. They were tired but milling around the room, all quiet. They had fought the battle all over again. Serling gathered his papers together.

Lieutenant Chelli approached him.

"Colonel, this isn't just the usual 'Lessons Learned' or post-action analysis, is it?"

"No." Serling thought a moment before he continued. "Captain Walden, the Huey pilot, has been recommended for the Medal of Honor."

Serling figured the information couldn't taint his inquiry at this point—and he was certain that he wouldn't have to come back to these men again.

Chelli took the information in, absorbed it.

"Well," he said, "I don't know if it was Captain Walden or who-ever—never met them, you know, but that Huey and her crew saved our lives."

"I wouldn't be here today." Thompson said it earnestly. "I know that."

"We all thought we were dead," added Egan.

"That Huey coulda climbed and just radioed in a location," Jen-kins offered. "We knew they went beyond their mission to help us."

"The Medal of Honor isn't enough for what they did." Thomp-son's statement received nods of assent from everyone.

"They ought to give it to every soldier on that Huey," Egan added, and everyone voiced an affirmation.

"Thank you, gentlemen."

Serling snapped his briefcase shut and headed toward the door.

One step outside the classroom and Serling almost collided with a civilian. He was a little guy, five feet four or five, barely coming up to the medals on Serling's chest. A baby face, thirtyish, but one of those men who would still look young in his fifties. He proba-bly still got carded if the bar was dark enough. Dressed in gray slacks and a blue blazer, white shirt and school tie, he could have wan-dered in from any East Coast prep school. The man's eyes focused on Serling's nameplate over his right pocket.

"Colonel Serling! Ed Bruno! White House Military Media Re-lations! Captain Banacek gave me your itinerary! I could have phoned, but I wanted to meet you one on one! Sorry I was too late for the first interview! How'd it go?"

"I'm not sure that's any of your business, Mr. Bruno." Not only did Bruno look like a kid, but he had the energy of a six-year-old on a sugar rush. It made Serling fidgety just standing next to him.

"Oh, right. Here's some paper, my authorization." Bruno shoved some papers at Serling as the men filed out of the classroom. Bruno scanned their faces.

"Wow, they're just kids."

"Men," Serling returned. "After what they've been through you don't call them kids. Look, Mr. Bruno . . ."

"Sorry—men. Men. But Christ on a crutch, look at those faces . . . Mom, apple pie, the whole goddamn Norman Rockwell ball of wax. A *People* magazine cover if I ever saw one."

Serling put the papers into his briefcase without even looking at them and started to walk toward his jeep. Bruno followed at his heels like a needy Chihuahua.

"Thought I'd tag along for the next couple of interviews and get some ideas for the press kit. Nothing intrusive. I'll be a fly on the wall—I swear. Always best to dig in with your own hands, don't you think? Get the *feel* of something."

"I really don't think that's a good idea." Serling turned to look into Bruno's eyes, to give him the full impact. "I don't want to inhibit anyone's testimony."

"Well, the official working relationship can be worked out, I'm sure. Right now I need some background on these kids—men. Make sure we don't have a wife beater or an illegal alien in the woodpile. Know what I mean?"

The rest of the men filed past them to the parking lot. Bruno looked at them, glanced at Serling.

"Brave men. *Brave* men. This must be particularly difficult for you, Colonel."

Serling felt himself stiffen involuntarily and it was an effort to keep the emotion from showing in his face.

"What do you mean by that, Mr. Bruno? *Exactly* what do you mean by that?"

Bruno smiled. He knew he had scored a point.

"Having me here. I know I'm an albatross."

Serling smiled now. Don't underestimate this little bastard, he told himself. Bruno babbled on.

"You ever see that Monty Python skit? Albatross! Cracks me up. I'm a pain in the ass. I know that. But it's my job—sort of. This medal . . . if Captain Walden wins the Medal of Honor—"

Serling interrupted Bruno. "No one *wins* the Medal of Honor, Mr. Bruno, they *receive* it. There are no Medal of Honor winners. It's not a contest."

"Right! Right! That's good, that's *real* good! See! That's what I'm here for! Can you say that again?"

And the little man thrust a tiny tape recorder into Serling's face.

Serling was trying to decide if he could get away with what he was thinking about doing with that tape recorder when he was saved by Lieutenant Chelli.

"Sir? You have a minute, Colonel?"

"Sure, Lieutenant," said Serling, glad for the interruption.

"Sir, you've had a remarkable career—before the incident at Al Bathra. I was wondering if perhaps you could give me a few hints in reference to getting on the fast track like you."

Chelli was worrying a large manila envelope in his hands.

"I wouldn't really know how to advise you on—" Serling began, but Chelli cut him off.

"I mean, they say, sir, that if it hadn't been for the incident at Al

Bathra you'd be a General now. I'm a full-tilt career ring-knocker, sir, and I plan on being the youngest General in Army history."

The young Lieutenant knew he had just said something that could target him for a lot of flak, but instead of backing off with an obsequious smile, he stiffened his back, ready to take whatever was coming.

Serling admired that.

"Well, Lieutenant, I don't know about any fast track. I know it's hard work and a little luck . . ."

"Sure, sure. I work harder than anybody. But if I can find me a rabbi like you got in General Hershberg . . ."

Now Serling was starting to not like him so much.

"I would hardly call General Hershberg my rabbi . . . ," Serling began, then stopped himself. Maybe the brash Lieutenant wasn't so far off the mark.

Serling glanced at Bruno, who was enjoying this interchange.

"But you're on his staff. He saved you from a court-martial."

Serling felt his face get hot.

"Where did you hear that?"

"Scuttlebutt, sir . . ." Chelli was backpedaling fast. He knew he had fucked up.

Serling waited a beat before he spoke, closed his eyes for a pro-longed blink, and imagined the words *Calm Yourself* on a black-board—a trick he had learned at Ranger school.

"General Hershberg did me no favors. Good luck on your ca-reer, Lieutenant. Fast track or not." Serling was pleased at how calm his voice sounded. "When you make General I'll send you a bottle."

Serling started to walk away with a glance at Bruno that dared him to say anything. Bruno was still smiling, but he could read faces well enough not to push Serling any further. A Washington, D.C., survival skill he had learned.

The Lieutenant hadn't learned it yet, though. He trotted back to Serling's side and thrust the manila envelope toward the Colonel.

"Sir, I almost forgot. I wanted to give you this."

Serling took the envelope. Chelli went on eagerly.

"It's an article I wrote for *Military Review*. It's an operational assessment of the battle at Al Bathra. In it, I propose three operational alternatives to your . . . the decision you made."

Serling looked at the envelope, then at Chelli.

"Only three?"

The sarcasm bounced off the Lieutenant.

"I thought you might like to read it."

"No." Serling tried to give the envelope back. "Thank you."

"I'm not being critical, sir." Chelli wouldn't take the envelope back.

"No?" Serling drilled the Lieutenant with his eyes, but Chelli kept talking.

"You don't want to read it, sir? I'm sure you've gone over the incident many times. There might be a solution here that you haven't thought of."

Serling almost smiled. But then, for a second, he saw the flames again. A tiny, frightening piece of The Dream.

"I doubt it. I doubt it very much."

Serling gave the envelope back. Chelli looked like a rejected suitor. Serling turned around to walk away and almost collided with Ed Bruno again.

"Lieutenant!" Serling called Chelli back.

Chelli was walking away. He about-faced and almost ran to Serling's side.

"Meet Mr. Bruno. White House, D.C. honcho. You're looking for a rabbi—he knows echelons beyond God himself. Mr. Bruno,

Lieutenant Chelli. The Lieutenant is an eyewitness to the Walden recommendation incident."

Serling left the two of them, Chelli launching into his story all over again and Bruno sputtering about back-story for the media.

SERLING asked the driver to take him to the Enlisted Men's Club over in the Bastone Gables area. She didn't ask why an officer would want to stoop so low. She had been to the Officers' Club and it impressed the hell out of her. It was the only moment in her short military career that she had even thought of putting herself through the high-octane Mickey Mouse of Officers' Candidate School. Just so she could have a seat at that big, long oak bar every night after watching a bunch of noncoms do all of your scut work.

Serling watched the beige buildings of the Eighty-second Airborne Division area peter out and be replaced by the brick structures of the Special Forces quarters. Then the driver headed north toward Pope Air Force Base.

The Enlisted Men's Club was a low one-story structure with a large parking lot. There were few cars in the lot, as it was still an hour before the establishment officially opened for the day.

PFC Quigley parked next to a large ten-year-old Wagoneer. Serling invited her inside but she declined, saying she had to study for her heavy-equipment examination.

Serling shrugged and went through the front doors of the club. Quigley went back to her Danielle Steele. She had been to this particular EM Club. It was not a fun place.

Serling walked into the club and almost laughed. It was the cleanest nightclub he had ever seen. The floor was spotless, the dark linoleum buffed to glistening swirls. The bar was immaculate, the bottles lined up as if for inspection, the glasses stacked so precisely and tightly they could have been carved from one piece of glass.

An enlisted man was on his hands and knees, marking the floor delicately with a felt pen. Tiny dots aligned with a taut string that ran across the floor from wall to wall.

Another soldier waited for the dot maker to finish, and then set the table in place, with each leg over a dot. The chairs were also dotted and aligned, the whole seating area in front of the dance floor laid out in one great perfectly symmetrical pattern.

Serling wondered what would happen on a drunken Saturday night.

The cause of this anal-compulsive table alignment was standing ramrod straight in front of the bandstand.

In his late forties, with a bearing that looked way beyond those years, wearing black pants and a khaki civilian shirt as if it were a uniform, was Jess Sidaris, mostly known as "Top." Anything he wore would look like a uniform. He had a jet black crew cut with sprinkles of brilliant white, and a face that could have been either Slavic or American Indian. High cheekbones, broad forehead, and deep-set eyes that could melt the silver right off a young Lieutenant's collar bars. Among the troops of Delta Company, those eyes were called the "laser targeting device." When they were in their active mode.

Serling learned to recognize it by a slight reddening of an already sunburned face. Then, the story went, the most you could do was bend over and kiss your ass good-bye, because your soul belonged to Sidaris.

Right now that famous glare was aimed at the bandstand, where five alarmingly thin and pale young men were plugging in or tuning their instruments. Heads of long, greasy-looking hair, scraggly goatees, and Salvation Army clothes seemed to be their uniform of the day.

Sidaris's arms were folded across his chest.

"Proceed!"

The band stumbled into a mighty noise. Serling couldn't recognize the style—Seattle grunge meets rap, then sideswipes heavy metal.

Sidaris didn't listen so much as tolerate the music.

The band played about four bars and seemed to be hunting for a chorus when Sidaris barked again.

"That's enough! That's enough! Cease! *Cease music!*"

That he was heard was a remarkable achievement; he hadn't moved a muscle, but then again Serling had heard that voice cut through the thunder of a battery of 105mm recoilless rifles.

The band stuttered to a stop. The lead singer, looking pained, stepped forward.

"You wanna hear another song?" He spoke with the same whining tone that he used for singing.

"No." Top Sidaris shook his head. "That's enough. My ears are bleeding as it is."

The bass player joined the lead singer.

"But you didn't give us a chance. We didn't even get to finish the first song, man."

Top Sidaris stepped up to the pair. They stepped back. It was an automatic reflex. Serling had seen twenty-year Ranger-qualified combat-experienced Staff Sergeants standing at rigid attention do the same thing.

"Don't get your shorts in a bind, son. You're hired. On one condition: I can't tell if you're any good, but you make enough noise and that's all that counts with this crowd."

"Hired?" The drummer grinned. "Cool."

The keyboard player was the smartest of the bunch.

"What's the condition?"

Top grinned like an Alpha wolf showing his teeth.

"You play at least one song that's on my jukebox. Deal?"

The band members looked at each other, held a brief, whispered conference, and walked over to the jukebox.

Sidaris watched them start reading the labels.

"Hey, Top!" Serling called out. "Need someone to wash glasses?"

Sidaris turned and recognized Serling.

"Major!" There it was. Sidaris's big toothy smile. That smile and a "Well done, soldier" could make young grunts charge a machine gun nest for this man—and it had on many an occasion.

"Oh, it's Lieutenant Colonel now. My apologies. What are you doing here, sir? Transferred out of that paper-pushing quagmire to a real Army posting?"

They walked toward each other and shook hands. There was an awkward moment, and then Sidaris opened his arms and they hugged.

"What the hell, sir, we've gone through a lot of flak together."

Serling felt emotion well up in his chest. The strength of his feelings surprised him.

"No, Top. TDY. Just doing a little legwork for General Hershberg."

"Shit-can that 'Top' stuff. Call me Jess. I'm a civilian now." Sidaris led Serling across the bar. "Come over here to my office—sort of."

Sidaris's office was a corner table with a calculator, a three-ring binder, a legal tablet, and a few pens. The two men sat.

The lead singer walked over to the table.

"Hey, mister," he whined.

"First Sergeant or 'Top' will do," Sidaris said.

"Yeah, First Sergeant, whatever . . . There's not a song on that jukebox after 1980."

"Seventy-five. You backing out of the deal?"

"No, sir."

" 'Top.' I'm not a 'sir,' either. I work for a living. No offense, Colonel."

"None taken . . . Jess. And call me Nat."

The scraggly kid was getting confused. He looked at Sidaris for a second and walked back to the jukebox, where another hushed conference began.

For some reason Serling felt the emotion well up in him again. He and Sidaris had gone through so much together. From his first posting at Fort Hood with the First Cavalry, just a First Lieutenant tanker, Sidaris had been his Platoon Sergeant. They'd risen in rank together, from Lieutenant to Captain to Major, Sidaris rising to First Sergeant. When Serling had returned to Fort Hood for Desert Storm there was Top. Desert Storm. Al Bathra. Serling and Sidaris. Top had been like a father to him, then later an equal, a friend, a hero, a confidante.

Serling fought the emotion back.

"Can a fella get a drink in this joint?" Serling smiled at Sidaris. "I'll buy you one."

"It's a little early for me, sir . . . Nat." Sidaris looked closely at Serling for a moment. But he rose and led Serling over to the bar, glancing at the guys huddled around the jukebox.

"I don't understand this Seattle grunge sound." Sidaris shook his head. "Goes right by me."

"That's probably the point. One generation separating itself from the previous one. Bourbon, neat."

Sidaris served it up himself. Serling took the glass self-consciously. He suddenly felt like a green Lieutenant again.

Sidaris could see that Serling was uncomfortable and he began to vamp.

"So how's D.C.? Forget D.C., we know how D.C. is every time we tune in to CNN or the Cartoon Channel. Fuck D.C. How's the family?"

Sidaris read the answer in Serling's eyes. He walked around the bar and sat next to Serling.

"The same." Serling shrugged. "I see you caught yourself a nice feather bed here."

"Well, hell." Sidaris looked around. "I retired and this thing came up. It's not too bad. The beer's cheap and it gives me more time to spend with my grandkids. My son's a WO Three now over at Fort Riley, Kansas."

"Good for him." Serling remembered the boy graduating from high school. It seemed so many years ago. "Sorry to see you leave the service, Top—Jess. Always thought you'd go for Sergeant Major. It wasn't because of Al Bathra, was it?"

"Naw." Sidaris shook his head but he wouldn't meet Serling's eyes. "Sergeant Major was never for me. Too much politics. I always said I wanted to get out if I ever had the chance at one last good fight. Desert Storm was that for me. After all those . . . mean years after Vietnam and . . . well, I went out happy and proud. Muller!"

A man whom Serling took for an employee scurried over and stood at near attention behind the bar under Sidaris's laser stare—the low setting, roast and broil.

"Yes, Top?"

"Muller, is that a bottle of Johnnie Walker next to the Bushmills? What are the standing orders for bottles behind the bar?"

Muller swallowed hard, glanced at the offending bottle, and turned back to Sidaris.

"Alphabetical order, Top," Muller began. "But I thought maybe since I get more orders for the JW I'd move it where it was handier . . . ?"

"And how am I going to do my inventory with any expedience? And all of the Johnnie Walkers go under the W, not the J. Black, then Red."

"You know, Top . . . ," Muller tried again. Serling figured Muller for a brave man. "I could do the inventory for you."

"It's my responsibility," Sidaris replied. "I'll do the inventory."

Serling had an image of Sidaris, this great modern warrior, the finest soldier he had ever met, taking inventory of cases of beer and bar nuts.

Muller knew the subject was moot and he started to remove the offending bottle.

"I'll take a hit off that Johnnie Walker before you move it," Serling said. His glass was already empty.

Muller brought the bottle over to the bar and again Top poured the drink himself and looked deep into Serling's eyes.

"What do you think, sir . . . Nat?" Sidaris was vamping again. "Alphabetical looks . . . unorderly. Maybe the bottles should be arranged by height, tall to short or vice versa?"

Serling smiled.

"Have you thought of setting them up by usage, most popular to least popular? For peak time efficiency?"

Muller glanced at Serling and Sidaris.

"I've had the thought once or twice. Of course the bar would look . . . untidy." Sidaris smiled. "Efficiency in a bar seems to be counterproductive. I'm in no hurry to make anyone drunk on their ass, but . . . Muller, why don't you draw up a list of liquor sales. I'll think on it."

Muller nodded. "Yes, Top, I'll get on it." Muller walked away smiling. Sidaris winked at Serling, who sipped his drink.

"Say, Top . . . Jess . . ." Serling tried to sound casual. "Have you heard anything from Patella lately?"

"He left the Army," Sidaris answered. "Settled in Florida, I think."

"A good man."

"One of the best gunners I ever saw." Sidaris confirmed Serling's estimation. "It's too bad what he's done to himself."

"What's that?"

"Last time I saw him he was climbing into the bottle so far he could have pulled the cork in after him."

Sidaris looked pointedly at Serling's drink. Subtlety was never one of Top's strong points. Serling couldn't meet Top's eyes.

The emaciated lead singer was suddenly at Sidaris's shoulder, with the other band members gathering behind him.

"Uh . . . mister, we found us a Sly and the Family Stone song we can cover."

"Good." Sidaris nodded. "Now one other thing. See this here VU meter?"

Sidaris pointed to one on the wall behind the bar.

"It goes in the red and I pull the plug." Sidaris walked over to the meter. "Like this."

He flicked a shiny toggle switch next to the meter. The stage lights were cut off. The power lights on the amps were suddenly dark and the microphone went pop.

But Top wasn't finished.

"And I got to recognize the jukebox song. Don't try to get away with any kind of musical camouflage. See you tonight. Nineteen hundred hours. Be on time or I dock your skinny asses."

The band wandered away, not quite sure what they had gotten themselves into.

Sidaris grinned at Serling.

"That's show biz."

The smile faded as Serling filled his glass again.

"Maybe I should visit Patella," Serling said.

"Maybe there's room in that bottle for both of you."

Serling looked at Top, shocked and embarrassed.

"Let me be blunt, sir . . . Nat, whatever . . . if I may."

"You may." Serling could hardly get the words out, his throat suddenly constricted. "Not that you ever needed permission."

"I mean blunt, sir. Now that I'm retired I seem to have this 'fuck you' attitude that goes with old men and young studs. I'd appreciate it if you let me decide which category I fit into.

"Let's talk about Al Bathra."

Sidaris looked directly at Serling, who suddenly felt very cold.

"You fucked up, sir. You made a command decision in a combat environment under hostile fire—and you were wrong. That's the chance you take when you make decisions. Nobody's perfect—not even the sainted General Hershberg. You make decisions and you hope you're right more than you're wrong. Just like any other job. Except when a combat officer fucks up, people get killed. It's a war, sir. People get killed. I repeat for the particularly dense: you are going to make mistakes. Some people will die. But you move on. You try not to make the same mistake twice. And you drive on."

He laid a hand on Serling's shoulder.

"You're a good officer, Nat. The best goddamn combat officer I've seen in my thirty-plus years. You belong with the troops. Get out of babble-land and back into the field. Get past this." He sighed and looked around the bar.

"Now *I* need a drink."

Sidaris grabbed Serling's glass and downed the contents.

Serling tried to smile at the older man.

"Thanks for the advice, Top, but you've said it all before."

"Well, hell, somebody's got to keep saying it until you hear it," Top replied. "Fuck it. I'm getting too salty for my old age. Stick around, sir . . . Nat. We'll talk about the good times. Shoot the shit. Smoke and joke."

"I have to get down to Benning in the morning. Early."

It was a lame excuse but Serling was afraid of staying around Top too much longer. He had come here seeking comfort and now felt only more pain.

Sidaris went behind the bar, opened the cash register. "Duty calls and all that shit."

There was a tap on Serling's shoulder. He turned and saw Ed Bruno beaming like a kid who had just entered the front gates of Disneyland.

"You're a hard man to find, Colonel." Bruno looked at Sidaris. "Bartender, white wine spritz . . . no, make it a beer, light."

Sidaris looked at Bruno without a smile.

"We don't open for another five minutes." And he began counting the money in the register.

Bruno looked at Serling's glass and went on without a hitch—he was bulletproof. He sat down next to Serling.

"You don't like me, Colonel. You don't want me around. I know that, but I'm going to be here, so let's find an accommodation."

Bruno leaned toward Serling conspiratorially.

"You do know that the White House didn't want you on this investigation because of your . . . history. But the General was adamant so I said what the hell. Walden wins . . . sorry, gets the medal, no one's going to ask who checked the bona fides. No one will give a rat's ass about you."

Serling smiled in spite of himself.

"Thanks."

"You're welcome." Bruno took Serling's smile as encouragement. "By the way, just to know where your sympathies lie . . . How do you feel about women in combat?"

"I don't look at Captain Walden as a woman, or as a man for that matter. She was a soldier. And the question is, does that soldier deserve the Medal of Honor? Plain and simple."

"Plain and simple . . ." Bruno chewed on that, letting his doubts show. Serling turned and faced him.

"Mr. Bruno, I don't think I can proceed on this inquiry, and do notice that I said 'inquiry,' not investigation, as you did, with your continued presence. The testimony of the various eyewitnesses and survivors is . . . I feel that your presence may be a hindrance to finding the truth."

"The truth . . ." Bruno mulled that over.

"So as for an accommodation," Serling continued, "this is what I propose. *I* conduct the inquiry. You don't."

"I don't think you understand the function of this inquiry."

"Oh, yes, I do. You're looking for your goddamn photo op. You don't give a damn about Captain Walden, what she did at Al Kufan, the brave men she saved, or what the medal means or stands for. All you care about is a photo of the President hugging Walden's daughter and handing over the medal to her parents because it will get you two minutes of free TV coverage on the six o'clock news. And how that translates into I don't know how many votes or approval rating points."

Serling wound down, reached for his glass, noticed it was empty, and set it aside.

"Videotape," Bruno said.

"Videotape?"

"Video. Still photographs are old hat," Bruno explained. "Video—we live or die by it. You're right, Colonel. I'm not ashamed of my job. That videotape will do us all a lot of good. The President, the Army, me . . . and you, too. Otherwise you wouldn't be here."

Serling nodded. "Then let me do my job. Alone."

"Well, to be blunt, Colonel, there are those who think you might have a personal bias in this inquiry that my presence could ameliorate."

"Bias?"

"Your Al Bathra incident."

Serling looked for Sidaris, wanting to order another drink, but Top was nowhere to be seen. He turned back to Bruno.

"That was then. This is now. I have a mission. I will accomplish that mission to my fullest ability. *No* bias."

"Let's do this, Colonel. Can I call you Nathan? You proceed with your inquiry and send me detailed reports of your findings. Be available for follow-up and keep an eye out for my angle on this. I'll stay scarce. Acceptable?"

Serling nodded. "Acceptable."

The doors to the club opened and Serling turned and saw Lieutenant Chelli and the rest of the survivors of Al Kufan enter the bar. They were a noisy group, full of camaraderie and good spirits. They took a large table in the back.

Sidaris appeared behind the bar and set a glass of beer in front of Bruno.

"We're open now."

"One more for the road, Top?" Serling pushed his empty glass toward Sidaris.

They looked at each other for a second, Sidaris disapproving, Serling entreating.

Sidaris poured the drink. "I said call me Jess."

"Thanks, Jess." Serling savored the burn as the bourbon slid down his throat. "And I'd like to buy that table a round."

Serling gestured toward Chelli and his men and pulled a twenty out of his wallet.

"Who are they?" Sidaris took the twenty.

"Heroes. Real heroes."

Bruno raised his glass to Serling in a toast.

"To heroes, then."

Serling looked hard at Bruno, searching for any mockery or sarcasm. He found none, so he raised his glass.

"Heroes," Serling acknowledged, and finished off his drink.

4

Serling walked through the Post. The sun had gone down. He had skipped lunch and typed up his report at an office provided by Eighty-second Division Head-quarters. The report had been pouched to arrive at the Pentagon and Hershberg's office the next day. Serling had a couple of copies made, one for himself and one that he would send to Ed Bruno as soon as the General gave his okay. He knew the approval would come, but he also knew that when it came to D.C. politics it was best to follow the Washington version of the Golden Rule—cover your ass.

The rest of Serling's time was spent making phone calls and laying track for the next couple of interviews—and fighting the urge to go out and find a place where he could get a drink.

A formation ran by Serling. Young soldiers, Rangers in T-shirts and shorts. They sweated in the damp, hot air, calling cadence.

> *If I die in a combat zone,*
> *Just box me up and send me home.*
> *Put my medals on my chest,*
> *Tell my mom I did my best.*

The pint of Jim Beam rattled in Serling's briefcase. He saw it as a reward for abstaining all afternoon. The drinks at Top's club he figured were a break in his morning vow, but he justified it to himself by the encounter with Bruno. He knew it was a bullshit rationale, but it helped salve over a bit of the guilt. Not much, but it was enough to help him buy the pint.

Entering the Bachelor Officers' Quarters, Serling was surprised at how tired he was. It was an effort to walk up just the four steps. Maybe it was because he wasn't eating right. He had skipped lunch and had dinner at his desk, a sandwich that a helpful SP/4 had gotten for him at the Commissary.

The door to his room opened a few inches when he turned the knob, but then it stuck. There was a manila envelope jammed under the door. Serling pulled it out. Written across the top was a note. "My article, just in case you change your mind." It was signed by First Lieutenant Michael Chelli.

Serling smiled. Persistent little bugger. He tossed the envelope onto the bed. Taking the pint out of his briefcase, he sat in the lone chair the room offered and unscrewed the cap. After pouching his report, he had told his driver to take him to the nearest ABC store and had her wait while he went inside and bought the pint. He slid the pint into his briefcase and felt embarrassed the whole time, like some kid with fake ID.

If you're going to become a professional drunk you're going to have to toughen up, Nat, he told himself.

He smiled to himself, then the humor drained away from him. Setting the bottle down, he paced the room angrily. What he was angry about he wasn't sure.

Serling sat on the bed, suddenly so very tired. It wasn't just physical, though even his bones ached with fatigue, but his very soul felt drained, too.

He was sitting on Chelli's envelope. Yanking it out from under him, Serling looked at it, opened the flap. He was familiar with the document format. He'd written a few of these himself.

"Incident at Al Bathra—Preventative Alternatives to Fratricide."

Fratricide. Serling hated the word. It followed his name more often than the appellation "Colonel." Still, it was better than the old term "friendly fire"—or the word that came up less often but cut him like a knife: murder.

Serling turned the offending cover sheet and began to read.

*

The eerie greenness of the world through the Starlight night scope always made Serling uneasy. Grateful as he was to be able to see in the pitch black darkness, to see the line of tanks that was his company, the crews scrambling around the tanks with last-minute battle preparation, the formation of Bradleys behind the Abrams—pleased as he was to see the readiness of his men, the very greenness of everything set him on edge. It all looked like some damned science fiction movie.

Serling turned the night scope and looked past the Abrams's big gun. The horizon was black, the green hillocks below were the enemy berms. That was what should have unnerved him. But it didn't. His men were ready.

Now he had to climb down from the tank and tell them.

On the ground below his command tank there was a huddle of Lieutenants and Top Sidaris. When Serling joined them they were taking one last look at the map, the red-filtered flashlight splashing off the map and onto their faces.

Serling scanned their faces, looking for any signs of trouble, too much doubt, too much adrenaline. They were fine. Boylar and Massey looked nervous, but that was their usual state on any training mission. Boylar looked a little more nervous than usual, but during previous exercises he always calmed down when the bell went off. Massey used his nervous energy to focus himself and his men. Nothing to worry about there.

Serling looked at Sidaris, who winked, then Serling looked at the map.

"Well, gentlemen, and I use the term loosely, this is it. Those aren't just grease pencil marks on a map anymore, that's the enemy. Saddam's best— but you're better. Don't underestimate the bastards, but remember this— you're better. Hell, we're just plain faster and smarter."

They smiled at those words. Good.

"Keep your intervals, stay on the horn, and roll." Serling looked at each man once more and made eye contact. "Move out."

Boylar was playing nervously with his West Point class ring, worrying it around and around his finger. Everybody got up to go to their respective tanks. Serling laid a hand on Boylar's shoulder. Boylar turned to face his commanding officer.

"I'm okay, Major." Boylar knew the question before it was asked.

"You're more than okay, Phil, you're the best." Serling smiled. "We've been through a lot together. Training, exercises, a few too many parties, and maybe one too many of Top's barbecues. You'll do fine. We're ready. Now let's show the world."

Serling took Boylar's hand and shook it. The Lieutenant nodded, grinned, and trotted off to his Bradley. Serling climbed aboard his Abrams, settled himself into his turret seat, put on his helmet.

Looking down, Serling saw Patella, his gunman, his face lit by the glow of the equipment dials in front of him. Don Patella was from Florida, but he couldn't tan. His pale white face crowned by black hair, he was one of those guys who looked good in a crew cut, but the contrast between the jet hair and his almost albino skin was striking. The men called him Andy Panda.

Patella had the big brown eyes to go with his nickname and he seemed to always have a new girlfriend. Below Serling's left foot was Joey Martinez, the loader, who kept licking the beginnings of a sorry mustache. Martinez had transferred from an Airborne unit, was Ranger trained, and should have been with a Bradley, but he had begged Serling personally for the loader's job—his heartfelt ambition was to be a gunner. Serling, always a sucker for enthusiasm, approved the transfer. Martinez had shined as a loader and was ready for the gunner seat, but there wasn't a slot open at the moment and Serling selfishly wanted the best men in his command tank for this occasion— real combat.

He rechecked his map overlays on the Multi-Function displays, particularly his Commander's Integrated Display, and scanned the sector one more time even though by now he had it all memorized. What was out there? Were they as ready for us as we were for them?

This was the hard part—the waiting. Serling made small talk with the crew. Martinez was thinking of investing in a dry-cleaning business in Austin with his brother. He'd be a silent partner, he said. No one had ever seen Martinez silent for longer than sixty seconds, so the comments flew. The driver, Mark Robins, kept glancing back at Serling from his cab up front, even though they were all hooked into the comm line. Serling knew that eye contact gave the men comfort, and he maintained it.

The tank engine rumbled pleasantly under his seat. Fifteen hundred horses of gas turbine.

It was cold. Bitter, mean cold and the sand was blowing, limiting visibility. Miserable conditions, but it was the same for both sides, Serling reminded himself.

Serling got the warning over the radio from HQ.

"Everybody set?" he asked his crew.

"Yes, sir!" Patella grinned. "Set to give ol' Saddam Insane a whole new way to hurt."

"A whole new paradigm of pain," Robins added.

"A virtual mother lode of pain." Martinez threw in his two bits' worth.

Serling laughed, looked at the sky. It was a deep black, no stars. A pall of black smoke from the burning oil fields of Kuwait blotted out everything; sometimes even the sun couldn't break through during the daylight hours.

There it was! A flare traced a lazy, pretty arc across the horizon to the left.

"Roll out!" Serling commanded. He hunkered into the thermal underwear Meredith had sent him, preparing for the cold night air to become a cold wind when the tank moved.

Robins ducked inside the tank, taking the hatch door down with him.

They began to move. Seventy tons of steel and depleted uranium armor. It was enough to make a soldier feel invulnerable—but they weren't. The Iraqis had a half dozen tricks in their arsenal to take out an M-1A2 Abrams battle tank.

Serling looked left and right. Under the flickering light of the flare he could see hundreds of tanks on line, rolling forward with a great roar of engines and clanking tracks. He felt pride swell in his chest. He was part of this huge land armada.

Checking behind him, Serling saw Boylar's Bradley waiting for their *interval to play out. The Bradleys were ungainly beasts, Serling thought. Snubby cannon, thin armor, and fast, but . . . Just not an Abrams. After the line of tanks had gotten a fifty-meter lead, the rank of Bradleys began to roll with the formation.*

Serling turned his attention to the front.

Just in time. Through the night scope Serling could make out the enemy tanks now, hulking beasts in a line facing the oncoming Americans.

Suddenly the night scope erupted with a long flash of brilliant green. Serling yanked his eyes away from the scope in time to hear the sporadic thunder of the enemy guns. The yellow flashes of HE rounds tore up the desert about three hundred meters in front of the Americans.

The enemy was skittish, firing way before the Abrams was in range. A waste of ammo.

"Hold your fire, hold your fire, gentlemen," Serling crooned to his crew and his company at the same time. "Wait for your range."

The Abrams chewed up the sand, rolling on relentlessly, the undulating terrain suddenly roughened by the sheer speed of the attack. Serling and his crew bounced around inside the tank.

"Patella." Serling still spoke softly. "Find me a target."

"Target, sir!" Patella had been locked on an enemy tank since it had appeared on his night vision.

"Sabot!" Serling called out.

"Up!" Patella called back.

They rolled on.

Another line of flashes erupted from the enemy lines. This time the impacts were much closer to the Abrams. A hundred meters or so. Serling felt himself tighten up. He knew the same nervousness was attacking his men.

Serling kept monitoring the range between the enemy and his tank, allowing himself a fifty-meter fudge factor.

The Abrams outgunned the enemy tanks and had more range. The trick was to fire within that safe zone and make that shot count.

"Fire!" Serling felt himself shouting.

"On the way," Patella returned.

BOOM!

The Abrams rocked with the recoil of the big gun. A millisecond later the other tanks on line fired. The concussion slapped at Serling's eardrums. For a brilliant second, the night became day.

Then a line of fire and flame exploded on the enemy tanks. Secondary explosions, ammo bays cooking off. A turret did a half-gainer into the night sky.

Serling looked into his night scope. Some of the enemy tanks were retreating—quite a few.

Patella was shouting to him.

"We got 'em! Got 'em! Got 'em good!"

"I can see that, Patella." Serling's voice was purposely calm. "Good shooting. Now settle and find me another target."

Patella went back to work.

"Sabot!" he yelled to Martinez.

The loader twisted to his right and banged against the ammo-door switch, which slid open the armored blast door that was supposed to protect the crew from the ammunition storage compartment in case it was hit. It was a good theory, Serling thought, but he wouldn't want to be the man to test it.

Martinez hefted a sabot round, releasing the knee switch and letting the door slam shut automatically. He rammed the round into the breech with his right arm and then, hand clear, yelled, "Up!"

"Target, sir!"

They loaded and fired three more times before the Abrams rolled past the first line of crippled enemy tanks.

The Iraqi armor was still burning. A few bodies were strewn across the battlefield. One of the bodies had flames dancing on the dead soldier's back. Serling hoped the man was dead.

Secondary explosions kept startling Serling. He remained alert for any enemy gunfire. An enemy tank to his right boomed deeply, and the back end flew fifteen feet into the air.

Serling monitored the traffic from Battalion and the radio talk from his own company, while Top kept them all in formation. Everything seemed to be going well.

Serling rolled on. Past the dead tanks. The enemy berm had been breached but there were hostile tanks ahead, fleeing the battlefield. Serling kept his eyes and instruments on them.

What Serling didn't see was the sand behind him writhing and shifting next to the tanks he had just destroyed.

And then, like giant creatures rising from the bowels of the earth, four tanks emerged from the desert behind Serling's line of Abrams tanks. T-55s, Russian made. Big, ugly, mean-looking chunks of steel.

The T-55 turrets swiveled and aimed their big guns at the very vulnerable rear ends of the American tanks that had just rolled past. They were in prime position within the American lines. The Bradleys were still coming up on them but the big Russian armor had little to worry about from the Bradleys' comparatively puny weaponry.

The T-55s fired!

A column of flame belched from each of the four cannons!

Serling was on the horn with Lagani, trying to reel in the eager Lieutenant who was in hot pursuit of the fleeing enemy, when the tank to his left blew up!

"Holy shit!" Serling shouted into the helmet mike. "Where did that come from?!! Black Four! Black Four! This is Black Six! Red Three was just taken out! Anybody see the shooter?!"

The radio was sudden verbal chaos. Tank commanders calling in with negative sightings, others wanting more information.

"Patella! You see where that came from?!" Serling was frantically scanning the horizon.

"I didn't see anything fire!" Patella was yelling. Serling didn't need the intercom to hear him.

Patella was peering through his optics, intent on spotting any sign.

"All I see is Arab butt, Major."

Serling looked left and right, searching for a stray ground trooper with a shoulder-mounted antitank weapon. Then he swiveled around to search the rear flank.

Just in time to see four points of light. Four blossoms of yellow and orange.

Before he could react, the Abrams to his right blew up! The tread flew off and the tank spun in a circle, tossing up a rooster tail of sand. He ordered his company to halt on line.

"Turn about! Turn about!" Serling ordered Robins, the driver. "Who's that firing at our rear?! I have cannon fire at my rear flank! Black Four! Black Four! This is Black Six! Is that our Bradleys?!"

"Black Six, this is Black Four!" It was Top Sidaris. "Our Bradleys haven't fired."

"Patella, what do you see?!" Serling called down.

The Abrams's turret was now facing the rear. Patella and Serling both peered into their night scopes.

"Hard to make out, sir," Patella returned.

Visibility was impaired by sand and smoke from the burning tanks.

BOOM! Four more orange bursts from the rear.

The sand exploded a few meters from Serling's tank. He ducked into the relative safety of his Abrams.

"Black Six, this is Black Four!" It was Top again. "Red Three says he

has enemy tanks in his lines. I say again: enemy tanks in our Red lines. Have engaged. Over!"

Boylar had the enemy inside his formation. Serling squinted into the dark. Robins had halted the tank at Serling's order, so it was easier to see.

Pinpricks of light, waving lines of red tracers, were the only signs of the firefight in progress.

"Nature of the enemy?" Serling asked.

"Think they're T-55s," was Top's reply.

Boylar was in trouble. Neither his armor nor his guns were any match for the Russian tanks.

"Patella, find me a target," Serling ordered.

"Got one, sir!" Patella called out, and added, "I think."

"I think?!" Serling repeated. "Do you or do you not have a target, Patella?!"

Peering out of the turret without instrument assistance but with his naked eye, Serling saw what looked like Bradley 25mm cannon fire. The T-55 boomed back. The Bradley fired again. Just spots of flame in the darkness.

"Got one, sir!"

Serling hoped Patella was right. He checked his instruments. He couldn't distinguish the T-55s from the Bradleys.

"Sabot!"

There was gunfire all across the battlefield. Battalion had ordered the assault to continue while Serling dealt with the sudden rear action.

"Up!" Patella called out.

Serling tried to see what Patella saw.

Machine gun fire ricocheted off his tank, the tracers glancing off and spinning lazily into the dark. Serling ducked reflexively, then came up.

"Sir?" Patella cried out. "Round up!"

Serling saw the Abrams on his right take another hit. He heard a man scream. Whether it was over the comm line or through the air, he couldn't tell.

"Sir?" Patella again.

"Fire!" Serling yelled.

"On the way!"

His Abrams's big gun bellowed. The tank lurched with the recoil. The muzzle blast kicked up a cloud of dust in front of Serling. He waited for it to settle, eyes glued to the night scope.

"Black Six, this is Four." Top's voice was flat. "We just lost Red Three."

Boylar. Serling tried not to let the information distract him from the job at hand. He had a company in danger.

"Target," Serling called out.

"Got one, sir!" Patella was as ready as ever.

Serling looked through the night scope at the burning vehicle they had just hit. It was on fire and the flames helped outline the target.

It was a Bradley.

Patella must have seen it at the same time.

"Oh, God . . ." Patella's voice was a whisper.

"Boylar . . ." Serling acknowledged.

"Patella, are you sure we aren't firing at our own Bradleys?!" Serling had to ask.

"They fired, sir!" Patella's voice was straining.

"At us or the T-55s?"

"At . . . oh, God . . ." Patella's voice broke.

BOOM!

A round landed fifteen meters from Serling's Abrams. His tank shuddered with the concussive impact. Shrapnel clanged off the armor.

"Sir, we're taking fire!" That was Martinez.

Serling looked through his night vision. He couldn't tell the Bradleys from the Russian tanks. If he fired again he might take out another of his own.

"Sir?!" It was Robins, the driver. He hardly ever spoke, but the worry was evident in his voice. Tension drew Serling's muscles taut, waiting for the next enemy round to come, this time on target.

"Black Four, this is Black Six!" Serling said into the comm line. "Order all Bradleys to turn ninety degrees and stop. Ninety and stop. Understand? Over."

"Ninety and stop. Roger. Out," Top responded.

"Patella!" Serling called below. "Target?"

Serling had his eyes glued to the Commander's Display. He saw some of the vehicles turn sideways, some not.

"Tank, sir!"

"Front on or side on?"

"Front on!"

"Sabot!"

"Up!"

"Fire!"

"On the way!"

BOOM!

The Abrams bucked. Serling heard the rest of his company firing, following his example. Top had heard what he was doing and he proceeded in kind, just as Serling knew he would.

This time there was less dust.

Serling saw a T-55 explode. Then another. All four enemy tanks took multiple hits.

"We got 'em, sir!" Patella grinned widely. There was also a lot of cheering on the radio traffic.

Serling was oblivious. He just stared through the dust, waiting for it to settle again.

THE sun was creeping up into a bloodred dawn, trying to burn through the smoke from Kuwait and the added haze from the smoldering tanks on the battlefield.

Serling rode his tank across the sand, not even looking at the crippled enemy tanks or the twisted remains of the dead.

One word to Robins and the Abrams stopped.

Serling climbed down and began to walk.

Toward the Bradleys.

They were still on line, where they had fought the T-55s. The Iraqi tanks had scored a few hits; some disabled American vehicles were dead in their tracks. Maintenance crews were already dragging one of them off the battlefield. Serling ignored these armored casualties. His focus was on one Bradley.

Roiling black smoke still tumbled out of the rent hole punched through the light armor by the Abrams's big gun.

An arm hung out of the hatch.

Medics were treating wounded on the ground near the Bradley. But none of the men were from Red Three. The crew from Red Three was dead.

Serling knew the wounded soldiers, he knew he should walk over to them, see how his men were doing. But he couldn't face them right now—and wondered if he ever could.

Serling walked up to the smoking Bradley, his eyes focused on the blackened arm, on the hand—and the ring on one finger. A West Point ring. Class of '90.

Boylar.

Serling felt his professional demeanor, the soldier face he had kept throughout the rest of the battle, begin to dissolve. He started to cry. Deep sobs wrenched from his chest. They came suddenly, surprising him, and he fought to remain standing as the naked emotion took the strength from his legs.

Serling tore himself away from the Bradley and faced the red dawn, letting the dust blow into his face, feeling the sting in his eyes and not caring.

He had killed four men.

His own men.

It was his fault.
And always would be.

✳

Serling partially awoke once during the night. Whether or not it was The Dream that had awakened him, he wasn't sure. He never awoke fully, he just surveyed the room with muddled perceptions, as if he were underwater. The lights were still on. He figured out where he was, glanced at Chelli's article. The white pages scattered across the floor were so brilliant they hurt his eyes. He pried off his shoes. His feet suddenly hurt where the laces had bitten into the skin. He unbuttoned his shirt, loosened his belt, and saw the pint; a half inch of amber liquid still remained.

He emptied the bottle down his throat, almost gagging from the burn. It satisfied something inside him to have emptied the bottle–completion. Hell, if you're going to be a drunk, be neat about it. "If you're going to be a bear, be a grizzly," was the way Top Sidaris used to put it.

Serling's mind drifted then, following Top Sidaris to their first assignment together–as Platoon Leader and Platoon Sergeant. It was love at first sight of an order that few civilians could understand. Serling had tried to explain it once to Meredith, but gave up. Top and Serling were made for each other–in a military way. Serling smiled at the thought. An instant team that magnified their respective strengths and filled in the gaps where each was weak.

And they had the knack of doing the same for their unit, platoon or company. They learned from each other. Serling's quick tactical mind, Top's ability to get men to follow him. Together they made a unit that could and would do anything assigned to them with enthusiasm and with dispatch. They were glorious.

Serling's mind did a roll call of the men he had commanded,

84

worked with, grown up with, or watched grow up. Boys who became men. Losers who took control of their lives. Incompetents who finally found their calling.

Risco, Faley, Cousins, the Gunther twins. Tomzak, Wong, Stelinger, Szebin . . . Faces that flickered by, most of them smiling for some reason.

Boylar . . . When the young Lieutenant had come to the company, he was on the verge of being cashiered out of the Army. "An attitude problem," was how Brigade had put it. Boylar's last chance. Top and Serling had taken the angry young man and had seen something in him. The men liked Boylar, but he couldn't relate to any of his superior officers. Serling and Top ran interference for Boylar, keeping him away from the brass, and they tried to find out what made the young officer tick.

They finally discovered that Boylar was just one of those anal types who needed to know the why and wherefore of everything before he could move. So Serling fed him information. Battalion Intelligence, Brigade tactics, Divisional theories, data that the line officer usually had no need for or truck with, but Boylar sucked it in until he was a consummate field officer. Serling was grooming Boylar for Brigade S-2 or S-3, Intelligence, or Operations, and the man's new attitude and record would guarantee the slot—when Desert Storm erupted.

Boylar . . .

One of Serling's success stories. There had been a few failures, but most of the time, between Serling and Top, anyone could be turned into a competent soldier.

Boylar . . .

Serling felt his eyes begin to tear up.

Boylar . . . one of the tribe. "The Tribe" was what Top had designated his and Serling's unit. The men took to the name, platoon or company. "The Tribe." Boylar had gone and gotten a flag made, which still hung in Serling's office in D.C.

Boylar . . .

Serling refused to cry.

He lay back on the bunk and closed his eyes.

Sometime far into the night he slept again, waking only once more to see if there was anything left in the pint.

There wasn't.

5

Serling awoke sluggish and tried
to shower the fog out of his head,
then dressed in civilian clothes
and took the shuttle van to the
Fayetteville Airport. From there
he flew to Atlanta and ran the vast
gauntlet of the Atlanta Terminal
to catch another little prop to
Columbus, Georgia. Both times
the plane was something called a
Brasilia 120 and on each trip he
bumped his head on the narrow
little cabin ceiling.

He used to travel in his uniform all the time. He was so proud of it: the medals on his chest, the rank on his collar. But these days he preferred civvies, mainly because the uniform usually instigated a conversation with the traveler next to him and the obvious questions came up.

"You in the Army?" That was the dumber and easier question to answer. "Were you in the Gulf War?" That was more difficult. "What did you do there?" That was impossible for him to respond to with any composure.

He shared a cab with three fresh-faced PFCs to Fort Benning. They were in their Class-A uniforms, pants bloused into their spit-shined jump boots, snappy Royal Artillery red berets. They let him have the front seat, though whether it was out of deference to his rank or age, Serling wasn't sure.

One of the paratroopers was a woman, tall and pretty, with a tattoo at the nape of her neck. It was a skull with a red clown nose. Serling was more than curious about her story, but he didn't ask. She seemed intimidated by his rank.

The Post seemed to go on forever. They drove miles beyond the WELCOME TO FORT BENNING sign before they even made a turn. Serling had the cab drop him at the Temporary Officers Billet, made a call to his liaison, and changed into his duty uniform. By the time he was dressed, his vehicle and driver were waiting outside.

The driver was a baby-faced Asian PFC. He wasn't talkative but he hummed constantly to himself and drummed on the steering wheel. Serling occupied himself trying to guess what the song was that the PFC heard in his head. Either Serling was more out of touch with current music or the PFC drove to a truly different drummer.

They passed the 250-foot red-and-white towers belonging to the Jump School, and Serling thought back to the miserable three weeks he had spent in Parachute School, capped off by the final glorious two days of jumping out of planes. He saw the Jump School students running all over the PLF course, trailed by the cadre shouting at their heels like angry dogs, and he felt great empathy with the poor Airborne hopefuls who were gasping for breath and grunting as they hit the ground, practicing their Prepared Landing Falls over and over and over.

Jump School had once been important to Serling. The jaunty cut of the garrison cap, the spit-shined jump boots, pant cuffs bloused into the boot tops. The Jump wings over his left pocket. Sometimes he thought he had joined the Army just for the uniform.

For a poor kid from Chicago who'd never had a set of new clothes—everything was either hand-me-downs or Salvation Army bargains—the crisp lines of the uniform with the medals and decorations always appealed to Serling. That's why he joined ROTC in high school. But even that uniform was used, bought off a kid who had dropped out. Serling's mother sewed, and she had taken in the shirt and jacket and it hadn't looked too bad on him.

When Serling had joined the Army right out of high school and attended college at Western Michigan, the new uniform issued at Basic Training seemed like the wardrobe of a prince. It made him special. And he had always wanted to be special, not just another poor kid without a future and without hope. Meredith had liked him in uniform; she said she fell in love with him when she first saw him in it, walking down the dirty streets of his neighborhood, the mean streets of North Lawndale, standing proudly on the corner of Sixteenth and Springfield.

The uniform *did* make him special. The Airborne wings and the patch only added to it. Ranger offered additional elitism, and Serling thought he was headed for Special Forces and the beret, the elite of the elite. But then Serling visited an old ROTC buddy at Fort Knox and had his first ride in an Abrams.

The tank was big, imposing, ugly. The noise was phenomenal compared to the pleasant stillness Serling cherished as he floated down to earth hanging from his parachute. Then the buddy let Serling take the cockpit. And there Serling found a home, a place he felt comfortable, a place where he felt whole, complete.

Serling immediately transferred out of Airborne Infantry and into Armor, giving up his jump status to get the assignment. He hadn't looked back or regretted it once.

The PFC driver took the HumVee along the runway to a far corner of Lawson Army Airfield, where the big lumbering workhorse C-130s were landing and taking off. A jet engine, off the plane and mounted on a fixed platform, was being tested. The noise was amazing, filling the air with an all-encompassing thunder that left room for nothing else. As Serling passed by it, the temperature of the air suddenly shot from the mid-eighties to a superheated hundred plus.

There was a company of soldiers lined up on the tarmac, their weapons and packs at their feet. Some read paperbacks, others smoked, but all waited for a C-141 Starlifter that was rolling down the belly door a few meters away.

The HumVee settled to a stop in front of a small pair of Quonset huts perched on the edge of the runway. Two helicopters, a Huey and a Blackhawk, rested on the baking cement in front, their blades hanging down as if they too were feeling the heat and the humidity.

A sign above the door declared, 264TH MEDICAL COMPANY—AIR AMBULANCE. Serling climbed out of the HumVee and opened the door. He immediately felt the cool relief of an air conditioner, a small one plugged into one of the windows and grinding away noisily.

The SP/5 behind the desk had to speak in a loud voice to be heard above the AC.

"Help you, sir?"

"I'm looking for Major Teegarden."

"In the back, sir."

The SP/5 jerked a thumb toward an aisle that led through the cubicle partitions. Serling followed the gesture into what looked like a ready area, where two long folding tables, a counter with the ubiquitous coffee machine, and a half dozen folding chairs stood.

Major Donald Teegarden, a tanned, balding man with a blond mustache and blue eyes that broadcast an immediate amiability, was playing a Gameboy with a Captain Byers. Byers was an African American with coffee-and-cream complexion; smooth, unlined skin; and hard eyes. He was soft-looking, but not overweight.

Serling waited until Teegarden turned the Gameboy over to Byers for his turn before he interrupted.

"Major Teegarden? Lieutenant Colonel Nat Serling. I'm doing the follow-through on your Medal of Honor recommendation for Captain Walden."

"Really? It's about time."

Serling liked the fact that Teegarden didn't seem embarrassed to be caught screwing around with a kid's game while on duty. The man was confident he had his company in order and could relax.

"Gladtomeetcha. This is Captain Dan Byers. What took you so long? I submitted that recommendation in '91."

"It had to find its way through the Pentagon."

"Nuff said." Teegarden smiled. "Coke? Coffee?"

Despite the AC chugging away at the other end of the building, Serling was warm. A cold Coke would have felt good, but he needed the extra caffeine from a cup of coffee to fight off the aftereffects of his bad night.

"Coffee'd be nice. Black."

Teegarden got up and performed the honors himself. Another

point in the man's favor as far as Serling was concerned. He hated officers who treated their staff like slaves. Serling took the proffered cup and settled into a chair.

"Can you break down the events of twenty-six and twenty-seven February '91 for me?" Serling began.

"Sure thing," Teegarden replied easily. Byers continued with the Gameboy, ignoring the two men.

"I'm on call if that's okay," Teegarden said. Serling nodded.

"Let's see . . . I sent out Dust-Off Two, Warrant Officer Fowler, at about ten-twenty hours to evac the troops from that vehicular accident. You're familiar with the file?"

Serling nodded again and sipped at the hot coffee, wishing he had gone for the Coke instead.

"We were getting ready to move forward," Teegarden went on. "To provide support for elements of the Eighty-second Airborne and the Twenty-fourth Mech."

"Captain Fowler's evac, it was a routine run?" Serling asked.

"Well, kinda routine. We were in Iraq by then. Captain Fowler couldn't fly above one hundred feet, that was our ceiling. Strictly NOE—nape-of-the-earth flying. So the fixed wings could go low for their bombing runs. Our radios lost contact below two fifty, three hundred. So we were deaf. And there was the dust and then the smoke from Kuwait, the oil-field fires. Visibility was nil, so we were blind, too. And sand everywhere—"

"Sandstorms, sand devils, sand-outs!" Byers suddenly interrupted vehemently. "Sand in the rotor, sand in the fuel, sand in the intakes. Sand in your eyes, sand in your nose, your ears, your food, your water, your mouth, up your ass, sand in places you didn't even know you had places. I'm still finding sand and I've been home for years. Sorry."

Byers seemed embarrassed at his outburst and he self-consciously went back to his Gameboy.

Serling and Teegarden smiled at each other.

"When did you realize that Fowler's ship might be in trouble?" Serling asked.

"Well . . ." Teegarden thought for a moment, got up, and went to a refrigerator and pulled out a Mountain Dew for himself. The can was frosted with drops of water, just like in the commercials. Serling took a gulp of coffee, looking for comfort in the caffeine.

"You sort of know how long a mission takes—how long en route, the pickup, how long to the MASH, how long to return. I give 'em some leeway. I gave Fowler almost an hour. Then I called HQ. They confirmed the pickup. Then I got the MASH unit on the horn and found out Fowler hadn't delivered. I wasn't that worried at first. A sandstorm could have put 'em down."

Teegarden looked at Byers as if he were the expert on sand and all its manifestations. Byers responded to the presumed role of authority.

"Sometimes the visibility was so bad you had to put down and wait it out. It usually blew over."

"But I called Air Rescue anyway," Teegarden added, and was about to continue when the SP/5 came into the room.

"Major, we have a possible heat exhaustion on the small-arms range."

Teegarden turned to Byers.

"Dan, grab that for me?"

Byers put away the Gameboy and grabbed his flight helmet off the wall as he hurried out the door. Through the window Serling could see a crew join Byers at the Blackhawk.

"Heatstroke can roll out of heat exhaustion," Teegarden explained. "Heatstroke can kill."

Serling knew that from experience, but he nodded.

"How did Captain Walden get involved in the search for Dust-

Off Two?" Serling asked, raising his voice over the noise of the Blackhawk revving up.

"She came to me." Teegarden turned to watch the Blackhawk lift off, then continued. "When she first came to my unit, Walden rode co-pilot with Fowler during her orientation. They were friends. They'd traded envelopes."

"Traded envelopes?" Serling asked.

"When we first got there—on the way over, actually—we each wrote a letter to . . . whoever. In case we didn't come back."

Teegarden looked at Serling, needing to explain. "We didn't know what we were getting into. Saddam's crack army, best in the world, in one war or another for years. We were . . . green. So we wrote these letters and traded them. You know, 'In case anything happens to me send this to my folks, my wife . . .' "

Teegarden stopped abruptly, shook off the emotion, and smiled tentatively.

"I actually found Captain Walden's letter in Fowler's footlocker when we packed his . . . effects. I sent it to her folks. I guess they didn't consider the possibility that they both might not come back. . . ."

Serling let Teegarden compose himself. "Captain Walden and Fowler were close." It was a statement, not a question.

"No closer than anyone else. No romance or anything, if that's what you're implying."

"I'm not implying anything." Serling kept his voice neutral.

"We were all close. Just the few of us, four choppers and their crews. Most of the time we were off by ourselves. We were . . . yeah, close. Combat close. Know what I mean?"

"I was in a tank unit in Desert Storm. I know how close you get— especially in combat. I'm sorry if I implied anything else." Serling wasn't sorry but he had other hard questions to ask. He continued. "So, Captain Walden approached you."

"We were all monitoring the rescue channels." Teegarden was mollified for the moment. "Captain Walden came to me. Karen knew Fowler, knew his flying habits, she thought she could retrace his route."

"You agreed?"

"Yes. We're Medevac. Rescue is our business, too."

"I'm not questioning your decision, Major," Serling said, backpedaling. Teegarden was a temperamental one—or he was hiding something. "So she went."

"Not right away." Teegarden was calm again, almost amiable. "I made her wait for an hour in case Air Rescue came up with something. Then I said okay. I made her strap on the extra fuel pods. She was not to attempt evacuation. There were too many on Fowler's Blackhawk for the Huey anyway. Walden's mission was to spot Dust-Off Two, go for altitude, and call in the location, then render what aid they could until the rescue team arrived. Those were my orders."

Teegarden looked at Serling eye to eye.

"Those were my orders," Teegarden repeated.

Serling met the challenge, knowing that silence was a better lever than any question he could pose. It was a contest.

A contest that neither man won as the SP/5 came in again.

"Sir, Medevac at Range Thurman. Bee sting."

Teegarden pulled away from Serling's gaze.

"Roger. On it," he said to the Specialist and turned back to Serling. "I've got to take this."

Serling couldn't tell if the Major was glad for the interruption or not. "Bee sting?" he queried.

Teegarden was already to the door, grabbing his helmet.

"For some people it could lead to anaphylactic shock. Could be fatal. Come along if you want."

Teegarden tossed a spare helmet to Serling. Another challenge? Serling took it.

Serling had to run to catch up with Teegarden on the chopper pad. The rest of the crew and the co-pilot were already climbing into the Huey. Serling watched them with pleasure. Working as a team. They had done this thousands of times. The Crew Chief helped Serling hook up his helmet to the intercom, then guided him to a bulkhead seat, and Serling buckled up. Serling listened in on the crew's bantering as they cranked up the big rotor. He was envious. He missed this so much, the synchronization of human endeavor toward one task, and he relished the apparent ease with which Teegarden and his crew went about their assignment.

The chopper lifted off. Serling's stomach flopped once, twice, then settled in for the ride—a definite E ticket, better than any roller coaster.

Once they achieved altitude, Teegarden came over the intercom to tell Serling he could continue if he wanted. Serling paused for a long moment. This wasn't the way he preferred to conduct an interview. He couldn't see Teegarden's face, just the back of his helmet, and he was afraid the communication system and helicopter noise disguised any nuance of language. But Teegarden wasn't under investigation here, he was just part of the inquiry. Serling thought it was all right to go ahead, but would keep the more delicate questions until he could see Teegarden's face again.

"Did Captain Walden file a flight plan?"

"Not as such," Teegarden responded. "But we discussed her route. She was going to follow the Euphrates, along the eastern bank. Fowler used to say he flew English style, on the wrong side of the road. Some kind of silly business designed to confuse the enemy. I used to tell Fowler that personally I thought *he* was confused, but . . ."

Even over the noise of the chopper and the static on the communications system Serling could hear the emotion choke up Teegarden's voice. The man cared about his men, at least he had cared about Fowler.

"Finally I told Karen, Captain Walden, that she could fly," Teegarden resumed, his voice composed once more.

"Finally?" Serling prodded.

"Well, to tell the truth, I was delaying her as much as I could, hoping that Air Rescue would come up with something. I suppose that's why by the time Walden went down, didn't report back, it was nearly dark and we couldn't . . . Anyway, Walden was insistent, so I said okay. Besides, I figured there couldn't be any harm in having another pair of eyes out there looking for Fowler."

"Are you feeling some reservations about your decision now?" Serling ventured.

"What the hell does that have to do with the actions of Captain Walden on twenty-six and twenty-seven February '91?"

No nuance lost there.

"None, Major. I just—" Serling stopped himself from apologizing. He was out of line, they both knew it. He didn't know where that question had come from. He tried to find a way back to the inquiry.

"Did you have any contact with Captain Walden after she left your base camp?"

He could see Teegarden shake his head.

"We lost contact after she was twenty minutes or so out. She was keeping low. Like I said, our ceiling was down to give the jets a lower profile. She put down just once because a dust storm degraded visibility."

"You learned this on the radio?"

"No. That I learned after the action."

"Please stay with what you personally witnessed. I'll be interviewing the crew later. Why did you send along Specialist Altameyer and the machine gun? Isn't that unusual for a Medevac?"

"Well . . ." Teegarden seemed to be scanning the area ahead, or maybe he was just searching for an answer.

"There'd been reports of aircraft taking ground fire along the Euphrates. Nothing of consequence. Could have been some trigger-happy Bedouins. Those people fire guns in the air like kids wave at trains. Plus, Walden's mission was not to evacuate, just locate and report, so she had the room. Call it CYA. 'Cover your ass,' you know. I hear everyone in the Pentagon has that tattooed on their chest."

The crew laughed. Serling didn't know if the joke was aimed at him, nor did he care.

"Where did you find Altameyer?"

"He was always hanging around the company area. He had a hard-on for choppers."

"Don't we all?" That was the Crew Chief. He winked at Serling.

The terrain below had shifted from endless acres of barracks and administration buildings to a rolling carpet of Georgia pine forest, interrupted by red clay access roads and the occasional firing range.

Serling remembered his days on the range himself. He never was a good shot, especially with the pistol, and qualifying had been hell for him.

They passed over one of the drop zones the Jump School used, a large patch of plowed field.

Serling didn't recognize it, but he remembered being dragged through the dirt and dust by a wind-driven chute, desperately clawing at his sand-filled quick releases, trying to set himself free.

The helicopter banked and circled the next range. Gravity pulled Serling toward the open door. Serling saw the yellow smoke first, then the four men who had popped it to mark the landing zone. The Huey began to descend. There was a small grandstand for classes and a group of soldiers had circled another who was prone on the ground, being tended to by a pair of medics.

Serling tried to remember his next question. "So the next time you heard anything of Walden's situation . . ."

"It was a rough night. As soon as the sun went down and neither aircraft had returned . . ." Teegarden seemed to have no problem flying and talking, as if he were driving to work on the Beltway.

"I don't think anyone in the company got any sleep. At first light, Division Intelligence and Search and Rescue reported that they had satellite infrared photos of what they thought might be our two birds. We cranked up and went in with the rescue party. I flew one Huey, Captain Liebman was in our other Blackhawk."

The Huey set its skids on the ground, kicking up loose foliage and a cloud of dust. Four soldiers started toward the chopper, toting an improvised poncho litter. Teegarden's medic sprinted toward them with his aid bag and they all huddled for a few seconds. Then the medic led the litter bearers back to the chopper.

Serling helped the Crew Chief and medic get the injured man aboard. The soldier was red in the face, his eyes swollen, cheeks puffing out, saliva running from the corners of his mouth, and he was gasping for air. The medic hooked his helmet back into the intercom.

"Let's get this dude to the hospital stat. He's swelling up like a blowfish. I've poked him with epinephrine, but we got to get him some serious help before his throat swells shut."

Teegarden rogered that and the chopper lifted off with another cloud of flying debris and dust. He called ahead to the Base Hospital and briefed them on the patient.

Suddenly the patient began pulling on Serling's arm, bloodshot eyes flicking around the chopper in panic.

"Hold him, sir"—the medic looked at Serling—"hold him still."

Serling held the man down while the medic reached into his aid bag and withdrew a scalpel. There must have been something in Serling's expression because the medic spoke to him again.

"It's okay, sir. He's not getting any air. I need to trach him. Hold him good."

Serling put all of his weight on the patient's shoulders and was nearly bucked off as the terrified man began to thrash around. His hands shot to his face, and his mouth went wide in panic, sucking for air that wouldn't come.

The medic calmly put the struggling man's head between his knees, and with a flash of polished steel cut a two-inch slot in the hollow of his throat.

There wasn't much blood, but the man's exertions increased. Serling couldn't hold him still. The medic was trying to insert a white tube into the slot, but the patient was fighting them both. The Crew Chief tried to help, but the man fought against all three of them with desperate strength.

Serling got down close to the man's ear.

"You're going to be okay, troop. Just relax. You're in the best of hands. Just relax. Help us here."

Slowly, the man settled down.

The tube went in.

"I got him now, sir. Thanks." The medic smiled at Serling, who went back to his seat and buckled in again.

"Any more questions, Colonel?" Teegarden asked over the intercom.

"Uh, yes, a few. Where were we? What did you see when you arrived at the crash site?"

"Two wasted choppers. They were so shot up they looked like termites had been at 'em. I was surprised anyone was alive."

"And the tactical situation?"

"They were encircled by a hundred, maybe more, enemy troops moving in under cover of fire. Oh, and a wasted tank on the northwest ridgeline. While the jet jockey and the gunships kept the enemy busy, Liebman picked up the Blackhawk survivors and I took the three off Walden's Huey. Once we were assured there were no other survivors, we lifted out of there."

"You called in the Willy Peter strike?"

"Yes." The answer was firm, immediate. "It was a hot LZ. We couldn't stay to retrieve the bodies without encountering casualties of our own. When Monfriez, Walden's Crew Chief, told me that Captain Walden and her co-pilot were both dead . . . Well, we all saw the footage on CNN when they dragged our dead boys through the streets of Baghdad. I wasn't going to let that happen to any of my people. Especially a woman. And don't think that's a sexist remark. I . . . cared about those . . . They died . . . bravely. I wasn't going to let anyone desecrate . . . So, yes, I called in the air strike. A cremation if you will."

"You never saw the bodies of Walden or Rady or the Blackhawk crew?"

"No, I didn't. I've seen enough dead people."

Teegarden was getting testy again.

"Nor did your Crew Chief or medic?"

"Negative, sir."

It was a formal no.

"We were under fire, sir." That was the Crew Chief again. Serling was surprised.

"You were there, too, Chief . . . ?" Serling looked at the Crew Chief's name tag: Daleski.

"Yes, sir." Daleski seemed pleased that Serling was surprised. "I've been with the Major since Hood. He can't fly without me. Something about proper ballast."

Serling heard Teegarden chuckle over the intercom.

"We took some hits on the rescue. One just missed the universal—millimeters away from it," Daleski went on. "WO Liebman's Blackhawk took some, too. They had a man wounded in the evac. Medic . . . Berg."

Serling nodded. The Crew Chief was trying to pull his pilot's fat out of the fire.

"Major Teegarden"—Serling wasn't going to let him off the hook yet—"when did you learn about the events that occurred on the Huey during the previous night?"

"At the MASH." Teegarden's tone was civil again as he surveyed the ground below. They were flying above barracks and paved roads again. "Altameyer, Ilario, and Monfriez started talking. That's when I wrote up the citation. I didn't expect the Medal of Honor would actually come through. Most of them get knocked down to a Silver Star or the Air Medal, but . . . I wanted everybody to know how extraordinarily this soldier had performed."

The chopper made a gentle touchdown on the pad in front of the Base Hospital. Doctors and nurses were ready with a gurney. They rushed toward the chopper, ducking under the whirling rotor blades. The patient was hefted out and wheeled into the emergency room. The medic went with them.

The rest of the crew remained in the Huey, the prop rotating slowly.

Serling took a moment.

Then he asked.

"Why did she do it?"

The question seemed to catch Teegarden by surprise.

"I . . . I don't know. Does anyone?"

"Was Walden . . . overly aggressive? Was she a hot dog?"

"No. Very conscientious. A highly motivated individual, but not a Nintendo jockey."

"Then why did she do it?" Serling asked the question again. "Why didn't she just go for altitude and call in the location?"

"And watch that tank chew up Fowler and his crew . . . ? The evac patients . . . People were in trouble. We help people in trouble. It's our job."

"Would any of your other pilots have done the same thing?"

"I don't know. Would I? I don't know. I hope so. I'd hope we all have in us whatever Captain Walden found that day. But . . . was she a hot dog? Was she Audie Murphy? Why did she do it? What does this have to do with the citation?"

"Nothing. Just curious." Serling tried to sound casual.

"Same here. Same here," Teegarden replied.

The medic came back toting five cans of Dr. Pepper. Teegarden lifted off with a Dr. Pepper in his lap as casually as if he were cruising for burgers down the local drag.

To Serling the cold soda was nectar. He was parched and, without realizing it, he emptied the can in seconds.

"You put Altameyer, Ilario, and Monfriez in for the Silver Star and Air Medal," Serling noted without a question in his voice, just probing.

"Yes." Teegarden's voice stiffened. "And they deserved it. They received them, too."

"Good men?" Serling asked.

"The best."

"Then why did you transfer them out of your unit after Desert Storm?"

"Well, Altameyer wasn't mine in the first place, he was an MP,"

Teegarden answered nonchalantly. "You'll have to ask his CO. Ilario and Monfriez requested transfer, for a variety of reasons—their own. I had no call to deny them. After what they'd done at Al Kufan it was the least I could do for them. The least."

They were returning to the chopper pad and Serling remained silent until they landed. The crew stowed their gear and everyone disembarked. The chopper blades ground to a stop.

"Did anyone hear any M-16 fire during the evacuation?"

Teegarden took off his helmet and looked at Serling.

"I heard all sorts of gunfire, big and little. Couldn't much tell one from the other. Except the Cobra's miniguns, never could mistake them."

"I heard M-16," the Crew Chief said. Serling turned to him.

"When?"

"When I ran out to help bring in Monfriez."

"How close did you get to Walden's Huey?"

"Not close. I could hardly see it, it was behind some rocks and shit. I wasn't looking for it anyway. There was enemy fire all over the fucking place, machine gun fire chipping at the rocks all around us. . . . I just helped get the evacuees into our bird so we could get the fuck out of there."

"But you heard an M-16."

"Yep. Distinct as hell."

"From where?"

"Who could tell? Like the Major said, the whole LZ was hot with gunfire. But I heard a sixteen, sure as shit."

"Thanks."

"Don't mention it."

Teegarden was waiting for Serling and they walked back to the Quonset hut together.

"Is she gonna get it?" Teegarden finally asked. "The Medal of Honor?"

"It's just a matter of rubber-stamping the paperwork as far as I can see," Serling answered.

"Good."

Serling turned and looked at Teegarden's face. "It always reflects well on a unit and, thusly, the Commanding Officer, when someone under their command is recognized. A career enhancement, they call it in D.C."

Serling could see the anger growing behind Teegarden's eyes. "You think that's why I did it? You . . ." Teegarden turned away and started walking, changed his mind, and stopped. He turned around and came back and got in Serling's face.

"I know something about you, Colonel." Teegarden's face was contorted in disgust and anger. "I recognized your name. Yeah, I know something about you, all right. And I can put it in one word. Fratricide."

Serling felt himself go dark. He felt his legs weaken and his shoulders sag. A huge weight seemed to press between his shoulder blades. He kept his expression frozen and waited a moment before he spoke.

"I wonder if that term is any better than the one it replaced." Serling was proud of how calm he sounded. "Friendly fire."

"You got no room to cast any doubt on the actions of Captain Walden and her crew. Or me, for that matter. Not one bit of room."

"No one knows that better than I, Major."

Serling gave Teegarden back the helmet and handed him the empty Dr. Pepper can and walked toward the waiting HumVee.

6

An old friend from Officers' Candidate School, now CO of a Quartermaster and Rigging Company, loaned Serling his office. They had lunch together at the mess hall earlier. The meal hadn't gone well. Serling had no appetite and his old buddy, at the back end of a bad divorce, wanted to talk about the good old days at OCS. Serling couldn't remember any. The constant harassment, inspections, class and study, plus the strain of physical training did not add up to pleasant memories for him. All he could remember was running everywhere and the pain in his knees when he tried to polish the floor to the cadre's satisfaction.

After lunch Serling had typed up his report on the interview with Teegarden. SP/4 Kane, a mousy woman with an odd, nervous laugh, was faxing the report to Hershberg as Serling picked up the phone and dialed.

Someone answered the phone announcing that he had reached General Hershberg's office. Serling identified himself and asked for Captain Banacek, who came on the line a few seconds later.

"Banacek here."

"Ban, this is Nat. Could you do me one? Run a check on the rescue helicopter armament for the Walden rescue."

"Her chopper?"

"No, the rescue on the twenty-seventh. Teegarden's, another Blackhawk piloted by . . ." Serling consulted his file notes. "Liebman, a captain. Check the gunships and the on-board personnel."

"What are you looking for, sir?"

"Any stray M-16s."

"Got it. You want to talk to the General?"

"Please."

"Hold one. I'll get him."

While Serling was on hold, SP/4 Kane brought him an envelope. Serling opened it. A "From the Desk of Ed Bruno" note was attached to a file folder. Serling looked at the folder and suddenly realized what it was. A 201 file for Walden, Karen E., and files on each of the three eyewitnesses, Altameyer, Monfriez, and Ilario. Serling couldn't believe it.

"Nat, how goes it?" The General was on the line.

"Fine, General. I just finished speaking with the CO who wrote up the citation. I've faxed you a written report."

"I'll look at it later. What was your impression of the man?"

"A little touchy. I yanked his chain a couple of times, but I think he's just the touchy type. Sincere. Not covering up or anything . . . just touchy."

"Chopper pilots. It's in their nature. They're just waiting to discover that, like the bumblebee, it is physically impossible to stay airborne. And at that point they crash. Where to next, Nat?"

"I'm still here at Benning. One of the eyewitnesses, Altameyer, is an instructor at the Ranger School."

"Well, keep me informed."

"I'll stay in contact, sir. By the way, sir, I'm forwarding an article to you written by a Lieutenant who survived the incident. It's an after-report on Al Bathra."

"Al Bathra." The General's voice sounded neutral, but it was full of incipient questions.

"Nothing new, sir, but well written."

"Is it the article or the Lieutenant that I should be concerned with, Nat?"

"The officer, sir. He's ambitious, intelligent, well spoken, and not afraid to speak his mind. He's your kind of officer, sir. And his actions in the Walden incident speak for his bravery."

"I'll look over the young man. And how are you doing, Nat?"

"Fine, sir. General, in reference to this Ed Bruno character, I've been holding back on any reports to him until you've had a chance to look at them."

"I appreciate that, Nathan, I dearly do." There was nothing the General enjoyed more than outmaneuvering a pesky politico.

"I was wondering if I could send the Blackhawk survivors' report on to him."

"I don't see why not. Go ahead."

"Any . . . typos or spelling mistakes I should correct, sir?"

The General laughed. "No, let it go as is. But I'm thankful for the opportunity, Nat. Is there anything else?"

"No, sir."

"How are you doing personally, Nat?"

That was the second time Hershberg had asked the question. Serling knew that the General didn't waste time or questions—and he didn't repeat himself by accident.

"I'm doing okay, sir. I'll report again when I interview the eye-witnesses."

"Do that, Nat."

And Hershberg hung up. That was how he ended conversations. No good-byes.

Serling hung up.

Serling looked at the 201 file he still held in his hand. Then he dialed the phone number stamped on Ed Bruno's note. There was a nice little drawing of the White House above the phone number. Serling took a pen and drew a face at one of the windows.

"Ed Bruno!" The voice was filled with boyish enthusiasm. This guy liked his job.

"Colonel Serling here. I'm forwarding the first report to you."

"I look forward to seeing it."

Serling would pouch a copy to Bruno after he was finished on the phone.

"I just received a package from you."

"Captain Walden's file, right?"

"And the others'. I'm not sure that I'm authorized to have Walden's 201 file. I'm not even sure you're supposed to have it. This is confidential information."

"Hey, we're the White House. We have a little muscle. How's it going, Nathan?"

Bruno was one of those men who called you by your first name

109

right off the bat. Serling had noticed the same thing with car and insurance salesmen. A phony affability and intimacy—it seemed to work on most people. But not Serling. It just irritated him.

"It's going as expected."

"Let's see . . . I've got your itinerary in front of me. You've just completed the Major Teegarden inter . . . inquiry. What's next? Altameyer? Tell me, Nathan, do you have any idea when you might be finished? A week? Ten days? . . ."

"I don't know."

"But you could give me a guesstimate. A day for Altameyer, a day for each of the other two. A day for travel, a day to write it all up . . ."

"You have a date set already, don't you? You've set up your photo op and your little media circus already, haven't you?"

"I won't lie to you, Nathan."

What had General Hershberg said once? If a politician says, "I won't lie to you," just cross your legs and make out a new will.

"There is a particular window in the Chief's calendar that is most auspicious for this kind of event, occasion, ceremony."

"I'll bet."

"None of this rigmarole has anything to do with your mission, Nathan. And in no way is it meant to influence your findings. You just keep on the way you're going. I'm only saying that sooner is better than later. You get me, Nathan?"

"I get you."

"I look forward to our next conversation, Nathan."

They both hung up at the same time.

Serling wiped the phone sweat off his hand on his pants. He looked at the files for a moment. Then he opened Walden's.

There was a photograph of Karen Emma Walden attached to her last evaluation. She was pretty, handsome, the all-American cheerleader type. Black hair, dark brown eyes, a smile ready on her lips. Forever young.

Serling looked at the picture for a long time.

A CHECK with the First Sergeant of Altameyer's Ranger Training Company directed Serling and his driver out to the Obstacle Course. There a group of young men with shaved heads was being run through the very organized hell that was Ranger School. The instructors barked at the men's heels like Chihuahuas on steroids.

The students looked haggard. The instructor cadre, in their starched fatigues and berets, looked like Army recruitment poster boys.

The driver finally parked next to a huge sandy field where the training equipment stood like giant medieval machines of torture—a comparison not too far off the mark.

The principal Ranger officer, Captain Ahlberg, sat on the bumper of his HumVee overseeing the training. Serling walked up to him and after identifying himself asked the whereabouts of Sergeant Altameyer.

The officer pointed up, and Serling, squinting against the sunlight, looked up to the top of the fifty-foot tower where the fast-rope training was in progress.

Fast rope was a sort of speeded-up rappelling, Serling remembered, to get off a helicopter as fast as possible so the aircraft spent as little time as necessary over a hot landing zone, where it would be vulnerable to enemy fire. Men were zipping down the rope one right after the other, some with more finesse than others. There were quite a few collisions at the bottom as men tried to scurry out of the way of those following, but didn't make it in time.

Way up at the top, Staff Sergeant Altameyer, a black tough,

harangued the men, his main focus being variations of faster and better.

"Get down the rope, soldier! Somebody's shooting at you! You're a sniper's wet dream hanging in the air like that! Go! Go! Go! You're slowing down the war! You're slowing down the man behind you! You're gonna get his ass wasted! This chopper's been in the air too long! You know how much these things cost?! Get down there! Move it! Move it! Move it! C'mon! What's wrong?! You want to live forever?! You scared?!"

The soldiers whipped past Altameyer and down the rope, most of them more afraid of Altameyer than falling to their death or breaking a leg.

Serling knew that at this point in their training some of them would have welcomed a broken leg.

Altameyer had a recalcitrant soldier at the top of the rope.

"C'mon, Federman. Chopper's taking flak. Chopper's leaving. The war's waiting on your skinny ass! What are you afraid of?! All you can do is break your spine! It don't hurt and you get a spiffy set of wheels."

Serling could see Federman, a pale man who looked tired or scared or both.

Altameyer hooked up to the rope next to Federman and suddenly plummeted the fifty feet. He didn't slide, but fell the whole way—headfirst. Altameyer put the brakes on for the last few yards, squeezing the rope between his legs, and came to a stop with his head only inches from the ground.

Federman, ashamed, came down the rope in fits and starts, feet-first, the prescribed way, with Altameyer watching all the time.

"C'mon, soldier. Let loose. Scare me!"

Federman finally hit the ground. The Ranger PI walked over to Altameyer. Serling couldn't hear them, but it was apparent that the

Sergeant was getting his ass chewed. Serling wondered if it was for his benefit, but he doubted it. The Ranger cadre knew what they were doing and they didn't have to put on a dog-and-pony show for a visiting Colonel. Hell, they trained Colonels. At the end of the dressing-down, the Ranger officer pointed out Serling to Altameyer and the Sergeant walked over to him.

Staff Sergeant Altameyer was a formidable-looking soldier. His dark skin was almost black, his body buff, and the veins and muscles in his forearms and biceps stood out in bold relief. There was a jagged, ugly scar on his left forearm. His fatigues were tailored, fitting his legs like jeans, and his V-waist and broad chest were hugged by the fatigue blouse.

Altameyer snapped to attention in front of Serling.

"Sir! The PI said you wanted to speak to me."

"Yes, at ease, soldier. I'm Lieutenant Colonel Serling from the Pentagon. I'm conducting the follow-through on Captain Karen Emma Walden's Medal of Honor recommendation."

Altameyer seemed surprised. There wasn't an obvious reaction, but Serling saw the man's eyes widen momentarily. Then it was gone.

"Something wrong, sir?"

"No. Just crossing every *t* and dotting every *i*. Can we talk?"

"Yes, sir. I've been let off duty for the rest of the day."

Serling led the way back to the parking lot and his HumVee. As they walked, Altameyer gave Serling sidelong glances all the way.

"I don't know what to tell you that I didn't already say. They got it all in writing."

"I read the transcript."

"Isn't that enough?"

"Not for the Pentagon."

"You talked to the other guys? Monfriez? Ilario?"

"Not yet, but I will."

Altameyer paused with Serling at the HumVee.

"This gonna take very long, sir? I was thinking I might go to the gym. I'm working out, trying to get on the boxing team."

"I don't know. I might need an hour or so."

"How about I drive us over to the gym? We can talk on the way. I can work out. I'll give you a ride to wherever you need to be after."

Serling looked at Altameyer. What was the Sergeant up to? Maybe nothing, but . . .

Serling knew the power of men talking under controlled circumstances, but he had a feeling that Altameyer was just a street kid like himself and that any environment that seemed like the principal's office would only lessen the likelihood of any openness and cooperation.

"Sure, anywhere you're comfortable."

Serling dismissed his driver, then crossed the parking lot with Altameyer.

"This here's my car." Altameyer looked at Serling to see if the Colonel was impressed. He was.

Altameyer opened the door to a 1993 Saleen Mustang convertible—turbocharged—black with a red interior. The muscle car of the nineties.

Serling got inside. Altameyer smiled and keyed the Saleen to life. The engine gurgled contentedly, the torque of the engine gently twisting the car frame. The Sergeant turned off the stereo in the middle of something that could only be identified as loud.

Altameyer stomped on the gas and peeled rubber out of the parking lot, then settled into the twenty-five-mph speed limit of the Post proper. Serling was reminded of a phrase Meredith often uttered as some hotshot in a Corvette zoomed by her on the Beltway. "The bigger the engine, the smaller the weenie." Overcompensation.

Serling smiled. Altameyer mistook Serling's expression and peeled more rubber at the next stop sign.

"You were an MP in Desert Storm."

"Roger that, sir. MPs. Didn't want to be no ground-pounder. Only combat I ever wanted to see was a bar fight on a Saturday night. Look where that got me."

Altameyer tried to smile, but it was a little weak. He was clearly nervous. Serling looked for the reason.

"You hung around the Medevac unit."

"I did. Some."

"You like helicopters?"

"Negative on that, sir. Don't even like to fly in planes. Didn't before my crash, don't especially now."

"But you did hang around the Medevac unit. Did you want to be a medic?"

"I wanted to hump a nurse once. Does that count, sir? I see where you're going. I'll come clean, sir. I play poker. Those Medevac folks had a lot of spare time on their hands between missions. Want to know a poker secret, Colonel? It'll make you a mint. The people you play against, find out what they're interested in, pretend you're interested. They start running off at the mouth, don't pay no attention to their cards. Those Medevac folks, they do love to talk about choppers."

Altameyer grinned again, more easily, and tapped the Saleen dashboard.

"Medevac folks bought this here auto-mo-bile. Yeah, I hung with the Medevac. I hung, I played, they talked, I won."

"Until February twenty-sixth."

"Well . . ." Altameyer's mood darkened. He pulled into another parking lot. The sign outside the lot declared the building to be the Post gymnasium. The hours were indicated below.

Altameyer got out of the car, grabbed a Nike bag from the back, and walked toward the building. Serling followed him inside.

Altameyer and Serling walked through the weight room. Altameyer was known here, exchanging high fives and macho greetings with the other soldiers. The few women who were working out did not greet Altameyer, Serling noticed.

Back in the locker room, the smell of sweat got stronger and there was a fierce amount of humidity from the nearby showers.

Altameyer undressed, hanging everything neatly in a locker. As his fatigue blouse and T-shirt came off, Serling could see another scar, a big pink slash across the black back. Altameyer caught Serling's look.

"I had some serious phys rehab time." Altameyer flexed. Big plates of muscle writhed underneath his skin. "Got into boxing."

"So tell me, how did you come to be on Captain Walden's helicopter?"

"Uh, let's see . . . Major what's-his-butt . . . Gardenparty . . ."

Serling eyed the Sergeant. Was he fucking with him?

"Teegarden."

"Right. He asked me. Said they were on a Search and Rescue and they might need some gun. The war had just got cranking and we didn't know what ol' Saddam Insane had in his pocket. I said okay. I wasn't seeing any action and I . . . you know."

"No, I don't. Tell me."

"Well, I was thinking . . . Get me some Air Medals or even if some raghead decided to bust some caps at the chopper I could get me a CIB or some shit like that."

"Some medals for the uniform. I can dig that." Serling wondered if he sounded patronizing. On the block you could say that, but a Colonel was supposed to be . . . dignified.

It blew right by Altameyer.

"Right. So I got me an M-60 and we bungied the sucker in one of the Huey doorways and we were good to go."

"Did you know Captain Walden before that?"

"Saw her around the area, but . . . not much. She didn't play poker for money, she said. She . . . was just another officer."

Altameyer turned his back on Serling before his last sentence and Serling couldn't see his face.

Altameyer pulled on his sweats, what was left of them. The sleeves were torn off the sweatshirt at the armpits, the pants chopped off above the knees. He began to wrap and tape his hands.

"The flight was uneventful up until . . . ," Serling prompted Altameyer.

"Up until . . ." Altameyer repeated Serling's last words and smiled sardonically. There was nothing more forthcoming from Altameyer.

"Soldier, I'm here to get your version of the events at Al Kufan and I intend to do just that. If it would help to go somewhere else to do this, we can leave right now."

Altameyer's smile faded and he nodded.

"Let's see. We set down once, dust storm. That and the oil fires. We couldn't see shit, so we hit the ground to wait it out, let it blow over. We were down for a half hour or so, then we went back up. God, I hate the dust. Hate the dust. Hate it."

Altameyer bit off the tape viciously. He sure hated something.

"How long before you spotted the crashed Blackhawk?" Serling asked.

"Half hour, forty minutes."

Altameyer stopped again and busied himself with his hands, punching one into the palm of the other harder than necessary. It was evident that Serling would have to prompt him again.

"So tell me what happened."

"Well, it all happened so fast at first. Then it seemed to take forever. We came around a bend in the river—and there it was. . . ."

Nervously Altameyer began to scrape a fingernail across the wooden bench.

✳

The helicopter sailed along the valley, a hundred feet above the river, as if the water were a rail and the chopper a roller coaster car. Cliffs and ridges rose on both sides, jagged peaks and raw rock scattered down the mountainsides. Occasionally Altameyer could see through gaps in the peaks to the desert beyond, an endless expanse of umber sand.

Altameyer rode in the left rear door behind Captain Walden, machine gun ready, finger edging the M-60 safety. Behind him sat SP/4 Ilario, Walden's medic. At the other door, behind the co-pilot, Warrant Officer Rady, sat the Crew Chief, Monfriez, ass on the deck, feet braced on a skid, M-16 across his lap.

And everyone was looking, searching the valley with their eyes, from the river to the mountain peaks, trying to spot the missing Blackhawk.

Captain Walden followed the meandering water as it curved around a bend in the river. It was the prettiest the country of Iraq had gotten for Altameyer, a welcome relief from the flat desert horizon and smoky skies, though the pall from the oil fires was still in evidence.

The chopper abruptly cleared the bend and they were on top of a battle in progress. Altameyer heard the big boom of the tank cannon before he could see it perched on a ridgeline above the river. He followed the end of the barrel to the target and found the downed Blackhawk, the olive drab fuselage cracked like a dry peanut shell.

The gunfire wasn't as loud. Under the thumping of the Huey rotors, the small-arms fire was just an irritating cacophony of clicking and snapping noises.

Altameyer saw puffs of smoke coming from the barrels of the guns and little figures scrambling over the rocks below the ridgeline.

The enemy saw the helicopter at almost the same moment and Altameyer could make out the features on some of their faces as they turned up and looked at him. He saw one man clearly and wondered how that soldier had gotten away without shaving. Didn't they have inspections in Saddam's army?

Then, suddenly, he realized that this was the enemy and he should be firing at them. He slipped the safety off the M-60 and pulled the machine gun butt into his side to steady his aim.

But by that time Walden was banking the helicopter and he had no target, only sky.

"There they are!" Ilario shouted needlessly.

"Fuck, a tank! They're in deep shit!" That was Monfriez, excited, but calmer than Ilario.

"There's your target, Altameyer. Get it." Walden spoke calmly and the chopper banked hard.

Altameyer stood on the skid and hung by his safety strap, waiting for his target to appear in the open void below.

For a few seconds there was only sky, then mountain, then suddenly the ridgeline and the tank.

It filled his vision. He fired.

The machine gun poured a line of tracers at the tank, the pink-red glow describing a lazy arc from the barrel down to the ground. Altameyer used the gun like a water hose and drew a line across the earth to the steel beast of the tank. The bullets hit the tank and harmlessly ricocheted off. Some of the tracers spun off, twirling like Fourth of July pinwheels. The tank driver ducked down, pulling his hatch closed behind him.

That was the only satisfaction Altameyer got as the helicopter continued the turn and he lost his target. But he could see the enemy firing up at them, sending muzzle flashes and green tracers zooming his way.

He felt more than heard the helicopter take a few hits. The dull clank as steel punched through the aluminum hull. Ilario jumped to the side as holes almost magically appeared at his feet.

"Holy shit! We're taking fire!"

Through the other door, over Monfriez's shoulder, Altameyer could see the tank again. The cannon fired once more and the concussion could be seen as the waves around it distorted the air.

Altameyer craned his neck and looked behind them. He saw the Blackhawk take the hit. The whole wreck shuddered and pieces blew off and tumbled into the air. Men were propelled out of the wreckage, tossed loose-limbed through the air, and landed limply nearby.

"I'll try another pass!" Walden yelled to Altameyer. "Get ready!"

"Won't do no good, Captain," Altameyer shouted back. "I might as well be pissing on all that armor!"

"What we need is an air strike!" Rady called out. "Bomb that fucker back to Baghdad!"

"By the time a jet jockey gets here . . . ," Walden began, but didn't finish the obvious thought. The Blackhawk, and all the men with it, would be destroyed by then.

"If we had a rocket . . . ," Ilario put in. "Like the Cobras . . ."

"We don't have a rocket, but we have a couple of bombs." Walden sounded excited. "Monfriez, unhook the aux fuel pod, port side, prepare to throw it overboard! Altameyer! Put a hold on that M-60! Get the flare gun from the survival kit."

"Throw it overboard?!" Monfriez stood there in confusion.

"What the fuck?" Rady was staring at Walden.

Altameyer caught on right away.

"Do it!" he shouted. "It's a bomb! Ilario, where the fuck's the survival kit?"

Monfriez got the idea and put away the M-16 and began to unstrap the big square fuel pod on the port side of the chopper. Ilario fumbled for the survival kit and Altameyer yanked it open. He grabbed the flare gun, a big, clunky piece of stamped metal. He found the catch and opened the chamber. Ilario handed him a flare.

Walden banked the chopper back toward the tank. They passed over the crashed Blackhawk. Desperate faces craned up at them. Altameyer saw their dirty, bloody visages and his heart leapt to his throat.

"Get ready." Walden's voice was calm again.

"Climb for altitude and call in our coords!" Rady burst out. "That's our mission!"

"After we slow down the tank," Walden replied calmly. "Otherwise there won't be anything for them to rescue. Target coming up."

Altameyer could see the tank ahead through the Huey windshield.

"Ready here." Monfriez was hanging on his safety strap as the fat fuel pod at his feet teetered on the edge of the Huey deck.

"Ready here," Altameyer echoed, not feeling ready at all. The unfamiliar flare gun felt heavy in his hand as he looked over Monfriez's shoulder.

Walden banked over the enemy tank.

The tank's machine gunner was ready this time. He spewed a stream of tracers at them. There was only one tracer for every five or six rounds on a machine gun belt. It was hard to conceive that for every round Altameyer could see coming at him, there were five or six invisible bullets behind it.

The arc of a tracer sent one right through the open Huey doorway, past Altameyer's and Monfriez's shoulders. A few other rounds slapped through the side door and front window. Altameyer flinched at every one, wanting to duck but not knowing which direction was safe. Then he realized that there was no safe place anywhere on the Huey.

"Choose your moment!" Walden called back to Monfriez and Altameyer.

Monfriez let loose the fuel pod!

The Huey lurched, suddenly a few hundred pounds lighter.

They all watched the slow-motion path of the fuel pod as it fell to earth. It landed twenty feet away from the tank, split open, and the fuel burst out upon the ground.

"Shit! Shit! Shit! Shit!" Monfriez's litany came across the intercom.

"We'll try it again." Walden was already banking the aircraft into a steep turn. "Prepare the starboard fuel pod. Right away. Rady, we flying?"

"All gauges reading normal! No damage yet! None that's stopping us!"

Altameyer could see a large gash in the windshield near Walden's head.

"Ready!" It was Monfriez who had pushed past Altameyer and un-strapped the starboard fuel pod.

"Altameyer!" Walden called out.

"Ready!" he called back, finding his throat dry.

"Have another flare ready in case you miss." Walden looked over her shoulder and caught his eye.

"I won't!" he called back.

"I got one." Ilario was ready with another flare anyway.

Altameyer looked at Ilario and Ilario gave him a goofy grin.

"Here we go." Walden yanked the chopper into a sharp turn. Altameyer could barely stand under the centrifugal force. "Pick your moment!"

"Allow for the speed of the craft." Rady tossed in his two cents' worth of advice. "The pod will drop at the same rate as—"

"I got it! I got it!" Monfriez hollered irritably.

Again, the tank was revealed under the open door of the chopper. The tank's machine gunner and the ground troops were waiting for them. Tracers chewed at the Huey! Ragged holes appeared in the hull.

Monfriez dropped the pod.

The chopper lurched.

Altameyer almost lost his footing.

The pod burst upon hitting the tank.

A direct hit!

Gasoline spewed all across the vehicle.

"Got it!" Monfriez shouted jubilantly. "Got the mother!"

The Huey spun in a tight circle.

Altameyer braced himself against the bulkhead and fired the flare gun.

The red flash made a beeline for the tank.

And the whole vehicle burst into flames.

Altameyer's earphones were filled with cheers and shouts of triumph.

But they didn't last long.

They were in trouble.

The helicopter was reeling. It pitched left, then right! Altameyer almost fell out the door. He grabbed his safety strap and pulled himself inside.

Something was wrong with the tail rotor—the Huey was spinning in circles! The engine sputtered and coughed a few times. Walden was fighting to control the aircraft.

"Grab something! Hold on!" she shouted to the crew. "Rady, call in a Mayday!"

Altameyer saw Walden look over at the co-pilot at the same time he did. Rady hung in his chair, supported only by his harness as blood poured out of his mouth and onto his chest in a slow, steady, bubbly red stream.

The windshield directly in front of Rady had been shattered by three bullet holes spaced closely together. A good shot group, Altameyer thought. Somebody down there either knows how to aim or he's damn lucky.

Walden began to yell into the radio herself, switching channels. Ilario was strapping himself into the folding seat against the back bulkhead. He tugged on Altameyer's sleeve to come join him.

"Mayday! Mayday! Dust-Off Three is going down! Mayday!" Walden kept repeating the words over and over as she fought the controls. The ground was coming at them fast.

Altameyer just stood there thinking, Do I survive better on my feet or sitting down? Maybe if I bend my knees I can absorb some of the shock. He saw Monfriez strap into a seat. *Stupid*, Altameyer told himself. *You're going to crash! Get into the fucking seat.*

Altameyer took a step toward the seat, but his safety strap yanked him back. He reached down to unhook it . . .

And they hit!

Altameyer didn't know if he had blacked out or not. He was just suddenly aware that it was quiet. Very quiet. Altameyer could hear a ticking sound—it was the Huey engine cooling.

He moved slightly. Dust fell in front of his eyes. There was a moan—it wasn't him.

Altameyer was hanging outside the chopper by his safety strap, his head mere inches from the ground. The M-60 dangled in front of him, the muzzle only inches from his face. The bore looked like a tunnel big enough to walk through.

Quickly realizing that he was on the wrong end of the gun, Altameyer skittered out of the way. It hurt to move. Hand over hand, he pulled himself back into the helicopter along the safety strap.

Altameyer looked around and saw that the Huey had crashed in a mostly upright position. The deck tilted to one side, but it was level enough for him to walk. The deck was sitting directly on the ground, the skids splayed out from the impact. Altameyer took a couple of steps. He bumped his head, turned, and saw the tail rotor blade poking through the ceiling.

Walden was already unbuckled and bending over Rady's injured body. "Ilario, come here," she called to her medic.

Ilario was fumbling with his straps. Monfriez was moaning and hanging out the other door. Altameyer helped him back inside.

BOOM! That got everyone's attention. Altameyer unhooked his safety strap, stepped out of Monfriez's door, and had a look. The enemy tank exploded again, secondary explosions as the ammo cooked off. The charred corpse of the tank commander still hung out of the hatch.

The enemy ground troops, scattered figures on the ridgeline, began to fire on the downed Huey. Altameyer ducked down behind the rocks that stood about four feet away, between the Huey and the ridgeline.

Bullets chopped pieces from the stone. A few pocked the engine and upper roof of the helicopter at points where it protruded above the rock outcropping.

"Altameyer!" Walden called. "Get the M-60 working!"

With Ilario and Monfriez's help, Walden unstrapped Rady from the seat and lugged the limp, unconscious man into the main cabin of the Huey. There was a big hole in Rady's flight helmet. Carefully Walden slid the helmet off Rady's head and a large flap of hairy scalp came with it. Altameyer shuddered.

Ilario went to work and immediately cut away Rady's Nomex flight suit and worked on the man's injuries.

Altameyer unbungied the machine gun while Monfriez fumbled under the backseat of the Huey for the M-16.

"Monfriez!" Walden called out again. "Check for fire!"

Walden went back to her pilot seat as Altameyer got the M-60 and his ammo pouch onto the rock outcropping. The belt had broken off in the crash. Altameyer reloaded as quickly as he could and began to fire back at the enemy soldiers. Long bursts at anything that moved. The Iraqis' heads went down behind the rocks and they slowed their advance on the Huey.

"This is Dust-Off Three." Walden was on the radio looking for help again. "This is Dust-Off Three. Acknowledge. All channels. This is Dust-Off Three." She clicked through the radio channels.

Altameyer, Ilario, and Monfriez looked at her, hope naked on their faces. She looked back at them.

"Ilario, what's Rady's status? Altameyer, easy on the ammo. We might be here awhile. Monfriez, report . . . please."

"No fire. Fuel tank's intact." Monfriez had the M-16 in his hands and he took a position next to Altameyer. He looked over the outcropping of rock.

"Ilario?" Walden turned to Ilario and Rady. "Rady . . . ?"

"He's in a bad way. Lung shot. Stable, but weak signs. Not much I can do here."

Walden climbed out of the pilot seat and made her way back to Ilario and Rady. She bent over Rady, who was laid out on the rear deck. Walden gently wiped the blood from the unconscious man's face with the tail of her fatigue blouse.

"The head wound?"

"Superficial," Ilario replied. "Radio?"

Ilario was scared now that he didn't have something to do, something to occupy his hands or his mind. He'd fixed up Rady the best he could for the moment.

"Dead," Walden said, and got up to survey their situation. She crouched behind Altameyer and peered over his shoulder at the enemy.

"They stopped moving in on us," Altameyer told her.

"Keep 'em that way, but conserve on the ammo."

Walden went to the other chopper door, looked at the wreckage of the Blackhawk. It was across the river, over maybe three hundred meters of rough terrain. There was no way to tell how deep the water was, and though there was a little strip of sandbar in the center of the river, it consisted of small, softball-size to basketball-size rounded rock. Some of it was piled up three or four feet high. Not the best ground for running.

A few men could be seen inside the Blackhawk, staring back at the crashed Huey. Farther up the river, Walden could see enemy soldiers working their way down the bank to the crash site.

"Monfriez, get that sixteen over here. Ilario, could Rady manage if we carried him to the Blackhawk?"

"I don't know, Captain." Ilario seemed relieved to be talking, to be busy with that for a moment. "It might kill him. He might die in the next fifteen seconds just lying here. I don't know."

"I'm not sure we could make it," Monfriez said, and pointed with the M-16.

Five enemy soldiers had floated downstream and climbed up on the rocky island between the Huey and the Blackhawk.

Someone from the Blackhawk fired on the enemy soldiers. They fired back. The shooting didn't escalate into a full firefight; both sides were just biding their time.

"We try to get there, we walk right into their guns," Monfriez observed. "Carrying Rady, we might as well just shoot ourselves and save them the bullets."

Walden went back to Altameyer and looked over his shoulder again. The enemy troops had stopped moving and found cover among the rocks below the ridgeline. Occasionally one of them would fire at the Huey. Altameyer responded with two- or three-round bursts, calmer now as he remembered what they had taught him in machine gun training.

Some of the enemy fire punched holes in the exposed portions of the Huey, but nothing got to the main body of the chopper. Altameyer noticed that no one ducked or flinched anymore when rounds smacked against the chopper.

"Ammo?" Walden asked him.

"I got this belt and another five hundred." Altameyer lifted the two hundred rounds still feeding the machine gun and kicked the box that Monfriez had retrieved from under the backseat.

"I guess we'll wait," Walden said finally.

"For what?" Monfriez asked.

"Search and Rescue," Walden returned.

Walden looked at the three of them. Altameyer didn't share a bit of her confidence. He didn't think she was as sure as she tried to sound. They were in big trouble.

Machine gun fire! A long, sustained burst. Everyone dived for the ground. Altameyer sighted up at the ridge. One enemy soldier without a live target to keep him occupied was firing at the tail of the Huey.

Fifty or a hundred rounds, one long blast that perforated the tail. The *chopper shuddered under the sustained impact. Then laughter from the ridge. Giddy, childish laughter. Then another fusillade.*

Altameyer got ready to return fire. Walden stopped him with a hand on his shoulder.

"Let him waste the ammo, we need ours. For later."

"For later . . . ," Ilario repeated, making the two words sound very ominous.

✳

Serling watched Altameyer's fingernail carve a groove in the wooden bench as he spoke about the crash and the aftermath. Altameyer saw that Serling was watching him and he stopped self-consciously. Serling smiled, trying to put the other man at ease.

"Tell me about that night."

"I never seen it get so dark. No city lights . . . just black. Black. It's hard to describe it to someone who wasn't there."

"I was there."

"Yeah? Infantry?"

"Tanks."

"Oh, yeah." Altameyer looked at the insignia on Serling's collar and nodded.

"You wouldn't get me in no tank. Death traps. There you are sitting on five hundred gallons of diesel fuel, a couple of hundred rounds of high-explosive artillery in your ass pocket, just waiting for some happy asshole with a rocket launcher. We saw a lot of dead tanks with crispy critters hanging out of them over there. Know what I mean?"

"I know what you mean." Serling tried to fight back the images that all too readily sprang to his mind. It was difficult.

"Tell me what happened during the night." Serling tried to direct the conversation back to his inquiry.

"Not much. The Captain put us on two-hour watches but there wasn't no need. None of us was going to sleep."

✳

Rady hadn't moved since they had laid him out on the rear deck. His breathing was barely perceptible. Now and then Ilario would check his vitals, but otherwise no one paid much attention to him. Altameyer couldn't look at Rady. The first time he had and he had seen that the flap of scalp covering his head wound had fallen away—Altameyer could see the glistening slickness of the other man's skull. It made him sick, even though there wasn't any blood, or maybe because there was none.

Altameyer sat in the doorway of the Huey, facing the rocks between them and the ridgeline. Ilario faced him, his Beretta pistol in his lap. Both men kept glancing out into the dark, for whatever good it did. Neither man could see ten feet beyond the chopper.

At the other door, Monfriez cradled the M-16 and kept an eye on the same dense blackness. Walden, pistol in hand, sat in the doorway with Monfriez, looking out into her own sector of the night.

"I wish the moon would come out." Ilario's voice seemed to be exceptionally loud after sitting there so long in silence. Walden shushed him.

Altameyer looked up. A silvery haze in the sky hinted at a moon when the clouds and smoke thinned out.

"We can't see them—they can't see us," Walden said.

"Yeah, but they know where we are. And they can move all over the fucking place. We're stuck—with him." Monfriez jerked the M-16 at Rady.

"You think Air Rescue will come tonight?" Ilario's voice was softer now.

"Most likely they'll wait for first light." Walden talked softly to Ilario, not because of the enemy waiting in the darkness, but in that type of kind voice she would use with a child. A scared child. "We'll just have to hold our water until morning."

"I can hear them out there, you know," Altameyer said. "Moving and talking. When you people aren't jawing."

"Then I suggest everybody . . . ," Walden started.

BAM! Walden raised her pistol and fired past Monfriez's head. An Iraqi soldier fell, firing off a reflexive burst from his AK as he went down.

Suddenly the Huey was under attack! From all sides the gunfire lit up the night with brilliant flashes. Sometimes Altameyer could see enemy faces illuminated by the muzzle flares.

Altameyer fired. He didn't remember at what or how often. It was just instant chaos. Everybody was shooting and the individual gunfire merged into one big noise.

Then it was quiet.

Altameyer had a flat ringing in his ears from the gunfire. He could barely make out the sounds of the enemy scurrying away over the rocks, only a few foreign words.

There was a metallic clatter as Walden tried to reload her Beretta. Altameyer quickly reloaded the M-60 and turned to see what was taking Walden so long.

Her left arm was shot up. Blood was quickly soaking her fatigue sleeve, and a white piece of bone poked through a ragged, blood-soaked hole in the fabric. Her right arm clutched her stomach and blood seeped out around that arm.

Walden got her Beretta reloaded with her lone right hand, then looked at the stomach wound as if she had just noticed it.

"Shit." That was all she said.

The one word seemed to rouse her.

"Ilario!" she called out. "You okay? Monfriez? Altameyer?"

"I'm okay," Ilario said, more to himself than to her. "I'm okay."

"My ear . . . ," Monfriez began. His ear was bloody, the tip shot off. He reached up and touched it, but jerked his hand back on contact. It hurt.

Altameyer felt a sudden stab in his side as he let the M-60 bolt snap forward, ramming a 7.62 into the chamber. Looking down, he saw blood on his side. He reached out and touched it and noticed the bloody furrow on his forearm. Then it hurt. One big burning blast of pain that made him dizzy. He almost fell over. Walden noticed.

"Ilario, take care of Altameyer."

"Rady's dead."

Everyone looked. Rady's body was still, his eyes glazed over. That was what dead looked like. Ilario got over to Altameyer.

"I'm cool." Altameyer felt the wounds on his rib cage. They hurt, but didn't seem deep. "Check the Captain out. She looks serious."

Ilario made his way over to Walden. Altameyer and Monfriez watched them. Walden seemed embarrassed to be wounded, or to have someone take care of her.

"Altameyer, Monfriez, keep a lookout." She gave the order through clenched teeth as Ilario looked at the stomach wound. It was one dark red hole pumping blood. "They might try again. How many rounds left?"

She drew a sudden sharp breath as Ilario examined her left arm.

"How many rounds? Report," she repeated.

"I loaded my last belt," Altameyer said.

"I've got one magazine left for the sixteen," Monfriez answered. "Beretta's full."

"Mine's empty." Ilario began putting a pressure bandage on Walden's stomach wound. "No more clips."

Altameyer remembered his Beretta side arm.

"I've got an extra clip." Altameyer tossed it to Ilario, who let it drop next to his feet. "Here."

Walden almost screamed when Ilario tried to splint her arm. She clenched her teeth and swallowed the scream. A primal animal-like keening deep in her chest was the only sound she made.

"Both of you . . . fire a couple of rounds off . . . let them know we're still . . . alive and kicking."

Altameyer pumped a couple of three-round bursts into the night at the *ridgeline. Monfriez fired two rounds randomly into the darkness on his side of the chopper.*

There were tears in Walden's eyes. She wiped them away with her bloody right hand.

"Now save your ammo for something you can see."

They all stared out into the dark.

✳

Serling watched Altameyer. The man was back in the desert, staring out into that fearsome night. The thousand-yard stare.

"The trouble was, you couldn't see a damned thing. You knew they were out there . . . sneaking up on you, ready to try again . . . but you couldn't see. . . . You couldn't see."

Serling was sorry he had to break into Altameyer's narrative, but it looked like Altameyer had run out of gas.

"The rest of the night went without incident?" Serling asked.

Altameyer took a deep breath and let it out. He was back in the real world.

"Yeah." Altameyer nodded emphatically. "Wasn't that enough for one night?"

Serling was surprised at his belligerent tone. Altameyer realized how he had spoken and he tried to cover it with a broad grin, though he kept nervously rubbing the scar on his forearm.

"We could continue this tomorrow," Serling offered. "If it's getting to you."

"What?"

"If these questions are getting too close . . . you know. We could finish up tomorrow."

"I don't get emotional about this shit." Altameyer was angry. "It's a gig, you know. My job. It's in the job description. You're gonna get shot at and shit on for chump change. But you get to travel to

132

the worst ass-wipe countries in the world, sample their worst diseases, eat the worst food, in the worst weather, the meanest bugs and snakes and crawly critters under the worst conditions known to man. Now ask me why I do it. C'mon, ask me. Ask me."

"All right. Why?"

" 'Cause I get to kill people."

Altameyer tried to give Serling a killer smile. It didn't faze Serling. He had been accosted by the biggest macho assholes in Chicago when he was growing up, and later in the Army. He knew the more you talked about it the less you believed it.

Altameyer's smile of bravado faded. He rose up on his feet and strutted out of the locker room. Serling followed him into the gym, one side of the building dominated by the boxing ring.

Altameyer walked over to a floor-to-ceiling mirror and looked at himself. Serling looked at the reflection, and not the man.

"Tell me what happened at dawn."

"Dawn . . . Why is it that people think only good things happen when the sun comes up? As if a little sunlight on the situation would make things better. We knew at first light that they were going to attack. And we also knew that if they did, we were dead men."

Altameyer looked deep into the reflection of Serling's eyes. He was searching for something—but he didn't find it.

"And woman . . . ," Altameyer added.

Altameyer stepped back and looked at himself, checking out his arms, his chest, and neck. He flexed his stomach muscles. Then he looked into his own eyes. "And woman . . ."

❋

The sun crept up over the mountains. In the growing light, the four people on the crashed Huey were still on watch, weapons ready. They were exhausted, their eyes heavy with the need for sleep, shoulders slack, bodies spent.

Altameyer saw it first.

"Oh, fuck me," he whispered. Ilario crept over to Altameyer and looked over his shoulder.

"Fuck us."

Silhouetted against the sun, enemy soldiers were descending from the ridgeline, where the tank still burned.

"How many?" Walden tried to talk without moving; only her lips formed the words.

"At least a hundred. More coming," Altameyer answered, supplying the information.

With the growing light of day, the ridge seemed to have an Iraqi soldier behind every rock large enough to provide any cover, and more soldiers were scrambling over the ridge itself.

Altameyer could see several enemy bodies left from the previous night's firefight lying just a few meters away, their blackened blood already drawing flies.

Walden tried to crawl over to look, but almost fainted from the pain the movement caused. Ilario helped prop her up.

Altameyer flexed his finger on the trigger.

"Wait 'til they get closer," Walden whispered between clenched teeth. "Make every round count."

Altameyer put the M-60 on single fire and wished he'd paid more attention on the machine gun marksmanship range. He wished he had packed another box of ammo. He wished he was on R&R. He wished a lot of things. . . .

"We're gonna need every bullet. Look." It was Monfriez pointing toward the river on the other side.

Altameyer and the others looked over to where Monfriez had indicated.

An Iraqi heavy machine gun crew was running along the spit of land in the middle of the river. They settled behind a large pile of boulders and began to set up. This was going to be a major assault.

"We're fucked." Ilario spoke for everyone.

They checked their weapons. Monfriez held up the M-16. "I'm empty. Used it up taking potshots all night."

Altameyer unholstered his Beretta and tossed it to Monfriez.

"Where's Rady's Beretta?" Walden asked.

Ilario pulled aside the poncho with which he had covered Rady during the night and yanked the dead man's Beretta and spare clip from the holster. He held them out to Altameyer, but Altameyer shook his head.

"Hang on to them. First to run out gets it."

"Glad to have you with us, Altameyer," Walden said. "Sorry about the circumstances."

Altameyer was surprised at the words. He was suddenly overwhelmed by emotion. He choked it back.

"What the hell. Who wants to live forever?" His voice was hoarse.

"I do," Ilario said, trying to make it a joke.

"Quiet!" Walden's tone was harsh.

"What the hell for? They know we're here. We know . . ."

"Quiet!" She gave the order again. "I hear something. Choppers."

That shut everyone up. They didn't move—they listened.

"I don't hear shit," Ilario mumbled nervously. "All this gunfire's made me deaf. My ears just ring."

"Shut the fuck up," Monfriez whispered.

They craned their heads upward, straining to hear.

And there it was—the distinct rhythmic stuttering of rotor blades. Helicopters!

The enemy soldiers heard it, too. They stopped maneuvering on the ridge. The Iraqi soldiers were looking toward the sky.

So were the four people in the Huey, desperately searching the sky for their saviors.

Then the enemy attacked. The Iraqis were determined to wipe out the survivors of both helicopter crashes before they could be rescued.

Gunfire rained upon the Huey from two directions. Bullets slapped into the hull, ricocheted off the rocks.

Altameyer returned fire in three-round bursts. He heard the Berettas firing; less effective, but comforting just the same.

Then the air was filled with a great roar as four helicopters and a pair of jets tore around the bend of the river and into sight. The Cobras immediately let loose with their miniguns, shredding the air into more noise.

The enemy troops between the two crashed helicopters felt the full force of two electric cannons spewing five thousand rounds per minute. Some of the Iraqis were literally torn to pieces.

One Cobra fired rockets at the ridgeline. The enemy troops started to run back the way they had come. Too late. The rockets created panic, and then the miniguns raked the ridgeline until nothing moved. The Iraqis were either dead, wounded, or cowering behind rocks.

A rocket hit the tank again!

The enemy fire was greatly reduced, but the Huey was still being hit by sporadic fire. It increased as the enemy reorganized. Altameyer emptied the M-60 at the ridge.

The Medevac choppers landed paired up, the Blackhawk next to its crashed counterpart, the Huey near Walden's UH-1.

Monfriez yelled above the din. "Let's get out of here!" he screamed, and slapped Altameyer on the shoulder to get his attention. He grabbed Ilario, too. "Ilario! Let's go! Help me!"

Monfriez got Walden by her good arm. He had to step out of the chopper to do it. Ilario took her bad arm.

Walden screamed in pain.

Monfriez went down! A bullet in the leg!

"Ilario! Help Monfriez!" Walden shook Ilario off. Ilario followed her order and hauled Monfriez back inside the Huey.

Altameyer emptied his Beretta over the rocks at the ridge and rushed over and grabbed Walden with his good arm. She pulled away from him, too.

"No! Help Monfriez!" she shouted at Altameyer. "I'm staying with Rady!"

"Rady's dead!" Altameyer yelled back at her, and tried to grab her again.

"I'm not leaving him behind! Come back with stretchers!" Walden gave him a cocky grin. "Two stretchers! Go! Go!"

Walden took Ilario's Beretta. With that pistol and her own she leaned out the Huey door, the pain of movement evident on her face.

"I'll cover you!"

And she began to fire out the door of the Huey at the enemy.

Altameyer grabbed Monfriez under the arms and with Ilario on the other side lifted him off the ground.

"No! No! No!" Monfriez protested and struggled, screaming. Altameyer thought they were hurting him, but they didn't stop. Monfriez would get plenty of medical attention once they were out of here. They ran toward the rescue Huey. They made it thirty feet and fell, the rocks underfoot making them stumble and collide.

They hit the ground hard and Altameyer's wounds sent hammer blows of pain up his arm and across his ribs.

"No! No! The Captain!" Monfriez was still yelling. "We gotta get the Captain!"

Altameyer turned and looked at the crashed Huey. Walden was half standing and half leaning against the fuselage of the Huey, firing the Berettas at the attacking enemy. One Beretta clicked empty and she threw it aside.

Then Walden was hit. Five, six rounds hit her body, tearing big, bloody holes through her. She slumped against the fuselage and fell over on her face.

Ilario got up and ran back to her. Altameyer followed and got to the Huey as Ilario rolled Walden over on her back. She was dead.

The enemy fire increased. They were attacking again. Bullets chipped the rocks around Altameyer and Ilario.

Boom! Mortar rounds.

The Iraqis were walking mortar rounds toward the Huey.

"Let's get out of here!" Altameyer had to pull the stricken Ilario away from Walden's body. He hauled him to his feet.

BOOM! The mortar rounds were landing closer round by round.

They ran back to Monfriez, who was crawling toward the rescue choppers. Altameyer and Ilario picked up Monfriez and sprinted toward the chopper. The medic and the Crew Chief from the rescue Huey darted out and took Monfriez off their hands.

Scrambling onto the Huey, Major Teegarden leaned over to Monfriez.

"Where's Captain Walden?!" Teegarden had to yell over the sounds of the choppers and the firing.

Ilario answered him. "Dead! Rady, too!"

Teegarden nodded sadly and looked at the wreck of the crashed Huey. So did Altameyer. They couldn't see inside. The rocks obscured the view.

Teegarden turned back to his controls and the chopper lifted off the ground.

Altameyer looked across the medic's back and saw the Blackhawk also clear the ground. Teegarden was on the radio.

The Tomcat that was circling high above the river banked sharply and came in low on a run.

Two bomb canisters fell lazily out of the F-14s and landed on each of the crashed choppers.

White phosphorus.

There was no mistaking the big white plume of smoke and brilliant fire. The choppers—and everything in them—were incinerated. Instantly.

Altameyer watched through the chopper door as the Huey circled and left. Soon there was nothing to see but the twin columns of white smoke. Then even that was gone.

✳

A weight lifter, big and V shaped, with thighs like Sunday hams, slapped white powder onto his hands, and Altameyer flinched at the noise. Altameyer punched his boxing gloves together. Serling had tied them for him. Altameyer looked at the Colonel.

"That was it."

Serling didn't say anything.

"Altameyer! You ready?" Serling looked for the source of the voice. It was a little man with a barrel chest and a long ridge of scar tissue across his forehead. He was standing near the ring.

Altameyer walked over to the man and Serling followed him.

"You were wounded again in the evacuation?" Serling didn't want to let him go yet.

"Yeah. Took a bullet. Didn't feel it until we got to the MASH."

Altameyer paused outside the ring. A Latino man was already in the ring, rolling his head around his shoulders, loosening up while he waited.

"Where's your brain bucket?" asked the man with the barrel chest.

"Don't need it," Altameyer replied.

"You don't step into my ring without one. I have to tell you again, you won't have a head to put it on."

The little tough guy grabbed a protective helmet off the floor and tossed the headgear to Altameyer. Altameyer grudgingly put it on. Serling stood next to the ring and the trainer looked up at him.

"Help you?"

The trainer didn't add "sir" or "Colonel." Serling liked the man.

"Lieutenant Colonel Serling. Just observing."

"McQuillen, Coach. Observe, then. Into the ring, Altameyer. Medina, you ready?"

The Latino nodded.

Altameyer stepped through the ropes and into the ring. The two men touched gloves and McQuillen yelled, "Ding! Dammit!"

The two men began to box.

139

Maybe "box" was the wrong word. Altameyer took a lot of blows, punching only when he wanted to provoke another onslaught from Medina.

"C'mon, Altameyer!" McQuillen called out with disgust in his voice. "Plant one before the season's over!"

McQuillen looked at Serling.

"No fire. No killer instinct, know what I mean? He's got something, though. Ain't scared. Wades in there, takes a lot of punishment. Eats a lot of leather, but he don't dish none out. Well, some . . ."

Altameyer took a brutal blow. Serling saw him reel from the impact and stagger back. But he shook it off and came at Medina, laughing. There was blood on his mouthpiece. He spit the mouthpiece out and began taunting Medina.

"That's the best you can do? That's the best you can throw at me? What are you, some kinda pussy? C'mon, Medina! You hit like a woman. My little sister hits harder than you. My mama hits harder. You some kinda fag?"

Medina came at Altameyer again, punching even harder, trying to shut him up. But the black boxer kept talking trash and egging on Medina.

McQuillen shook his head.

"Maybe he thinks he can win by wearing the other fella out. If he don't bleed to death first."

McQuillen climbed through the ropes and pushed between the two fighters. Altameyer protested. McQuillen picked up the bloody mouthpiece, wiped it on Altameyer's sweatshirt, and jammed it back into Altameyer's mouth before he motioned the two men to continue.

Altameyer was a human punching bag. It wasn't that he couldn't hit, but he only did it to incite Medina. He just took blow after painful blow. Serling watched in horror.

He wondered what was wrong with Altameyer. Up to now he had thought that the man was more or less telling the truth. But this masochistic behavior was a sign that Altameyer was more than troubled by something. Maybe it had to do with what had happened that night on the Huey.

Serling tried to recall what he had read in the file Bruno had sent him. Altameyer was from Detroit, Michigan. He had joined the Army right out of high school, like Serling. His mother had been a bus driver with the Detroit City Transit System. He had a brother in prison in Jackson and a pair of sisters, one in college at Western in Kalamazoo, the other married and living in Indiana. The brother in prison bespoke the kind of life the family had lived. That Altameyer had gotten through high school without a police record was a credit either to his mother or Altameyer himself or both.

Serling had recognized the home address; he had been to Detroit to visit two of his cousins many times and he knew the area. To be African American and grow up around Warren and East Grand Avenue and not get arrested for anything was a major accomplishment. Just walking down the sidewalk in that neighborhood could put you in the backseat of a black-and-white.

Altameyer's military record was nothing spectacular but it was clean. He had spent some time in Korea, got good marks on all his evaluations, and had taken a special leave from duty at Fort Leonard Wood in Missouri to go home for his mother's funeral. He was smart, his test scores were high enough to get him into OCS if he wanted, but he seemed to lack the ambition. His record showed a well-adjusted soldier proceeding through a respectable if unremarkable career as an enlisted man. The backbone of the Army, men like him.

But this beating Altameyer was subjecting himself to indeed was provoking. . . . Nothing usual about that. Serling wondered if there was some kind of Post-Traumatic Stress Disorder diagnosis that would explain this behavior.

Serling saw Medina land a round so hard that blood shot out of Altameyer's nose in a long red spurt. Altameyer just grinned with a bloody, gruesome smile and continued to egg on Medina.

Finally McQuillen stopped the slaughter and sent Altameyer to the showers.

AFTER the bout, if anyone would call it that, Altameyer's responses to Serling's questions were monosyllabic and of no help. Serling finally told the beaten man that he would wait for him at the car.

It was one of those balmy nights again. The humidity hung lightly in the air and there were wisps of fog that snuck around corners and down the street, slipping under the lights like ghosts.

Serling leaned against the Mustang and thought about Altameyer and his version of the events at Al Kufan. He checked the original document. Altameyer's story fit the eyewitness account that he had given to Teegarden and that had accompanied the award submission. In fact it was almost word for word. That in itself was a problem. Usually there was some variance in details, misrecollection, confusion in battle.

Altameyer came out of the gym and walked over to the Mustang. His face was bruised and a bit swollen, his eyes bloodshot, his hair still wet. He tossed his bag into the rear of the Mustang and climbed behind the wheel without a word to Serling.

Serling got into the passenger seat and Altameyer eased the Saleen out of the parking lot and onto the street. He asked Serling where he wanted to be dropped off. Serling directed him to the BOQ.

The ride back across the post was more sedate this time. Altameyer was withdrawn and quiet. Serling looked at him.

"What kind of officer was Captain Walden?"

"Female. Kinda short." Altameyer tossed it off as a joke. Serling ignored that.

"Did she display any . . . characteristics that . . . gave you any idea she would perform the way she did in combat?"

"I didn't know her." Altameyer looked at Serling with suspicion. "I was just on for the one gig."

"During the incident . . . did she display any fear . . . any doubts when she had to make those . . . perilous decisions?"

" 'Perilous decisions' . . ." Altameyer thought about it for a moment. "No, she just made them."

"Just like that?"

"Just like that."

Serling was left with his own thoughts. He let the silence work on him for a moment.

Altameyer pulled up outside the BOQ. Serling didn't get out of the car even when Altameyer turned and faced him and raised his eyebrows with a "What are you waiting for?" look.

Finally Altameyer spoke. "Walden was okay. She was . . . What you're gonna do will make her a hero, right? She . . . deserves it."

Serling didn't answer, letting the silence stretch out.

"I just wish . . ." Altameyer stopped himself. "I just wish . . ."

"What?"

"I just wish I could be left out of it. I don't want to tell that story again. Not one more time."

"Why?"

"Living it was enough. You don't know what I mean . . . but . . ."

"I do."

Serling got out of the car and walked around to the driver's side. He looked Altameyer in the eyes.

"One last thing." He saw Altameyer tighten up. "The M-16."

Altameyer met Serling's look, eye-to-eye, mano a mano.

"The M-16?" he asked, looking as innocent as he could.

"When did it run out of ammo?"

Altameyer paused. "What did I say?"

"I don't remember, that's why I'm asking."

"No, no. You're trying to make some kind of point, Colonel. You're pulling some kind of 'Columbo' shit on me. The M-16 ran out of ammo sometime in the night."

"No one aboard your Huey fired an M-16 during the rescue on the morning of the twenty-seventh?"

"That's affirm . . . *Sir.*"

"You're sure?"

Altameyer couldn't hold Serling's gaze any longer. He looked away and Serling glanced at Altameyer's hands. His knuckles were pale, the veins in his hands prominent as the man squeezed the steering wheel tightly.

"That's most affirm. Definitely." Altameyer's voice was near anger. "We had no ammo for the M-16. That it, sir?"

"No."

Altameyer's head snapped back at Serling, his jaw muscles flexing as he gritted his teeth.

"Was there ever any talk of surrender?" Serling asked.

"No, sir." Altameyer bit off the words. "None."

"Not even during the night? When Rady needed medical aid? When you were surrounded, out of ammo . . ."

"No, sir! Not ever, sir!" Altameyer was reverting to that Ranger robot response. No matter what Serling asked now he would get a flat "Yes, sir!" or "No, sir!"

Serling slipped a card out of his wallet and gave it to Altameyer.

"That's it, Sergeant. Thanks. Here, call if you have anything to add to your statement. They'll get a message to me. By the way, the Medal of Honor doesn't make anyone a hero. It just recognizes the fact."

Altameyer tossed the card on his dash and backed out of the parking space, then peeled rubber out of there.

Serling watched Altameyer's taillights fade, then walked toward the BOQ. An illuminated sign across the street caught his eye. The Officers' Club.

Serling changed direction and crossed the street.

Inside the Officers' Club, Serling took a seat at the bar, noticing that the bottles behind it didn't seem to be arranged in any particular order.

The bartender finally wandered over to Serling and he ordered a bottle of George Dickel to go. The bartender politely told him that because of state ABC laws he couldn't sell liquor by the bottle. Serling slipped a twenty across the bar and asked the man if he had a bottle of mouthwash he could sell him instead.

The bartender smiled as Serling laid his briefcase on the bar and snapped it open. The bottle of George Dickel fit nicely inside, and the twenty disappeared as if it were a prop in a magic trick.

"Sure you don't wanna drink it here?" the bartender offered. "We got popcorn and chicken wings."

Serling looked around the club and felt a deep depression come over him. He had been in too many places like this in the last six months—make that over a year. How time flies when you're having a breakdown.

"No, thanks," Serling told the bartender. "I drink alone."

"That's a bad sign, so they say."

"Tell me about it."

Serling left.

Reaching the BOQ and walking to his room, Serling passed a room of lieutenants playing loud poker, their cigar smoke hanging in a light blue cloud above their table as they told bad jokes, taunted each other with macho put-downs, bet quarters and dimes as if they were thousand-dollar chips, and solved the world's problems in a sentence or two.

Serling envied them. There was a certain innocence there that he had lost. He wanted it back. Maybe that could fill this big black hole in his soul that was getting bigger every day.

There was a note stuck to his door. He let himself inside, then retrieved the note. It was a message from General Hershberg that said to call him at home.

Serling looked at his watch, not yet nine o'clock, not yet too late to make the call. Serling walked down to the pay phone at the end of the hall with his address book in hand.

He looked up the number and dialed. The phone was answered by Hershberg's wife Donna. She was a little woman, not five feet tall but full of energy. She taught in college, microeconomics, ran three or four charitable organizations, raised five children, was totally active in their lives, and danced through the social life of a D.C. three-star General with what seemed to be joy. She made every woman around her feel lazy and inadequate. Meredith had said that she could have hated Donna Hershberg if she didn't accomplish all she did with such a cheerful spirit and childlike enthusiasm, that it could give you a contact high just being in the same room with her.

Donna berated Serling for not visiting in the last six months, then put the General on the line.

"Nat?"

"Sorry it's late, sir, but the note said to call anytime."

"No problem, Nat, I'm glad you called. How's the Walden inquiry going? Are we all playing from the same sheet music?"

"I thought we were, but a few of the Blackhawk survivors mentioned hearing some M-16 fire during the rescue. Possibly coming from Walden's Huey. According to the eyewitness accounts the lone M-16 was empty. Teegarden didn't hear it so I wrote it off, but when I asked Altameyer about it he twitched."

"He did now . . ." The General fell silent. Serling could hear a movie playing in the background. It sounded like Bogart's voice. "What are you going to do?"

"Push that button on the other two eyewitnesses."

"Well, you do that . . . and tell me what you get. This Bruno character giving you any static?" Maybe Hershberg was getting pressure from the White House.

"We've made an accommodation."

" 'An accommodation,' " the General repeated with a chuckle. "Well, keep your legs crossed and keep me informed. Press those buttons like they were missile launchers. With prudence. You know what I mean, Nat?"

"I do, sir."

"You never know when one of those bastards will blow up on the pad."

Serling paused a moment. "Sir, why would a man, a hero, punish himself? Literally beg to be hurt?"

"Who are we talking about, Nat?" The General's question wasn't a casual one. The General's tone of voice had shifted into a personal mode.

"Altameyer, sir. He got into a boxing ring and begged to be beaten. Just asked for physical punishment."

"Altameyer . . . You should know the answer to that one, Nat."

"I should . . ." Serling was suddenly angry and braced himself to argue with the General. He didn't know where the anger was coming from.

"Think about it, Nat." The General's voice was now strictly military. "That's why I assigned you to this mission. Night, Colonel."

"Good night, sir."

They hung up together. Serling walked back to his room mulling over what the General had said.

7

Serling sat in the room on a chair with weak springs and stared at two things on the coffee table—the Walden 201 file and the bottle of George Dickel. He sat there for a long time.

He unscrewed the cap from the bottle, then tightened it back down. He took out a legal tablet and wrote up a report on Altameyer, printing neatly so that someone else could type it for him.

Debating with himself about how much to tell Bruno, not wanting the little man to overreact, Serling wrote the report without holding back anything. If he decided to censor the report to Bruno he would just make changes in the typed copy.

When the report was done, he put it and the Walden file into his briefcase. All that was left on the table was the bottle.

FORT Benning was quiet, even peaceful, at two in the morning. Serling walked aimlessly, just wandering, relishing the cool, damp air. He strolled through the middle of the Physical Training Course, past the apparatus and raised platforms for the supervising instructors.

The bottle was in his back pocket, a constant reminder.

The field was dark, but at one edge stood a phone booth that was lit from inside. In the light fog that was drifting across the ground the phone booth glowed. A beacon for a lonely man.

Serling walked across the field and over to the phone booth and stepped inside under the light. He took the bottle from his pocket and put it on top of the phone and dialed.

There was a rattle and a clunk on the other end.

"Hello?" The voice was slurred with sleep.

"Hi, hon."

"Nat?! Where are you?" Serling liked Meredith's voice when she first woke up. There was a bit of little girl in it and a bit of a sexy rasp.

"Still at Benning. I'll be in San Antonio in a day or two. At a hotel. I'm tired of BOQs and Fort Sam is limited in accommodations. I was thinking of stopping at the Alamo, get the kids T-shirts. I thought I should ask you about the sizes."

"Nat, you know their sizes better than I do." The sleepiness that was in her voice at first was gone now. "What's going on?"

Serling looked at the bottle before he spoke.

"You always call me on it, don't you?"

"And you do the same for me. That's how it's always worked."

There was another moment of silence. Then she spoke softly.

"What is it, Nat?"

Serling's thumb worked at the remnants of the plastic seal on the bottle.

"Nothing. I just wanted to talk to somebody who doesn't salute, I guess. A halfway friendly voice."

"Well, do you want me to rattle on for a minute?"

"Please."

"Let's see. Something's wrong with the new fridge. The light doesn't come on when you open the door. And no, it's not the bulb. Lynn lost a tooth. We did the whole tooth-fairy bit, she found a quarter under her pillow. So I catch Roger with a pair of pliers trying to get little Barry Kravel to yank a few of his bicuspids. They were going to split the proceeds. By the way, Lynn wants to wear a wig to school."

Tears welled in Serling's eyes. He felt himself choking with emotion. Meredith continued, unaware.

"Oh, I have to drive twelve blocks, all the way over to Wagner so Louie can practice riding his bike 'cause he's afraid to fall in front of his friends and he won't let anyone see him riding a bike with training wheels."

"I have to go." Serling could barely get the words out.

"Talk to me, Nat."

"Gotta go. I'll call you later."

"Nat . . ."

Serling hung up on her. He looked at the bottle, grabbed it, and fled from the phone booth.

8

The lake was still, flat, with barely
a gentle rolling ripple undulating
across the mirrored surface. There
was no breeze and the humidity
hung thickly in the air, full of
mosquitoes, which surrounded
Serling as soon as he stepped out
of the rental Ford.

Serling waved the mosquitoes
away and walked to the shack,
which was perched precariously
over the water. Half of the structure was on land and half of it

hung out over the lake on wood pylons that looked to Serling as if they were half-rotten.

Along one side of the building a dock ran another twenty feet into the water. The dock looked as shaky as the shack. So Serling was surprised at how clean and neat the interior of the store was when he stepped inside.

After all, it was a bait shop, that was what the hand-painted sign in front of the building had advertised. He didn't know what he was expecting—something repulsive, buckets of seething worms, smelly tanks of minnows.

But the worms were in covered basins, labeled neatly: RED WORMS, NIGHTCRAWLERS. And the minnows swam in a large metal tank that burbled pleasantly as a pump recycled and aerated the water. The lures, bug repellent, fishing line, and other myriad fishing accessories were hung neatly on pegboard displays. There wasn't a trace of dust and the floor was swept.

The only odor in the air was of cookies, peanut butter, freshly baked, and the old woman behind the counter was taking one cookie sheet out of the oven as she put another one in. She had a hardworking walnut of a face, as did the man who was skimming the dead minnows from the tank. He picked the dead minnows out of the hand net and tossed them to a pair of cats, who watched his every move with an intensity that fascinated Serling.

Serling walked over to the old woman who was using a spatula to skin the cookies from the sheet and onto a plate. There was a clear plastic dome next to the plate with a sign that said HOMEMADE COOKIES $1. Serling figured the price was a steal, the cookies were each the size of salad plates.

"Coffee's over there. Milk's in the cooler there with the soda pop." The woman pointed out the coffeemaker and the cooler for Serling. "Help yourself. Don't touch what you ain't gonna eat."

Serling walked over to the cooler and got himself a carton of milk.

"Mrs. Patella?"

"Yes?" Her eyes narrowed a bit. "Folks call me Sharlene."

"I'm looking for your son Donald." Serling picked up a cookie and took a bite, then a drink of milk. The milk was so cold it hurt his teeth, driving a frozen knife into his headache. The peanut butter cookie was still warm. It tasted so marvelous that he had to pause a moment and savor it before continuing.

"I was at the clinic, they said he was here."

She looked Serling up and down. He was dressed in civilian clothes, jeans and a chambray shirt, wearing his favorite penny loafers. The supervisor at the Topping Drug and Alcohol Abuse Clinic had stared critically at the pennies in the loafers. The supervisor, a Mr. Fedder, had been dressed so nattily in a big green suit that Serling figured the pennies were some kind of fashion faux pas. But Cheryl, Serling's oldest girl, had put the pennies in the shoes with a child's simple logic that penny loafers had to have pennies.

On an impulse that morning, Serling had called Top Sidaris and asked him more specifically about Patella's whereabouts. Top thought that a reunion between the two men was a great idea and he asked for a half hour to make a couple of calls. Exactly thirty minutes later, Serling had the address and phone number he needed. Donald Patella was a patient at the clinic in northern Florida. Serling canceled his flight to San Antonio and rented a car. He made the drive in more than two hours, and was delayed by a huge hangover headache, only to have Fedder tell him that Patella had checked himself out of the rehab center and gone back to his parents.

It took a little talking, but Serling was able to finally pry the address from Fedder. He could have called Top again, but he felt he had asked too many favors from him already. After showing his military ID and listening to Fedder's opinion of the Gulf War—against—and Colin Powell—for—Serling had the address of Patella's parents, both a home address and their business, the bait shack.

Serling stopped at the house first, but no one was home even that early in the day, so he drove over to the lake. He got lost twice and stopped to get directions from a cashier at the local 7-Eleven—wrong directions—and asked a man pushing a shopping cart full of soda and beer cans—correct that time.

"Who are you?" Mrs. Patella's question wasn't voiced rudely, just cautiously.

The old man who Serling assumed was Mr. Patella walked over from the minnow tank and stood by his wife. The cats followed him. The old man had the wrinkled red leather skin of years spent outdoors, but his pale blue eyes looked like they belonged in a younger face.

"Lieutenant Colonel Nat Serling."

Both the Patellas recognized the name at once. It didn't send them into any joyous celebration.

"He's out at the McCaffrey place painting their cabin," Mr. Patella answered. "Hope to hell he finishes it before summer."

"Could you give me directions?" Serling asked.

"Sure. Draw you a map, too. Know how you military types get all het up over maps."

Mr. Patella tore off a strip of cash register tape and began to draw. His wife smiled nervously at Serling.

"Have another cookie?"

Serling wasn't finished with the one he had. He mumbled, "No, thank you," as he chewed another bite of the peanut butter cookie. The milk wasn't as cold now, but it still tasted good as he took another drink. He ate the rest of the cookie while the old man drew the map.

Mrs. Patella came out from behind the counter and edged over to Serling.

"Donald admires the hell out of you, Colonel. Maybe you could talk him into going back to the clinic."

"He didn't stop drinking?" Serling asked.

"It's not the drinking. Everybody drinks," Mr. Patella said.

"Not like that," she tossed back at her husband.

Mr. Patella shot her a hard look, then looked at Serling as he spoke. "It's . . . let me put it this way, Colonel. I done hid all my guns. I don't want the boy to be alone in the house with a gun around. You catch my drift?"

Serling nodded slowly.

"Can you read a map?" Mr. Patella slid the strip of cash register tape across the counter to Serling.

"The Army taught me how."

The old man grinned.

"Then I'll try to explain it to you so you don't get lost."

Mrs. Patella shrugged at Serling. "My husband was in the Marines."

THE directions and the map were perfect. Mr. Patella had been very precise, using hundred-foot measurements with multiple local landmarks and signposts. All in all, the ride to the cabin was very pleasant as Serling circled the lake past sparkling neat cottages, green lawns, and long stretches of narrow road overhung with trees that created a green dappled tunnel. He ate another cookie with another pint of milk, the Patellas not allowing him to pay for either.

The McCaffrey cabin was a small, narrow one-story clapboard building on a quarter-acre lot with fifty feet of lake frontage. A Japanese mini-pickup was parked in front of the garage. The pickup bed was filled with paint cans—some new, some empty—used rollers, a few brushes, and a few hundred beer cans.

Serling walked down the narrow gravel pathway that wound between the cabin and the A-frame cottage next door. The cabin was half-painted, the formerly chipped white surface now being covered with yellow—a too-bright neon yellow that Serling thought was awful, but it wasn't his house. Maybe the McCaffreys thought it was a cheerful color. When the sun struck the yellow at the right angle the glare sent a laser beam into Serling's headache, which, up to this point, had been diminishing.

Serling called Patella's name a couple of times. There was no answer. The lake itself was hidden by a couple of huge jade plants. Serling walked toward the sound of the lapping water.

Then he heard the shot!

Serling ran down the yellow paint–spattered path and almost tripped over the paint can and roller laid out on the plastic drop cloth. Clearing the jade plants, he saw a figure at the end of the dock that poked out into the lake. Remembering Mr. Patella's words about guns around the house, Serling ran harder.

Another shot!

Serling suddenly slowed, seeing that the man at the end of the dock had a rifle to his shoulder. It's hard to commit suicide holding a rifle that way. The man fired again. Serling watched for a moment. He was firing at the water. The bullet made a neat little splash.

Serling stepped onto the dock and walked toward the man, still not sure it was even Don Patella. The man seemed so thin. Then he felt or heard Serling's hollow steps on the boards of the dock and he turned.

It *was* Patella. Emaciated, bearded, sunken eyes peering from under the bill of his ChrisCraft gimme cap. The face scared Serling. Patella looked haunted, like a man one step away from the grave.

"Major!" Patella straightened up and extended a hand toward Serling. The rifle hung in Patella's other hand and Serling heard Patella flick on the safety. Good soldier, he thought.

They shook hands, and then on Patella's enthusiastic instigation they hugged. Serling felt a little awkward in the embrace and when they parted he thought he saw Patella catch his discomfort.

"Patella, it's good to see you." He wasn't lying. It was good to see the man, as bad as he looked. For a moment Serling felt a camaraderie with him.

Patella sat down on the end of the dock. Serling joined him. The dock was high enough that their feet didn't touch the water. A case of beer separated them. Patella took out a bottle, opened it, and took a long swig, then held it up to the light.

"Ever wonder why they call an empty bottle of booze a dead soldier?" Patella didn't look at Serling.

"Yes," Serling admitted.

Patella took another bottle from the case and offered it to Serling. "Have one."

"No, thanks." Serling wanted the beer, but he was supposed to be here to talk Patella back into rehab. Patella took another drink and looked at Serling.

"Don't tell me you ain't drinking, Major. I can smell it on you. And you got to be drinking some for it to come out of your pores in the morning."

"I'm trying to quit."

"You're not going to lecture me, are you, Major?"

Serling didn't answer. He wanted to say a lot to Patella, but the only words on the tip of his tongue were, "It's Lieutenant Colonel, I've been promoted." Serling swallowed those words, feeling that whole subject was trivial.

Patella emptied the beer and tossed the bottle into the lake. He raised his rifle and clicked off the safety and fired at the bottle—missed it. So that was what the shooting was about.

"No, I won't lecture you. But I will pass on a word from your mother. She wants you to go back to rehab."

"No way. It's worse than the Army. Had to make my own bed in the morning. Had to pull KP."

Patella fired at the bottle again, hit it. It plinked and sank.

"They don't understand, Major. No one does."

"I know."

Patella opened another bottle, drank long and deep.

"I don't like to drink, never did." He looked at the bottle and scraped at the label with his thumb. "Before . . . Before I never was much of a drinker. But booze is the best way of coping now. Until they give me something better, I'll stay with the booze."

Patella drank the beer down in one, two, three fierce swallows, then tossed the bottle into the water again and fired—he hit it. The bottle sank.

"Have you tried to do without it?" Serling asked.

"Yeah. You?"

"Yes."

The word was a sad defeated answer that took the strength out of Serling's body.

"Find anything better yet?"

Serling didn't answer.

"Obviously no."

They were silent for a moment. Patella emptied another bottle and once again tossed it out into the lake. He reached for a fresh brew and pulled another out and handed it to Serling, who accepted the beer this time.

Patella fired at the floating bottle, missed.

"You still in uniform, Major?"

"Not a Major anymore." Serling nodded and drank. The beer was warm. He didn't like beer. It took too long to get drunk and you had to piss too much. "Lieutenant Colonel."

"You'll always be a Major to me, sir." Patella laughed.

"And Blackburn will always be a Sergeant. I'm stuck in time like some fucking 'Twilight Zone' episode. I can't get past twenty-two hundred hours, twenty-six February 1991. It's like I didn't live before that night. And I sure haven't lived past it. Blackburn, Sacks, Boylar . . . I hardly knew Pittman but now I remember every moment I spent with the poor bastard. His ugly laugh, the picture of his ugly girlfriend. His fucking bad jokes. I can even see his face when I killed him. I wasn't there, but I see him. I'd have to be in his tank to see that, right? And if I was in the tank I'd be dead. But I'm not dead and I wasn't in the tank, but I see his face."

Patella's lower jaw trembled. Serling turned away before he was overcome himself. He remembered Boylar's crew. Each one of their faces was vivid in his mind. Dead men. Men he had killed.

The light shimmered blindingly bright on the lake, but Serling stared into it, letting the reflected sun blast his eyes. It was like looking into fire.

Finally Serling spoke, forming each word carefully.

"You didn't kill them, Patella, I did. I gave the order."

"I pulled the fucking trigger. I targeted them."

"The investigation cleared us of all blame. We didn't know that the target signature of a tank being hit was the same as one that was firing. We never trained under live fire. How could we have known?"

"How could we?" Patella repeated Serling's words. "Yeah, how could we, Major . . . Colonel?"

Patella fired at a new bottle—missed.

"Major?"

Serling looked at Patella. He could barely stand the pain on the other man's face.

"They weren't on the same radio frequency as us, were they?"

"No," Serling replied. "Why?"

"I keep hearing them scream. I swear I heard them scream. I still do."

"So do I."

"You poor bastard."

Patella offered Serling another beer. Serling shook his head.

"Mama says the booze will kill me." Patella laughed again, a sick little chuckle. "She don't get it, does she?"

"No."

"No one understands but you, Major."

Patella laughed harder, a little hysterical, a little out of control. "My mama thinks I'm drowning and the man she sends to save me can't swim. Sorry, Major."

Serling couldn't help but laugh, too. He took the second beer, emptied his first and tossed the bottle into the water. Patella shot and missed. The two bottles bobbed lazily on the surface of the water.

Patella offered the rifle to Serling. It was a nylon Remington 66. Semi-auto, plastic stock. It looked like a toy.

"No, thanks."

Patella shrugged, aimed, and fired. Two shots, two hits. The bottles disappeared. As many beers as Patella had ingested, he was still sober enough to shoot straight. He had always been a good shot. That was why Serling had picked him to be his gunner. That was why they were here.

Serling looked out across the lake. He thought about taking his kids and Meredith to a place like this.

"Don't kids swim here?" Serling asked Patella.

Patella looked at the water.

"Shit. Oh, fuck." Patella seemed genuinely distressed. He put down the rifle, took off his shoes, cap and shirt, then jumped into the water.

Serling waited. The ripples made by Patella's entrance into the lake died away. The waves stopped slapping against the dock. It was quiet.

Serling quickly got worried. He looked at the water. Not a ripple, not a sign. He looked down at the spot where Patella had gone in. It was green and opaque.

Serling toed off his loafers, took his wallet out of his back pocket.

Just then Patella broke the surface and set some broken glass on the dock. He saw Serling in his socks, wallet in hand.

"Scare you, Major?" Patella asked, smiling.

"Yes."

Patella's smile dropped, suddenly sad.

"Sorry."

He dived again.

It took a dozen dives for Patella to be satisfied that all of the broken glass had been retrieved. There was a small cairn of brown and amber shards on the dock.

Somewhere along the line Patella had cut his palm. It was a long gash, not deep, but bleeding freely. While Patella sat on the dock next to him, Serling bandaged the gash with a strip of cloth torn from an old pillowcase he had found in the house.

"This I can fix. I've been trained." Serling smiled at Patella, who smiled back.

"All them OCS medic courses?"

"Four kids . . ." Serling couldn't hold the smile any longer.

Patella looked at Serling while he finished the bandage. "Damn, Major. You came to me looking for some kind of answer, didn't you?"

"I can't deny it."

"Oh . . . I'm so sorry, Major. So damn sorry."

"So am I."

The two men looked at each other, seeing the same thing. A sad, lost man without one idea of how to be happy again.

They worked on some small talk, Patella abandoning the rifle and beer to pick up a roller and return to his painting. But they had little more to say, trying to stay away from any discussion of the past.

Serling watched Patella paint and remembered one day at Fort Hood when the much too young SP/4 spent over an hour explaining the proper way to skin an alligator, laughing the whole time, while they waited for their stalled Abrams to be towed off the field. He missed that young man. Finally, after an uncomfortable silence, Serling made an excuse about catching a plane to San Antonio and Patella walked him back to the rental car.

As Serling got into the driver's seat Patella saluted him with the bandaged hand.

"Major, you get any clue, you let me know."

"You do the same, Patella."

Serling returned the salute, then started the car and drove away. In the rearview mirror Patella became smaller and smaller until a curve of the road wiped him out of Serling's sight.

Serling's sadness found a profound new low. At one point in the drive back north, he had to pull over onto the shoulder and take a breather, collect himself and try to stop the images of Al Bathra from overwhelming him. He was short of breath.

Finally he was calm enough to continue driving. Two things kept him going and he tried to focus on them. His family, Meredith and their kids. Somehow he had to get himself back on track before he lost them.

And Karen Emma Walden. She represented everything he wasn't. A hero, a leader, a true soldier. And Serling was going to see this inquiry through to its finish. He was going to see that she got her medal.

Then what? he asked himself. Then what?

He didn't know. He didn't want to think about it.

9

The hotel room in San Antonio
had a balcony that hung out over
the river. Serling had thought that
a hotel room would make him
feel better than the BOQ, offer a
little comfort in the bustling city.
But it somehow made him feel
even more lonely.

It was a beautiful night. The
running of the water beneath his
balcony had a sweet sound, and
tourists and lovers walked along
the riverbank under the swaying

trees. And Serling felt more alone than he had since he left home for Basic Training. He was a tough kid back then, but he had never been more than a few blocks from his parents' comfort. He used to sneak out of the barracks late at night and call home just to hear their voices. They were both dead now: Dad from cancer, Mom from losing Dad. He thought of calling Meredith again, but after hanging up on her in the middle of the last call he felt that he had transgressed too far. Meredith would forgive him, though. He just couldn't forgive himself.

The loneliness ate at his heart and his chest was a big hollow place that nothing could fill. The solution was to numb it all.

He went looking for a bottle.

And found one.

AFTER Bragg and Benning, Fort Sam Houston, in the midst of urban San Antonio, seemed to be a sedate, almost genteel Post. Completely appropriate for a base where the main task was to train healers, not killers. Every medic, doctor, and nurse who enlisted went through Fort Sam Houston's Academy of Health Sciences.

The buildings were all a yellow beige that matched the native clay, and most of them had Spanish-style red tile roofs. The old Officers' Quarters, still in use, were Georgian Revival, with white columns and second-story balconies.

On his way to the Brooke Army Medical Center, the old main hospital, Serling was struck by the number of buildings in disrepair. Mostly old wooden barracks, but a few concrete structures with peeling paint, broken or missing windows, sagging roofs, all looking decrepit and neglected.

He had noticed the same thing at Bragg and Benning, too. It was a sign of downsizing and military budget cutting, abandoning structures that were of no use or redundant, and replacing them with a smaller, post-Cold War military force.

But it still saddened him and reminded him of his Chicago neighborhood, where such neglect was a sign of poverty. He was proud of the Army, he wanted it to be able to look as powerful externally as it was internally.

And like most of Serling's problems lately, he didn't have a solution, just a resigned state of regret.

Serling shrugged the feeling off and followed the map to the massive yellow brick building that was now the old hospital. He had read somewhere that it was soon to be decommissioned. He hoped that it, too, wouldn't be abandoned.

Walking across the parking lot, he felt a bit nauseated, not hung over exactly, and this time he didn't have a headache, but he felt weak and vulnerable. He had missed his morning run, sleeping past his wake-up call and his own alarm clock.

The nurse at the desk, a male SP/5, gave Serling directions to the pharmacy.

There was a line of a dozen soldiers at the half-open Dutch door and SP/5 Ilario was dispensing vials and bottles to them. He was a small man in his early thirties, his eyes hidden behind Ray Charles-style horn-rimmed glasses with the lenses tinted light brown. He had deep lines in his forehead and at the sides of his mouth. Too deep for a man so young.

Serling got in the back of the line. The man in front of him, a Sergeant, looked at Serling's Lieutenant Colonel insignia and tapped the man in front of him, a Staff Sergeant. They whispered to each other and the Staff Sergeant also looked at Serling, then they both stepped out of line and left.

Serling watched them go and turned his attention back to Ilario.

"Here's your fungicide, but I'm telling you, in the morning when you shower just piss on your feet. Urine will kill that athlete's foot in no time. Next! Here's your Hismanal, Sergeant, but you want to get rid of the allergies—bee pollen pills—and no coffee or chocolate. Caffeine makes allergies worse."

"If I give up coffee they might as well discharge me now." The Sergeant cracked a smile and took his pills with him.

And so it went as the line got shorter, Ilario dispensing the prescribed medication with little remedies of his own advisement. A few more soldiers, two men and a woman, seeing Serling in line, left abruptly. They could have been just goldbricks, slacking off to avoid duty, but Serling doubted that very much.

Ilario didn't look at any faces, he just kept his eyes at chest level noting the name on the tag over the right pocket, then finding the appropriate prescription on his clipboard.

When he came to Serling's name tag he froze. Slowly raising his eyes, he looked at Serling. "Can I help you, Colonel?"

"Anything for an upset stomach?"

"Tried any Tums?"

"What? No homeopathic alternative?"

"You know about alternative medicine, sir?"

"My sister is a believer. Me, I believe in aspirin."

"So do I. Take one every day."

"Altameyer call you?"

Ilario was taken aback, but only a notch.

"No. Monfriez. Altameyer called Monfriez. He called me."

"That's nice. You three still stay in contact. Friends?"

"Not exactly. What do you call people who shared something like we did?"

"Heroes?"

"Survivors, more like it. So where do you want to do this?"

"Anywhere you feel comfortable."

"You smoke?"

"Not anymore."

Ilario grabbed his cigarettes and a Zippo and turned to an SP/4 behind the Dutch door.

"Rowtero, take over. Sick Call's done. I'm going to feed my cancer genes."

Ilario led Serling out of the pharmacy.

Serling and Ilario approached a bench on the grounds outside the hospital where an old man in a hospital robe spoke with an agitated old woman. Ilario walked away from that bench and went in search of another. Serling followed and observed the medic.

William Ilario had been born in Bayonne, New Jersey, and was raised in Philadelphia, where his family had moved to when he was seven. He had been the youngest of five children and his mother died of a heart attack when he was eleven. His father was a plant maintenance manager for Monsanto. Ilario was smart enough to receive a scholarship to Notre Dame as a pre-med student, but he quit to join the Army. He had performed remarkably well in Grenada and Panama and his record was exemplary in all respects.

That file information provided by Bruno didn't exactly fit the nervous, fidgety SP/5 whom Serling watched today. Ilario couldn't even decide where to sit, flitting from one bench to another, rejecting one because the sun was too glaring, or the slats were cracked, had splinters, and so on. Serling followed him patiently.

Finally Ilario moved on across the street toward the Post swimming pool. The pool was fenced in and there were a few benches outside, along the fence.

The pool was populated by a few dozen children whose ages Serling estimated were from eight to ten. They were happily shouting and screaming and splashing under the supervision of several swim-suited women. Mothers, teachers, or swimming instructors—Serling couldn't tell.

Ilario lit up a cigarette.

"Do you think this is how the Nazis got started? Banning smoking?"

"I doubt it."

"A bit totalitarian, though." Ilario took a few drags on the cigarette. It seemed to calm his nervousness. "So what do you need to know?"

"How long were you with Captain Walden?"

"Over four years. Four years and a couple of months. Stateside at Fort Hood—can't seem to get out of Texas. Then over in Saudi."

"That's a long time. Did you know her well?"

"As well as you get to know any officer, I guess."

Serling didn't know what Ilario meant by that. He knew that in some small units the relationship between officers and enlisted men got very close. Especially units like helicopter flight crews or, as Serling knew all too well, tank crews.

"What was she like?"

"She was okay. Wasn't on my ass too much. What's this got to do with the Medal?"

"Nothing. Just curious."

Ilario had smoked his first cigarette nearly down to the filter. He lit another off the butt. He looked at Serling, at the medals on Serling's chest, focusing on the Gulf War ribbon.

"You were in Saudi? See any combat?"

"Yes. Tanks."

"You lose any men?"

Serling nodded and wondered how much Ilario knew about his past. Ilario didn't pursue it.

"Have you noticed . . . ? I have, since I came back . . . that there is this . . . closeness with other combat vets? This . . . thing?"

"My Sergeant Major said it's because we've all faced the tiger. We've all been tested. We know our limits."

"Yeah? I don't buy into this 'bond of war' shit, but we all do know something that no one else knows. Can't explain it to a civilian, not even another soldier if he hasn't been under fire. It's a secret. We never share it. We can't."

"A secret . . ." Serling pondered the words. Ilario looked away. "Tell me about the crash and everything as you saw it."

"You talked to Altameyer. I stick by whatever he said."

Ilario still wouldn't look at Serling.

"I'd rather have your point of view."

"I wrote it down once. Didn't you read my statement?"

"I did. All three statements are remarkably consistent."

"They should be. It's what happened." Ilario now looked at Serling, emphasizing the last sentence with a determined expression.

"It doesn't usually work that way. Usually there are quite a few discrepancies."

Ilario looked away again, lit another cigarette.

"You can't force me, sir." Ilario spoke in a whisper. Serling almost couldn't hear him.

"No? I could order you, but we both know that's a joke. However, I could make things damned unpleasant for you."

"Unpleasant?" Ilario's laugh was an unpleasant sound. "What do you want, Colonel?"

"The truth."

"I don't think so."

"Try me."

"You won't like it."

"I don't have to like it."

"You're going to hate it. It might just stop this whole Medal of Honor thing."

What was Ilario implying?

"I'm prepared for that."

"Really?" Ilario looked at Serling, judging him. From the expression, Serling took it that the SP/5 doubted Serling's readiness. "Where do you want to start?"

"It's your story."

"Okay . . . Let's see . . . the dust storm. We were forced down by a dust storm."

"I know."

*

Ilario loved flying. Not being a natural risk taker, he found it a constant thrill. The supreme rush of the ground roaring past at low altitude, the breath-holding scare of banking at a ninety-degree angle and feeling that you may fall out of the chopper at any moment. It was something he had never experienced in civilian life growing up in Philadelphia. He joined the Army and became a medic merely as an excuse to escape Pennsylvania and the demands of his father's plan for him to become a doctor. His lie was that he would come home after three years and get a job with the Sheriff's Department as a paramedic. The disappointment of his father and some of his brothers and sisters was evident. They had always had such high hopes for little William. But he was never going home again and he was never going to give up the opportunity to fly in a helicopter for free.

But then there were the clouds. Sometimes—rarely, but often enough to make him wary—a low cloud cover or an unusually high flight pattern required that they fly through a cloud. That scared him. It touched something deep inside of him and plumbed the depths of his fear. Maybe it was not being able to see the earth below or the sky above, or maybe just the unique opacity of a white mist that had no end. The pilots called it losing ground reference.

So when they set down to wait out the dust storm, Ilario started to become frightened. The dust blew and swirled around them, cutting visibility to a few feet at best. No sky, no horizon, he couldn't even see the ground, and he knew it was less than three feet below the deck.

And the noise. The constant shrill blowing of the wind, the wicked hiss of the sand buffeting the hull, the darkness with fleeting glimpses of half light as the whirling dark wall of dust and sand attacked the Huey in large waves. All that combined to wear away the meager bit of courage he could muster, much in the same manner that the sand stripped the paint from the aluminum skin of the helicopter.

Captain Walden turned and looked back at him. He looked to her for some comfort as he had so many times before, but he couldn't find it now. She looked as scared as he felt.

"I think we should go back." She said it to all of them. "This sand isn't doing the aircraft any good. If it continues up north we'll never be able to see Fowler's Blackhawk."

"I say we wait until this blows over," Rady offered. "They always do, then try a few more klicks upriver before we go back."

"Yeah, Cap'n, let's try a little longer," Ilario added, trying to bolster Walden and his own confidence.

Walden looked at Monfriez.

"I'm for going ahead," he volunteered. "The ship can take it."

Walden turned to Altameyer for his two bits.

"I'm just a passenger." Altameyer shrugged a little too cockily and nonchalantly. That irritated Ilario.

✳

Ilario lit another cigarette and lined the butt of the last one neatly next to the others on the bench between him and Serling.

Serling took a moment to see if Ilario was going to continue of his own accord.

"She was reluctant," Serling stated for Ilario.

"Well, she wasn't all fired up about going ahead. Then, when we spotted Captain Fowler's Blackhawk . . ." Ilario looked at the pool, at the kids, the sky, his own feet, and then finally at Serling. He took a big drag from the cigarette.

"I knew those people, every one of them. Fowler, Halligan, Terry Balkum, the medic. Balkum and me . . . ah, fuck it."

Ilario took a long breath.

✱

Ilario looked out the door past the strut to watch the river flash past beneath the belly of the Huey. The view was making him dizzy, so he looked up through the door, and as they turned the bend in the valley he saw it—the crashed Blackhawk.

"There they are!" Ilario shouted, but by then everyone else had seen Fowler's Blackhawk, too.

The tank fired! By then the Huey was over the ruins of the Blackhawk, and Ilario saw the impact of the round. The Blackhawk shuddered as if hit by a giant fist. Ilario could see faces, none he recognized immediately, some looking up at him. Faces in anguish, in terror.

There was cursing over Ilario's headset. Monfriez with a steady stream of epithets.

Altameyer was shouting. "Get me around! Get me around so I can fire!"

Walden banked the Huey and Altameyer stood on the skids and poured a steady stream of 7.62mm at the tank.

Ilario looked past the machine gun and saw the tracers bounce harmlessly off the vehicle armor.

In turn tracers arced upward from the ground toward the Huey. Ilario felt their impact vibrating through the deck under his feet as a few hit their mark. Walden banked away.

"Turn around! Turn around!" Altameyer shouted. "Let me have an-other shot at it!"

"I'm going for altitude!" Walden yelled back. "Call Search and Rescue!"

"Those guys will be meat by the time Search and Rescue get here!" Ilario was surprised at the loudness of his own voice.

"We can't do anything against a tank!" Walden shouted back.

"Call in an air strike!" was Rady's suggestion.

"Take too long!" Monfriez countered.

"I'm going for altitude." There was no confidence in Walden's voice. "We'll call in our posi—"

"Wait one! Wait one!" Rady interrupted her. "We got two bombs of our own on board! The spare fuel pods! Monfriez, unstrap one! Altameyer, get the flare gun!"

"It won't work!" There was a strain in Walden's voice.

"Let's try it!" Monfriez was already unstrapping a fuel pod.

✳

Another cigarette butt joined the rank on the edge of the bench. Ilario stared out at the pool full of screaming kids but he didn't see them, didn't hear them, his eyes were focused somewhere beyond all that.

Serling had to admit to himself that for a moment he too had gotten lost in the valleys of Iraq.

"So it was Rady's idea to use the fuel pods?"

"Yeah." Ilario nodded. "I helped unstrap them. Captain Walden turned the chopper around when the first one missed."

✳

Ilario was excited, adrenaline fueling an instant high as he watched the fuel pod tumble out of the Huey and toward the tank. When it missed, he instantly felt his hopes crash, as if they, too, had hit the rocks with the fuel pod.

Walden circled away from the tank. More thumps reverberated as once more, enemy fire found the Huey. Ilario saw a hole appear near his left foot. He scuttled away from it as far as he could get.

"That's it!" Walden shook her head. "I'm going for altitude. I'm getting us out of here!"

"No! Once more!" Monfriez began to unstrap the other fuel pod. Ilario didn't help him this time, he was still pressed against the bulkhead, trying not to stare at the bullet hole but finding his eyes pulled toward it again and again.

The tank fired again! Ilario didn't see it; he just felt the concussion of the big gun. He did see the Blackhawk explode and a body sail through the air.

"Please, Captain!" he cried out. "Please!" He didn't know if he was pleading for the people on the ground or for his own safety.

"I can get it this time!" Monfriez begged. "One more!"

Ilario felt the pull of centrifugal force as Walden turned the Huey about.

"All right! One more! Then we're going for altitude! This is not our mission!" Walden's voice was taut, straining.

"Not so Rambo, huh, Colonel?" Ilario looked Serling square in the eyes. "Rambette, whichever. Doesn't make as good a story. I gotta take a piss."

Ilario jumped up suddenly and entered the building adjacent to the pool. Serling watched him go, feeling suddenly tired, hollow, as if a big part of him had been carved out and left empty. He tried to get past this fatigue and begin to analyze what Ilario was telling him. But Serling became distracted as a child suddenly appeared in front of him. A little boy holding up his sagging, soggy trunks with both hands. He looked to be about four years old.

"Mister, tie me?"

Serling smiled, gathered the limp, loose strings, and began to tie them. "Here's a nice double knot."

Serling looked around for the boy's parents and saw no one in view. That worried him and also sparked the beginning of a warm anger. People who let their kids wander around unsupervised.

"I like double knots. Like on my shoes. I can't do knots good. Don't like tying knots."

"Me, too. There you go."

The boy looked down at the knot and tucked the ends into his waistband.

"Jimmy! Jimmy! Where do you think you're going?! Huh, little man?" A plump woman came bursting out of the glass doors and ran over to the little boy. She looked at Serling.

"He won't let me take him to the bathroom anymore. Has to go by himself and into the men's room. No more."

She hustled the little fellow back inside as Ilario came out, walking briskly. He sat back down on the bench and nervously fumbled out his cigarettes and lighter and set one afire. His hands were trembling and he fidgeted with the Zippo, flicking the cover open and shut, open and shut.

Ilario saw that Serling was watching the lighter. He put the Zippo away and stared out at the pool.

"I come here all the time. Know why? No, not to rubberneck the women in bikinis. The kids. I love watching kids. Sometimes I sit on the porch of my cabin, watch them dive into Skull Lake. . . . There's something about them. They do the damnedest things, never think about the consequences. Talk about brave."

"I don't think oblivious risk-taking is necessarily brave."

"But can you imagine going through life without thinking about the consequences? It's not the doing that gets you—it's the consequences. Deep, huh?"

Ilario shut up, maybe recognizing that he was talking too much.

"What happened during the night?"

"The night . . . Oh, the night. *That* night. We argued mainly. Captain Walden wanted to surrender at first light."

Ilario looked at Serling to check his reaction. Serling kept his face blank and waited for the other shoe to drop.

"Because of Rady, she said, him being wounded so bad. Her responsibility was to get him medical care, she said."

"And after Rady died?"

"She still thought surrender was a good idea."

"And the rest of you?"

"Altameyer said he wasn't giving up until he was out of ammo or some kind of macho shit like that. He's a Ranger now."

"How about Monfriez?"

"He wanted to fight."

"And you?"

"I . . . didn't know. I was . . . scared. Really scared. You know?"

"I know."

"Do you?"

"Yes, I do."

"Sure." Ilario's voice was filled with doubt and sarcasm. Serling didn't argue the point. What was he going to do, join in an "I was so scared I . . ." contest?

"What happened during the evacuation?"

"Well, there we were, right? On the left a big-ass rock, and on the right an extremely hard place, and the two John Waynes stroking away until their wad was shot and me and the Captain trying to . . . maintain . . ."

✳

Ilario watched Teegarden's Huey and Liebman's Blackhawk roar overhead. A huge wave of relief washed over him, overwhelmed him, and brought him to tears.

He and Monfriez were struggling with Walden, holding her by the arms as she fought to break free, intent on running out of the cover of the helicopter.

"Wait for the Cobras!" Monfriez yelled.

Altameyer was firing away with the M-60, trying to keep the enemy at bay. But he was only one man and the Iraqis had them surrounded. Bullets chipped away at the rocks around them and ripped into the body of the Huey.

Teegarden lowered his Huey to a landing midway between them and the crashed Blackhawk.

Walden tore free of Ilario and Monfriez and made a dash for Teegarden's aircraft. She got only a few yards when she took a tumble. Ilario thought she had tripped.

He ran over to her, discovered Monfriez running at his side. Enemy fire intensified around them. They grabbed Walden and began to drag her back to the Huey. She screamed. Ilario saw the bloody patch in her stomach, then the dark hole. She screamed again and then he noticed that the arm he was holding was bent at the forearm. A splinter of white bone stuck through the torn and bloody sleeve.

Ilario wanted to change his grip, he knew he was causing her pain, but he was afraid he would drop her.

Then Monfriez collapsed, clutching his leg.

Ilario dragged Walden back to the downed Huey on his own, with her screaming all the way. Monfriez hopped, then staggered back by himself and collapsed on the deck of the chopper.

Ilario went for the first-aid kit inside the Huey. The Cobras strafed the ridgeline and river bottom with their miniguns. The surge of noise was deafening. Ilario turned to Walden with a compress bandage and tried to concentrate on his job as a way to keep his wits.

Altameyer ran out of ammo, cursed, tossed away the M-60.

"Let's go!" Monfriez yelled.

The enemy fire decreased sharply after the Cobras attacked. Ilario tossed aside the bandage and grabbed Walden again, this time higher on her arm, under her armpit, trying not to hurt her any more than necessary.

Altameyer tried to help Monfriez, but Monfriez pushed him away.

"Help the Captain! I can make it!" Monfriez hopped to his feet. "Let's go!"

Altameyer grabbed Walden's other arm and he and Ilario tried to lift her.

But she began to fight them, yanking herself away from Altameyer, pulling against Ilario.

"I'm not leaving my aircraft! It's not safe! It's not safe!" she screamed.

Walden fought the two men. She was completely hysterical. Tearing away from Ilario's grip, she flailed at him with her good arm. Altameyer tried to grab both of her arms, but she kicked him in the chest. He fell back against Monfriez, who screamed and went down, too.

Ilario helped Monfriez up. When they were on their feet again they turned toward Walden.

She had the M-16 and it was aimed at their chest level. The barrel wavered, but her finger was on the trigger and they were only a few feet from death.

"I'm not leaving my aircraft!" she screamed again. "Go on! Go on!"

Ilario, Monfriez, and Altameyer backed away almost by reflex. It wasn't enough for Walden. She fired at the ground in front of their feet. A short burst, it spat rock and dirt into their faces.

They backed away a few more feet, this time on purpose.

The enemy fire increased as the Cobras flew past the target area and went into a turn for another run.

Suddenly the Huey was peppered with gunfire. The three men dived for the ground. Walden was hit with a fusillade of gunfire. Her body was buffeted by the bullets and then she collapsed limply, lax muscles failing to support her anymore, and she fell into the dirt.

The three men low-crawled under the gunfire to Walden's side. Ilario got there first.

She was dead.

Monfriez looked at her last.

"Let's get out of here."

Ilario and Altameyer grabbed Monfriez under his arms and ran to Teegarden's rescue helicopter.

Ilario got closer and closer to the chopper, one refrain running through his brain over and over: "I'm going to live. I'm going to live. I'm going to live."

*

Serling was silent for a long time. Ilario waited and smoked.

"So why did you lie to Major Teegarden?" Serling finally asked.

"We felt bad for her. We were trying to be . . . nice. I . . . I . . . I didn't want her folks to know she . . . cracked. Her folks are nice people, live in Abilene. They used to come over to Hood, watch Walden's kid when we went out on exercises. . . ."

Ilario was getting into an area he didn't want to think about and he pulled himself back.

"That's the way it went down, Colonel. We made up a story to be . . . nice to Walden and it . . . got out of hand, I guess. So just forget the medal or leave it as it is. I don't care. I gotta get back to my duty station."

Ilario rose from the bench, collected his butts, and took them over to a trash can and dumped them. With a last look at Serling, he headed back toward the hospital.

Serling rose to his feet and watched Ilario's retreating back. Ilario glanced back over his shoulder a couple of times, then entered the hospital.

Sitting back down on the bench, Serling looked around for something to focus on, some kind of visual anchor as his mind flitted about, a thousand thoughts, a million new questions.

Serling centered on a little girl of seven or eight, about Roger's age. She climbed up to the high board and cannonballed into the water. Brave or oblivious? he wondered.

SERLING sat in front of the typewriter and stared at the blank page he had rolled into the platen more than an hour before. He didn't have writer's block, he knew what to write, he just didn't want to write it. A few times he had raised his hands and they hovered over the keyboard, but he couldn't bring himself to type the first letter.

Looking away from the terrible accusation of the blank paper, he glanced at Walden's open 201 file and his eyes fell on her photograph. She was a coward.

A PFC interrupted his reverie.

"Sir, the fax is all yours now."

Serling jerked out of his stasis, nodded, and began to type. And the longer he typed, the more disturbed he became—and the more depressed.

SERLING drove over to the Quadrangle, part of the original fort, a huge enclosed area surrounded by tall yellow brick buildings with a small park inside. The grassy area used to be a parade ground when it was built in 1876, but now it was a peaceful area for tourists to wander and various birds to patrol, begging for bread crumbs. The nasty squawks of peacocks and the rude honking of geese were the only sounds to interrupt Serling's thoughts.

He sat in the shade and pondered Ilario's testimony. Walden was a coward, the eyewitness accounts a fabrication. He felt dizzy and confused, not able to focus on anything. He remembered how once, as a kid playing in Lake Michigan, he had waded out and suddenly stepped into a drop-off. There was nothing underfoot but water, and he couldn't swim. He screamed and got a mouthful of water, which panicked him further, and he flailed at the water, reaching out desperately for something to cling to, something to grab on to to pull himself to shore. He kicked out with his feet, madly trying to find some solid sand to step onto, but went under, feeling the water shoot up his nose, choking, screaming, crying, until his older sister Lisa caught his hand and pulled him to shore.

She almost had to carry him, he was so weak, and his mother worried over him the way she did when he had the flu. But there was no Lisa to pull him out now—no mother to comfort him.

Serling was drowning and there was no one to save him.

He walked over to his car and drove off the Post and back to his hotel. There was a bar downstairs.

WHEN Serling left the bar three hours later, it was dark and he was drunk. He knew he was drunk. He tried in vain to walk with some equilibrium but bumped into a light pole once, and almost fell as he stumbled his way down a short flight of steps. He was determined to find a restaurant and get something solid in his stomach to ameliorate the effects of all that alcohol. He couldn't find the restaurant the bartender recommended and said to himself, "Screw it." He wasn't hungry anyway. He got lost twice when he made wrong turns on the way back to his hotel.

Serling found himself walking along the path that bordered the canal, past the strolling tourists, past lovers walking hand in hand, past the open-air restaurants where happy people laughed and chatted. Occasionally a small boat floated down the canal.

All of a sudden Serling felt weak and dizzy. Leaning against a tree, he felt a surge of bile rush from his stomach and into his throat. He fought it back. He opened his mouth and took several quick deep breaths, and in a moment he was better, with only a sour taste left in his mouth.

Trying to step away from the tree, he suddenly lost his balance and fell. Grabbing the tree for support, he slid down the trunk and into a sitting position.

And instantly he was vomiting into the canal, heaving up the bitter, burning contents of his stomach into the water below. He waited for the convulsions to subside. He wasn't in control of his body so he let it take over. Twice more he threw up. Finally he took inventory, and all systems seemed to be at rest. He wiped his face and looked up to see two children staring at him. Ice cream cones in hand, they were obviously brother and sister, around five and six.

"You sick, mister?" the girl, the older one, asked him.

"He's not sick," the boy chimed in. "He's drunk. Drunk as a skunk." The boy said the words as if he had learned the phrase by rote.

"Skunks don't get drunk."

Serling looked at the children, feeling wretched and disgusted with himself.

"I got kids," Serling mumbled, trying to explain himself, trying to tell them that he wasn't a drunk all of the time, that he was a father, that his kids loved him, that he bought them ice cream, too, and took them on trips. . . .

A woman, the children's mother, walked over to them. She looked at Serling, revulsion evident on her face.

"I got kids," Serling said it again, this time to her. It was a plea for understanding or forgiveness, he wasn't sure which.

"A lot of good you're doing them right now," the woman said, and walked away, the kids in tow.

"You're right." Serling nodded. "She's right." And he fell into a deep well of self-pity. Serling found himself sobbing. On his knees, with the smell of vomit all around him, he wept.

People walked by, pointedly ignoring him. He didn't blame them. He wanted Nat Serling not to exist anymore.

10

Serling woke in his clothes, his body aching all over. He rose from the bed, and the pain that shot up his neck and exploded behind his forehead made him gasp. Taking in the air made him breathe in the smell of vomit, which permeated the front of his uniform. That made him sick again.

He heard a knock at the door. Maybe that was what woke him.

"Later!" Serling called out,

thinking it was housekeeping. The loudness of his own voice startled him.

The knocking became pounding.

"Okay, okay, okay," he yelled, but more softly this time. "When's checkout?"

Serling glanced at the clock—7:41 A.M.—and groaned under his breath. The groan that came out of his mouth when he stood was much louder. He leaned against the wall for a second and waited for his balance to return and his eyes to focus. Muttering a few of his favorite cusswords, he made his way to the door and opened it.

Ed Bruno stood there as fresh as a morning bloom.

"You . . ." Serling was caught by surprise, amazed at the anger that Bruno aroused in him. "You little . . ."

Then he caught himself and tried to blink himself into full consciousness. Bruno strode into the room, right past Serling.

"Christ on a crutch, Serling, you look like ten pounds of shit in a two-pound bag. And you smell like a bus-station toilet."

Serling closed the door and went into the bathroom and splashed cold water on his face.

"What the hell do you want, Bruno?" Serling looked down at his shirt. It looked as bad as it smelled, and he stripped it off.

"So! She's a coward!" Bruno crowed. "The bitch cut and run!"

Serling froze in front of the mirror. He opened his toilet kit and took out a bottle of aspirin and ate a handful, then chugged them down with water straight from the tap. His face twisted at the bitter taste, but it did take away the vomit breath.

He walked out of the bathroom and found Bruno rummaging in the courtesy refrigerator.

"That's what Ilario stated." Serling took off his sleep-wrinkled pants.

"You believe him?"

"I haven't spoken with Monfriez yet. I reserve judgment."

"I don't." Bruno found a can of Dr. Pepper and a jar of macadamia nuts. "It's done. As far as I'm concerned, if one eyewitness calls her a coward, she's a coward."

"Not necessarily." In his years in the Army, Serling had dressed and undressed in the presence of a lot of men, but doing it in front of this little pipsqueak made him angry. He buttoned his clean pants and sat down facing Bruno.

"True, but we certainly can't give her the fucking medal if we have a loose cannon like Ilario rolling around the deck. We could wind up looking down the muzzle. How do you like that military metaphor?"

"Spiffy. But I'm not done with my investigation."

"Inquiry."

Serling wanted to wipe the superior grin off Bruno's face with his fist. "There's something hinky about Ilario," he said instead.

"I don't care."

"I do."

"Of course you do. You want her to be a hero. Hell, you *need* her to be a hero. She's the hero you weren't. If she's a coward . . ." Serling shot him a look. "Okay, a fuckup, then she's just like you. And then there's no hope, right? No hope."

"Don't apply your Kmart psychoanalysis to me, Mr. Bruno." Serling stood up and looked down at Bruno, seething with anger. To his credit, Bruno didn't back off.

Serling walked over to the window and pulled the curtains aside. He squinted into the light just to have something to do while he calmed himself down.

"I fucked up. Nobody knows that better than I do. I was cleared of any charges. It was an accident. *I've* moved on. I wish to fuck everybody else would."

"You moved on. Uh-huh. Does that mean you were a degenerate drunk *before* Desert Storm? Good for you."

Bruno's cutting remark struck Serling deeply. He whirled around, his anger burning.

"I'm continuing with my assignment." Serling spoke through clenched teeth.

"I wouldn't book my flight. I say this is over. And if I say it, the President says it. The President says it and your boss says it. I'm surprised your orders haven't come in yet. Maybe they have, if you'd been conscious enough to take your messages—or my calls. See you back in D.C."

Bruno got up and headed for the door, taking the Dr. Pepper and the nuts with him. Pausing with the door open, he turned back and faced Serling. "Just to satisfy my own curiosity, were you drunk that night in the desert?"

Serling advanced on Bruno, his hands clenched into fists. "You talk about cowardice. . . . You political weasels have a lot of room to talk. You've never made a decision without a committee, a think tank, two consultants, and a nationwide poll behind you. Or had to stand by a decision. You guys flip-flop more than a goldfish out of his bowl."

Every angry sentence took Serling another step closer to the doorway and Bruno. But little Ed met anger with anger.

"You're done, Serling! Go home! Or climb back into the bottle, whatever suits you!" Bruno slammed the door in Serling's face.

With Bruno gone, Serling collapsed into a chair, suddenly tired and weak in the legs. He looked around the room, his eyes falling on the telephone. The message light was blinking.

It took Serling a while to shower, dress, and pack. His movements were not hampered by a hangover, which seemed to have been ameliorated by the encounter with Bruno, but his lethargy came more from a lack of direction, a lack of focus. He didn't know what he was packing for or where he was going next.

When he checked out, the clerk handed him his messages. He had continued to ignore the light on the phone and he threw the messages away unread.

He made the decision when he reached the airport.

THE Arch swept across the St. Louis skyline. Serling drove his rental car across the Mississippi River, enjoying the rumble of the wheels on the deck of the bridge with a childlike delight.

On the other side of the river was Granite City, Illinois. It wasn't hard to find Kane and Greene Guns. As soon as he entered the city, he stopped at a 7-Eleven for a doughnut and he looked up the number in the Yellow Pages. He called and got succinct and accurate directions from a gravelly voice on the other end of the line.

Serling bought a few more doughnuts and by the time he found the gun shop they were gone. He didn't know he was that hungry, but for the last few days he had eaten nothing but junk food. He hadn't had enough energy or patience to endure the nuisance it would have been to make a decision on a restaurant, figure out what to order; it just seemed like too much trouble. Food had become a low priority—it was just fuel for his body. There was powdered sugar all over his jeans as he got out of the rental car.

He brushed off the sugar and entered through the two formidable steel doors that protected the store. The inside was just like every other gun store he had ever been in. Racks of rifles, glass cases full of pistols. Serling liked guns but he generally disliked gun shops. He liked to shoot, had even taught Meredith and planned on teaching the kids, but most gun stores seemed to be the haven of right-wing macho assholes with a lot of opinions they insisted on spouting without much provocation—sometimes none.

Serling walked through the store. There were a few customers and three countermen, each of whom wore a pistol. Serling didn't know which one was Del Monfriez until another clerk called him to the phone. He left his customer in front of one of the pistol cases and took the phone.

"Yeah, still got it." Monfriez waited. " 'Til nine. Like they say at the girls' school: lights out at nine, candles out at ten."

Monfriez hung up and went back to his customer.

Serling took his time and looked Monfriez over. He was in his late thirties or early forties; a balding, solemn-looking man with red hair and brown eyes with huge bags. He took a boxed pistol from the case and put it on the counter. The customer, a fat man with a slight handlebar mustache, picked the pistol out of the box and aimed it at the wall, holding the gun sideways.

Monfriez grabbed the customer's hand and turned the pistol vertically.

"Where'd you learn to hold a pistol?" Monfriez's tone was sarcastic. *"Boys 'N the Hood?* You seen too many of them black gangsta flicks. They're always holding it like that, sideways, no wonder they never hit nothing. Always full-auto, of course. You hold a pistol like that, you ain't gonna hit nothing. That's why they need them splatter guns, MAC-10s and shit. That's where the sights are, on top." Monfriez demonstrated for the customer. "No wonder they have so many drive-bys that kill innocent people. They can't hit nothing, yanking the weapon like they were pulling their pud."

Monfriez took the pistol back and demonstrated an exaggerated gangsta grip, then gave it back to the customer. He looked over at Serling, still waiting and watching him.

"Help you, mister?"

"Lieutenant Colonel Nat Serling. You've already heard about me."

Monfriez gave Serling the once-over, looked him up and down.

"Yeah. Let's go out back. Browder! Take over here. Man's looking for something for his mother."

Another clerk took over and Monfriez led Serling through the store, into the back storage area, and past the boxes of inventory to a small indoor shooting range. There was no one there, but the smell of cordite hung in the air.

A Ruger revolver, a quick-loader, and a box of .357 ammo sat on the bench in front of the targets. Monfriez checked out the pistol, then turned to Serling.

"Hey, Colonel, you heard about the Polish proctologist, uses two fingers so he can get a second opinion?"

Monfriez waited for Serling to laugh, saw that he wasn't going to, and sat down at the bench and tossed Serling a pair of ear protectors.

"I know why you're here." Monfriez loaded the Ruger. "I'm telling you straight out—I made my statement. It's in writing. I don't gotta say diddly more. I don't work for Uncle Sam these days. I got this store, half of it anyway. You know how they make Mexican shish kebab? They shoot an arrow into a garbage can."

Monfriez took aim and shot at the target fifty feet away. Serling didn't know if Monfriez was trying to provoke him or amuse him with the ethnic jokes. He did know he didn't like Monfriez on sight and he was trying hard not to let his dislike of the man get in the way of what he was trying to do.

"Why did you leave the service after fourteen years?" Serling asked. "Why not pull the full twenty?"

"If you can ask the question, you ain't been in the Army long enough to understand. Know the definition of a Jewish nympho? She does it once a month whether she wants to or not."

Monfriez fired at the target again, then made a slight adjustment in the Ruger sights.

"I'd like you to tell me what happened, what you actually saw."

"Like I said, you got it on paper. I got nothing to add."

"Can I ask you a few questions?"

"Go ahead, but remember what the bride said on her wedding night. Don't ask me no questions, I won't tell you no lies. Heard about the Polack who bought a rowing machine? He woulda drowned if the lake hadn't been frozen over."

"How long were you Captain Walden's Crew Chief?"

"Just a few weeks. When she got to Saudi her regular Crew Chief got the chicken pox the second day over. She kept a clean ship, though. I came from the Two Thirty-second. Me and Walden didn't hit it off, I'll be honest."

"Why not?"

"There's this kind of woman, you don't just meet them in the Army. They want a man's job, they figure the way is to be tougher than a man. I don't fault them none. It's a tough row to hoe, but they end up being one thing . . ."

Monfriez looked to Serling for the end of the sentence but saw he wasn't going to fill it in for him.

". . . a bitch." Monfriez finished it for himself. "You know, like that Margaret Thatcher. A full-tilt flaming bitch."

Monfriez shot again. Then, as an afterthought, a punctuation mark, once more.

"Was she a good officer?" Serling persisted.

"She was all right. Hey, she could fly. That was her job. But, hell, you can train a ten-year-old to fly a UH-1, that don't make them Norman Fucking Schwarzkopf. She got on my ass, but I put her right."

Monfriez reloaded and held the gun out to Serling.

"Here, try it."

Serling hesitated a moment, then took the Ruger and aimed quickly.

BAM! BAM! BAM! BAM! BAM!

Then Serling flicked the safety on and handed the Ruger back to Monfriez. Monfriez pushed a button on the bench that brought the target up to him.

The holes were gathered together in an area you could cover with a silver dollar. Serling had never been good with a pistol, but he had just gotten lucky—or his focus on Monfriez had transferred to his gun hand.

"Nice shot group," Monfriez noted. "Yeah, after I sighted it in. You done with your questions?"

"No."

"Yes, you are. You're done now."

Monfriez got up and walked out, carrying the Ruger. Serling followed him back through the storage area.

"Why did you make up the statement you gave to Teegarden?"

"Look." Monfriez paused and gave Serling a quick, angry glance. "The other two weepy ass-wipes talked me into it. Okay, she gets the medal. Fine. Fine by me. Lotta good it's gonna do her. Shit, maybe I can sell my story to *People* magazine. Maybe a TV movie or something. Otherwise this whole thing ain't worth the hole in a chicken's ass. Good-bye."

Monfriez continued into the front of the store and he handed the Ruger to the clerk named Browder.

"Browder, call Dr. Witkin. Tell him his pistol's sighted in. He's got no more excuses."

Monfriez didn't look at Serling; he had been dismissed and he was being ignored.

But Serling didn't take his cue and leave. Monfriez finally motioned him around to the customer side of the counter.

"Is that why you did this, Monfriez? To make yourself famous, make some money?" Serling asked. "Was that your plan?"

Monfriez looked around to see if anyone had overheard Serling's questions, then he leaned across the counter and spoke in a low tone.

"Colonel, you know what to do if you get a hang fire?" he asked. "When you pull the trigger and the round doesn't go off?"

Serling was willing to play along, maybe the punch line would help him.

"Wait with your weapon pointed to the ground."

"You know why? Sometimes the primer just cooks. Could be a slow burner. It could still go off. And if you open your weapon to take the round out . . . ? It might blow up in your hands. Ruin your whole day."

Monfriez leaned an inch farther and got in Serling's face.

"Leave the round in the chamber, Colonel. Leave it be."

Serling smiled. That made Monfriez uncomfortable.

"You just threatened me, didn't you, Monfriez? I work at the Pentagon so I'm kind of slow on the uptake, but I do recognize a threat when I hear it. Let me respond this way."

Serling leaned closer. Monfriez flinched; their faces were an inch apart.

"I may be an officer and therefore a gentleman by proclamation, but before I joined up I was a Chicago street kid. I fought my way to school every day and fought my way back home every night. I lived in a battle zone, gunfire was just background noise, and firefights were just traffic hazards."

Monfriez turned away, but Serling yanked him back—hard!

"So now that I'm in civilian clothes and declaring myself off duty I have no compunction whatsoever about taking you outside and tearing you a new asshole."

Serling was suddenly a very scary man. Monfriez's hand slid toward the gun in his holster. Serling's hand shot out and grabbed Monfriez's wrist.

"And if you think that gun is going to help you—don't. Because I'll break your fucking arm before you can clear the holster. You'll be hearing from me, mister."

It was suddenly very quiet in the gun store. Everyone, clerks and customers, was staring at Serling and Monfriez. One of the clerks had his gun out. Serling released Monfriez and walked past them all and out of the store.

Once on the sidewalk, Serling got into his rental car and sat for a few minutes waiting for the adrenaline to leave his system, for his breathing to steady itself. He hated getting angry, he felt that whenever he did he had somehow lost something.

When he was finally calm and his breathing was normal he started the car and headed back to the airport.

Once he reached the airport he headed for the bar and had a scotch—to decompress, he told himself—and he tried to figure out what to do next. The Monfriez encounter hadn't cleared the waters that Ilario had stirred up. In fact they were muddier than ever. Serling opened his briefcase and took out the Walden file.

Once more the photograph drew his attention. Who was this woman? Was she a coward? A hero? Monfriez called her a bitch. Was Bruno right? Had Serling invested too much in proving this woman a hero? Yes, he had. But now he just wanted to know for himself. Who was she? What happened in the desert in February of 1991?

Serling looked through the file again, hoping to find a clue, a hint. Not to what happened; he had read and reread the file, weighing every word. Even searching between the lines, he had come up with nothing. No, now he looked for some kind of direction, what to do, where to go.

He didn't want to go back to D.C. He couldn't. He couldn't go home, either, not until he solved his own problem. Somehow that problem had become linked with Karen Emma Walden.

Serling put the file back together. Walden, Karen Emma, Captain. DOB, 7 September 1963. POB, Abilene, Texas.

SERLING changed into his uniform when he arrived in Abilene. He was worried about his appearance and he even got out his shaving kit and went over his chin once more. He wanted these people to like him. The Waldens were in the phone book, the same address as in their daughter's 201 file, but he had checked the phone book anyway.

The house was as he had imagined it. A two-story brick with a touch of aluminum siding at the eaves. The siding looked new. Serling imagined that Karen had lived there all her life until she went away to college and then the Army.

The Waldens were a bit uncomfortable with Serling at first, but everyone relaxed over iced tea in the living room. Serling wasn't at his easiest. He wasn't even sure why he was here.

They talked about the weather, the black currant tea blend versus Lipton orange pekoe. Mrs. Walden brought out Rice Krispie Treats she had made for Ann Marie and her friends. They munched on them for a while and reminisced about childhood junk food for a moment. Serling praised the Rice Krispie Treats too much, but he didn't know what else to say.

The Waldens were short people, had grown to look like each other as old married couples often do, but both had vague, shadowy physical echoes of the photographs of Karen that were arranged around the room. Her mother's eyes, her father's nose and chin. There was enough of a resemblance to further unnerve Serling.

Then three girls, ten or so, began playing in the front yard. They drew chalk outlines of each other on the sidewalk. One would lie down and the other two drew the chalk silhouette. When they rose and stood back to look at their handiwork, Serling couldn't help but be reminded of the chalk outlines of murder victims. He fought back the thought of dead children.

He needed a drink.

But he watched the girls and tried to tap into the happiness of their laughter, to ride the slipstream of their innocent fun. Then that brought thoughts of his own children and the feeling that he should be at home with them.

The Waldens also watched the girls, vicariously immersed in their play. Serling envied them all.

Mrs. Walden, Geraldine, was speaking. Serling had been so involved in his own thoughts that he had missed her first couple of sentences.

". . . better than Joel or me. Sometimes she wakes up in the middle of the night and asks if her mama's come home yet. Otherwise . . . I read somewhere that if a child doesn't see a person die or dead, like in a casket, that the person isn't really dead for them. That would be nice, wouldn't it?"

Serling nodded. It's time to get to it, he thought.

"I don't know how to ask this properly," he began. "But did your daughter have a . . . background of . . . heroism?"

Serling hadn't told them what either Ilario or Monfriez had said about Walden's being a coward.

"No. No." Geraldine shook her head. "Just an ordinary girl. Just our Karen."

"A little more stubborn than most." Joel added that. "Got that from her mother's side."

Serling smiled.

"I'm just trying to . . . understand her."

"She wasn't a remarkable girl . . . woman." Geraldine corrected herself with a wry smile. "To us she was special, of course, but by most standards, I guess . . . nothing much remarkable about her."

"Well, she was a female helicopter pilot," Serling noted. "That's still rare enough to be remarkable."

"That's my fault," Joel stated. "We took her to the fair when she was . . . eleven."

"Twelve," Geraldine corrected. "Seventh grade."

"There was a helicopter there, a small one with the bubble up front. We called it a whirlybird back then. Used to be a TV show called that," Joel remembered. "The fella, the pilot, was selling rides. I bought Karen a ticket 'cause her rabbit had just won a ribbon; she bred flop-ears—Four H. It was just a short ride, but when she came down . . . I don't think she ever came down actually, if you know what I mean. After that first ride she was . . . up there."

"She went back every day for the rest of the fair," Geraldine continued. "Used up all of her Four H savings."

"She didn't say much after the fair was over, hardly a peep," Joel said, picking up the verbal baton. "Didn't go collecting models of helicopters or go to air shows or nothing."

"Just showed up at the dinner table one day, second year of junior college." Geraldine put another Rice Krispie Treat on Serling's plate as she spoke. "She'd joined the Army, she was going to fly helicopters. I was pushing her to be a nurse. She was always so independent."

"Got that from her mother, too," Joel put in.

The two old people looked at each other, half smiling and with a communication of love so long standing that it cut Serling to the heart. He missed Meredith more at that moment than he had in months.

"She was so proud when she got her wings." Geraldine looked toward the photograph on the end table. The Waldens with their daughter between them, their smiles so broad that they lit up the room. "We went to the graduation."

The Waldens were quiet for a moment, transported back to that time in their lives when everything was great, when there was hope and a life to embrace it. Serling let them stay there as long as they wanted and wished he could join them.

The reminiscence was interrupted by the entrance of their granddaughter, Ann Marie, who rushed into the living room breathlessly and then stopped, frozen in her tracks and staring at Serling.

The little girl looked so much like her mother that Serling held his breath.

Serling tried out a smile on her. But she gave him such a hard, serious stare, a look that was so brutal for such a young child, that Serling was shocked.

Ann Marie looked at her grandmother.

"Grandma, can I make some Kool-Aid?"

"Sure, honey." Geraldine smiled fondly at the girl. "You know where it is."

Ann Marie cast another hard look at Serling, then ran off into the kitchen. They could hear her clattering around in there.

"I'm sorry." Geraldine, having seen the look her granddaughter gave Serling, apologized to him. "But the young man who came to tell us about . . . Karen was dressed just like you. She misses her mama."

"I understand," Serling said. "I have kids of my own."

"Her father is in Michigan," Joel explained. "He and Karen divorced after only a couple of years. He wanted Karen to quit the Army. Fat chance there. My thinking, he never got over Karen not taking his last name. We have custody."

Serling could feel an undercurrent of hostility about the ex-husband.

"Thank the Lord." Geraldine smiled. "Ann Marie is our saving grace. You have children. You know. They are what we live for. What we do it all for. Treasure them while they're here, Colonel. While you can."

Serling didn't have anything more to say. He ate some more of his Rice Krispie Treat, drank some more iced tea. Children's laughter filtered in from outside.

"God, how I love that sound," Joel murmured.

Serling looked at him. Joel smiled weakly, embarrassed somehow by his confession. Serling reached out and laid a hand on the man's knee, afraid to say anything but wanting desperately to communicate his agreement and understanding.

Joel placed one hand over Serling's and patted it. That small physical gesture moved Serling almost to tears. He gently removed his hand and drank the rest of his tea.

The Waldens walked Serling to his car. Serling was careful not to step on the chalk outlines. Geraldine forced him to take the rest of the Rice Krispie Treats, swearing she would make another batch for the girls.

As he opened the door of the rental car and reached for the keys, Joel spoke. "If she gets this medal, will we meet the President?"

Serling couldn't look Mr. Walden in the eye. He wondered if

he was leading the couple on by not revealing his doubts about the medal being awarded to their daughter now. He decided to go along with the lie of omission.

"Probably."

"I have something to say to him." The old man set his jaw.

"Joel . . ." Geraldine's tone was cautioning her husband.

"I know that Kuwait thing wasn't his cross to bear. I know that. But I want him to know something. If he gets ready to send our kids off to fight, he better have tried everything he could to avoid it first. I'm talking negotiating like it was his own life—or his kids'. It seemed after Vietnam for a while there we thought twice before sending our kids in harm's way. Lately, though, it's more like every time some half-assed politician starts dipping in the public-opinion polls we invade some piss-pot country. And American kids die. If he's going to do that, it damned sure better be worth every life. Damned sure."

Joel stopped abruptly, surprised at his own passion. He calmed himself down, then spoke more softly. "That's what I want to tell him."

Serling reached out and shook the man's hand.

"I think you should," Serling said.

There was a child's scream. Serling and the Waldens jerked their heads toward the back of the house. The three little girls ran out from behind the house yelling, "Snake! Snake! Snake!"

"I'd better go check." Joel was already on his way. "Probably just a garter snake, but . . . Nice meeting you, Colonel."

Serling and Geraldine watched him approach the three girls.

"I'm sorry about Joel's little speech, Colonel," she said as soon as Joel was far enough away not to overhear them. "He . . . he just doesn't want Karen to have . . . died for nothing."

"I know," Serling answered her. "She didn't, though. She saved all those men's lives. I wish you could meet them. They . . . they appreciate what your daughter did."

"I'd love to meet them, actually." She paused, then added, "There *is* a possibility she won't receive the medal."

Serling was surprised at the statement. Had he given something away? Mrs. Walden, for all her grandmotherly ways, was a very perceptive woman.

"Yes."

"Well, then, in that case, could you give this to . . . Oh, I don't suppose you can give it to the President himself, but to someone who will . . . treat it with the proper respect and attention."

She dug into her apron, looking to see if Joel was watching them, and handed Serling a wrinkled, weathered, crinkled envelope. Serling stared at it, still held in her outstretched hand, not making a move to take it. He knew the stationery: Fort Hood PX issue.

He also knew what it was.

Mrs. Walden didn't have to tell him, but she did. "It's the letter Karen wrote to us before . . . The one she left with Captain Fowler. Captain Teegarden sent it to us with Karen's things."

She reached out and took Serling's wrist and thrust the letter into his hand so that he had to take it.

"Someone who is . . . responsible," she continued. "They should read it. Get it to them. Please."

"I'll do my best."

There was another squeal from the girls and Serling looked up to see Joel dangling a little snake toward them in one hand to their squeamish delight.

Geraldine impulsively hugged Serling and then he was allowed to climb into his car and drive away.

The letter sat on the seat next to him, filling the car with a presence that few living people could imagine.

Serling drove halfway to the airport before he had to stop and pull over in a Handy Andy Market parking lot and read the letter. The handwriting was delicate, almost flowing. The message wasn't. He read it only once; the words stayed with him. It was a half hour before he could move again.

11

Serling sat in the hotel room and stared at the coffee table in front of him. Arrayed on the table were a half-eaten Rice Krispie Treat and the crumpled foil it had been wrapped in, the letter from Walden to her parents, and a bottle of George Dickel, the seal as yet unbroken.

After reading the letter in the parking lot, he had stepped out of the car to get some fresh air, to stretch, to get away from the experience he had just gone through.

Walking into the store and buying the bottle was done almost unconsciously. Suddenly he was back in the car with the bottle. And since he didn't know where he was going next and he had the bottle, the logical action seemed to be to check into a Holiday Inn.

Now he sat there, not able to read the letter again and not wanting to open the bottle and drink from it.

So he picked up the phone and dialed.

Meredith answered after the third ring.

"Hello, Serling residence. Chaos is our middle name."

"Cute."

"Nat." She sounded cautious. "How are you?"

"What's going on there?" He could hear kids in the background, loud and animated.

"It's raining. Been raining since last night. The Gomez kids have been here all day. *All day*. Ten kids. At full volume. How are you, Nat?" She repeated the question.

She tried to toss off the last casually. It didn't quite work. He could hear the concern in her voice.

"Fine. Fine. I guess."

"You guess? . . ."

There was a moment of silence while Serling tried to figure out why he had called and Meredith waited for her cue.

"Mer . . . ," he began. "I have a bottle of George Dickel in front of me. I don't want to drink any of it, but . . ."

"Well . . ." Meredith was vamping, trying to come up with the right response, just as she did when the kids asked one of those difficult questions. "Mommy, why do men have nipples?"

"That's a step in the right direction, Nat. That you called."

"I guess so. That doesn't help me not drink it."

"You could toss it out the window."

"I'm not sure these windows open."

"You know what I mean."

"Yeah. But I'd go buy another. Or I'd go to the bar downstairs."

"Then the secret's not in the bottle but in why you need it. Tell me that one."

Serling tried to answer that, hoping that it was right there on the surface of his thoughts. But it wasn't. So he dug deeper, as deeply as he could. Then he stopped because it hurt too much.

"I can't, Meredith."

"Why not?"

"I don't know. Because I'm not sure I know the 'why' yet."

"Bullshit." The Chicago street kid came out in her. "Tell me."

He was silent in response.

"Guess what I'm eating," he said after a moment.

He could hear her sigh over the two thousand miles of wire or fiber optics or whatever they were using these days.

"What?" She played along.

"Rice Krispie Treats."

"Really? We made some today, the kids and I . . . me. Lasted ten seconds. Synchronicity."

"A nice old couple gave them to me. I'd like us to be a nice old couple, Mer."

"So would I, Nat."

Her voice was filled with emotion. Serling felt himself choke up, too.

"But you know, Nat," Meredith continued, "drinking from that bottle would not help us in that direction."

"I suppose not."

"You suppose not. That's a chickenshit answer, Nat."

"It is," he agreed.

"You're not a chickenshit kind of guy. Never have been. Don't start now. And, no, the kids aren't around to hear me say 'chicken-shit.' I'm in the bedroom sorting socks."

Serling had an image of that and he wanted to be there so badly that it was a physical ache.

"Thanks, Mer."

"What? I helped? What are you going to do with the bottle?"

"I'm going to flush the contents."

"I believe you. I really helped?"

"A lot. Thanks, Mer."

"Anytime."

"I gotta go now."

"Will I see you soon?"

"Hope so. Gotta go."

He had to hang up soon or he was going to cry.

"The kids miss you. That's not blackmail, just a fact."

" 'Bye." It was as much of an answer as he could manage.

" 'Bye . . ." Meredith drew it out; she didn't want to hang up, either.

Serling hung up first, feeling as if he had done something wrong to the woman he had loved for more than fifteen years.

Before he could reconsider and change his mind, he grabbed the bottle and took it into the bathroom, breaking the seal on his way. He poured the contents into the toilet, holding his breath so he didn't inhale the fumes. He knew that if he got a good whiff he would be in danger of drinking it, he wanted it so much.

The bottle gurgled empty and he flushed the toilet, then rinsed the bottle out in the sink just to eliminate any residual odor of liquor. He tossed the cleaned bottle into the wastebasket.

Back on the sofa, Serling sat and looked at Walden's letter again. He was suddenly cold. And lonely, but he couldn't call Meredith again, he didn't want to pile his grief onto her. He had to deal with this alone.

It was going to be a long night.

SERLING was up early, dressed and at the Abilene airport before seven in the morning. In spite of the early hour, the ticket counters and baggage check-ins were busy.

He dialed a pay phone and braced himself for the coming conversation.

"General Hershberg's office." Banacek was as crisp and authoritative as usual.

"Ban, it's Nat Serling."

"Nat! The General wants to talk to you ASAP! Hold on!" Banacek couldn't hide the urgency in his voice.

Hershberg came on the line quickly, but calm and subdued with just a hint of iron in his voice. No greeting, just a firm question.

"Where are you, Colonel?"

"Abilene." Serling felt like a kid caught by his father doing something bad. "I'm about to buy a ticket. I just spoke to Walden's parents. I was also in Illinois. I interviewed Monfriez, the third eyewitness."

"I see." Serling could tell by the tone of his voice what the General saw. A miscreant Lieutenant Colonel. "Then you somehow missed my message."

Serling paused and considered whether or not to lie.

"What message was that, sir?" It seemed safe enough to ask that.

"Calling off the Walden inquiry. I read your Ilario report. It doesn't exactly–"

Serling jumped in and cut the General off abruptly. "I don't think, sir, that Ilario was all that truthful in his responses. Something stinks in this, sir. And the same goes for Monfriez. He's also hiding something."

"So you have *two* of the three eyewitnesses who don't support the recommendation? Nat, you just reinforced my reasons to call this thing off. I want you—"

"Sir, I'd like to pursue this a little further."

It was quiet on the other end of the phone line. Serling was scared. He knew he was on dangerous ground, a career minefield.

"Nat, listen carefully. You will not, I say again for clarity's sake, you *will not* interrupt me again."

"Yes, sir." Serling felt a moment of relief. If the General was just warning him, he was okay. Well, he wasn't in the best of situations, but it was better than if the General remained silent.

"I understand your trying to help out Walden, Nat, but if there is one shaky eyewitness, then the whole medal is tainted. Sounds like you may have two. You know we can't allow any, *any* doubt when it comes to the nation's highest . . ." Serling heard the General's exasperated sigh. "You know what I'm talking about, Nat. Come home."

It wasn't exactly an order, it sounded more like a recommendation. Serling took hope and pushed on.

"But, sir, even if she doesn't qualify for the medal, I feel there should be an inquiry as to what these men are hiding."

"If you say so, I will initiate such an inquiry, but that is another department and another day. Nat, don't press me on this."

Serling knew he had to be very careful now.

"Begging the General's patience, sir, I will press. Do this for me, sir. Give me three days. A pass . . . on my own time . . . unofficial. A three-day pass, sir. Give me that, sir. Please. This is important to me, sir."

There was a long silence on the other end of the line.

Serling couldn't stand the quiet. He would try another tack.

"Sir, you said you gave me this assignment for a reason. I think I am getting close to something that seems to be . . . very important to me. To my future in the Army. To my . . . It's important, sir."

Still more silence. Serling wondered if he had oversold himself.

"The pass is granted." It was the General's command voice. No fatherly tone, no friendly camaraderie. "But hear this, soldier. In three days I want your ass at attention in front of my desk, and brace yourself for a thorough examination of your career possibilities and your role, if any, under my command. Do you understand me, Colonel?"

"Yes, sir," Serling responded in kind with his best cadet voice. "Most definitely, sir."

And the General hung up.

Serling didn't know whether to feel elated or if he should really begin to worry about his future. He decided to favor the upside. What he had told Hershberg about his future in the Army and the Walden affair was true. His career, his marriage, his life . . . they were all on the line, and it all pivoted on Karen Emma Walden and what she did in the desert one night during the Gulf War. He had to know the truth.

12

The Rangers were being run through the Obstacle Course by the cadre. A muddy field with rows of concertina wire and tangle wire, culverts, railroad ties, and anything else that would make the going difficult had been arranged on the ground.

Adding to the physical impediments was a force of cadre tossing quarter-pound blocks of dynamite into the puddles and wielding M-16s full of blank ammunition.

This was possibly the most unpleasant one hundred yards, short of actual combat, that these men would ever traverse in their life.

The Rangers scrambled through the Obstacle Course in teams. One team leader made it to the end drenched in mud, half-deaf from the explosions, exhausted, but proud of his accomplishment. Altameyer soon corrected that as he got into the team leader's face.

"What the fuck are you doing, Ranger? Where are your men?"

The team leader turned to show his men, four muddy, bedraggled, grossly fatigued soldiers. But Altameyer pointed back on the course. One lone soldier was hopelessly tangled up in the barbed wire, left behind.

Altameyer went berserk.

"You don't leave a man behind! Look at me, Ranger! You never leave a man behind! Never! You're brothers! He depends on you! You depend on him! American soldiers never leave one of their own behind! Never!"

Altameyer began to jab the Ranger in the chest for emphasis. The student took it, one hard poke after another of Altameyer's knuckle.

Serling stepped toward them, about to intervene. Physical abuse was taboo. No training cadre ever physically assaulted a student.

Before Serling could reach Altameyer and the Ranger, the principal instructor stepped between them. Serling saw the PI dress down Altameyer and send him off the Obstacle Course. Serling ran to intercept him.

Altameyer was angry and bitching to himself—and he was visibly shaken to see Serling.

"You lied to me, Sergeant." Serling didn't see any reason to soft-pedal the encounter. He decided to use shock and bluntness to his own purpose.

"What are you going to do, sir? Make me join the Army?" Altameyer decided to play it tough.

"It's a court-martial offense to make false statements on awards documentation. But we don't want to dance to that tune, do we, Sergeant?"

"What do 'we' want to do, Colonel?"

"Talk."

Altameyer looked around suspiciously.

"How about we talk someplace private. I'll drive."

Serling, not on official status this time, didn't have a driver or a car. In fact he had taken a cab to the base and hopped a ride on the company water wagon when he found out where Altameyer was assigned that day.

He followed the Sergeant to the parking lot and the Saleen Mustang. Serling tried not to show his reluctance as he got into the passenger seat. Altameyer drove out of the parking lot.

Neither man spoke for a while. It wasn't until Serling saw that they were heading off the Post that he broke the silence.

"Where are we going?"

Altameyer ignored the question.

"Might lose my gig with the Rangers," he said instead. "PI's pissed at me. Says I'm . . . fuck it. They'll probably send me to the regular Infantry now. Ground-pounder. My own fault. I changed my primary MOS to get the Ranger assignment. That's okay. Infantryman. It's not a career, it's a shitty job."

Altameyer reached under the passenger seat behind Serling's legs and pulled out a pint of Jim Beam, uncapped it with a practiced one-hand, and took a long drink.

He saw Serling watching him and misinterpreted the look.

"Don't give me any shit about drinking and driving, sir. I'm not in the mood. Have some."

Altameyer offered the bottle to Serling.

"No, thanks, I'm trying to quit." In truth, Serling hadn't had a drink since the day before on the flight to Abilene. He wanted a drink, needed it even more. But he shook his head.

"Me, I'm going to quit, too." Altameyer smiled and drank again. "After this bottle."

Altameyer laughed. Serling didn't.

"Are we going to talk, Sergeant?"

"As soon as I figure out what I got to say, sir, I will promptly relay that information," Altameyer said, mocking Serling. Then he got serious. "You ever kill anyone, sir?"

The big question. Serling wondered if Altameyer knew the ramifications the question had for him.

"Yes."

"You know you can talk about killing somebody. Wolf talk, you know. 'I'll kill you, motherfucker, I'll waste your ugly ass.' We all say it. But killing somebody . . . it's a hard thing to do. Easy to pull the trigger. Hard to live with. Know what I mean?"

"I know exactly." Was Altameyer playing with Serling?

"I killed people that day. That night. Out in the desert. I don't remember much about them. Little figures falling over. I saw a couple of faces, but none stayed with me. A raghead with a big mustache. I can remember him if I try. But Captain Walden's face . . . Her face . . . she's looking at me whenever I close my eyes. Nothing gets rid of her. Dope, booze . . . praying. Even tried that. Nothing works."

Altameyer emptied the bottle, tossed Jim Beam out the window. It was getting dark.

Serling's mind was racing. What was Altameyer saying? Did he kill Walden? Is that what these three men were covering up? Why would he kill her? What did he have over the other two to keep them quiet, to scare them into lying?

"Are you telling me that you . . . ?" Serling ventured.

"I'm telling you shit!" Altameyer interrupted him loudly. "Just shut the fuck up and listen . . . sir."

Altameyer tried to laugh again, but he failed and the laughter died on his lips. He was having a hard time. Altameyer looked disgusted, not at anything in particular around him, but at himself.

"You know, it's the gray areas that get you," Altameyer continued. "Right or wrong, black and white . . . I can deal with that. But who would ever think that killing would be a gray area. It's wrong to kill someone. Flat out. That's one of the black and whites, one of the Ten Commandments. Then you get in the Army. You kill people. It's part of the job, they say. You kill someone, the Army says it's okay, then it's okay. Maybe that makes it okay for them, but it don't make it okay for you. Know what I mean?"

"I think so."

Altameyer looked at Serling, desperate for help or understanding. He was desperate for something.

"Tell me, sir, tell me," Altameyer pleaded with Serling.

"It's a struggle every day finding out what's right or wrong. Most people don't even want to wade into those waters. That's why we have religion, Codes of Conduct—to sort it out for us."

"But they don't help a bit when it cuts to the bone, do they?"

"Well . . . they . . ." Serling found he couldn't lie. "No. What does this have to do with Captain Walden?"

"Everything." Altameyer's voice was a whisper. "Everything," he repeated.

Altameyer reached under his seat. Serling figured he was going for another bottle.

But he pulled out a pistol instead.

It was a Colt .45 automatic, Model 1911, old Army issue. In the intervening years it had been replaced by the Beretta 9mm. Altameyer aimed the pistol casually with his right hand—at Serling's chest.

Serling stiffened. He looked around. There was nowhere to run. They were cruising at fifty-plus down a tarmac road that appeared to be sparsely populated. Every half mile or so they zipped past a shotgun shack or a mobile home. That was all.

Train tracks ran parallel to the road and the Saleen gradually approached the rear of a slow-moving freight train.

Altameyer punched the gas and the Saleen shot ahead, passing the freight train in a few moments. The .45 didn't waver from Serling's chest. Altameyer twisted sideways to keep an eye on both Serling and the road. He glanced at the train.

Serling thought of jumping Altameyer then, but wrestling with the driver of a speeding car and what he had to assume was a loaded pistol didn't seem to be sensible right now.

"I always liked trains," Altameyer mused casually, as if he weren't holding a gun on Serling. "Since I was a kid. They're big, black, strong, tough. Like me. Iron. If I ever boxed pro I was going to call myself Howard 'Night Train' Altameyer. What do you think, Colonel, don't that have a nice ring to it? 'Night Train.'"

The Saleen was ahead of the train now, well ahead by a mile or two. Suddenly Altameyer made a sharp turn down a dirt road and stopped on the tracks. Serling couldn't see the train itself, but the light on the engine was a small white flare in the darkness.

Serling slipped one of his hands toward the door latch.

Altameyer jabbed him in the side with the muzzle of the pistol.

"Altameyer . . . ," Serling began.

"Shut up!" Altameyer growled. "Sir . . ."

The train whistle sounded. It might have been a routine procedure in this stretch of track or because the engineer had seen the

Mustang on the tracks, Serling didn't know and couldn't guess. The sound had a frightening urgency to it.

"I do love trains." Altameyer cocked his head and listened to the whistle. "Ain't that whistle pretty? Listen to it."

Serling listened. The shrill sound wasn't pretty to him. To tell the truth, it scared the piss out of him. And it was getting louder.

"But a train off its tracks ain't worth shit, is it, Colonel? It's just . . . scrap iron."

Altameyer pulled the gun out of Serling's ribs.

The train was roaring toward them down the tracks. Serling could see it now, even the engineer was visible at the window shouting and gesturing to them.

"I lost my track, sir. There in the desert. Get out."

Serling was surprised. What was Altameyer trying to do? Commit suicide? Serling wanted to talk him out of it.

"Altameyer . . ."

"Get out!" Altameyer screamed the two words.

Serling opened the door and got out. Altameyer pulled the Saleen around and faced the oncoming train. Serling grabbed the door handle on the driver's side, not knowing what he was going to do, but determined to get Altameyer out of the car.

Altameyer stepped on the gas.

The Mustang leapt ahead down the tracks.

Serling's grip was torn from the door.

The Saleen engine kicked in the turbo. Serling heard the whine over the grinding rush of the oncoming train. The train whistle keened.

The Mustang and the train met—head-on.

The crash was an awesome, thunderous clash of metal. The Saleen disintegrated on impact, exploding into flying pieces of steel and plastic.

Then it blew up! A giant fireball engulfed the train engine.

Serling ran and dived into the trees lining the tracks to try and avoid the tumbling wreckage.

The train was trying to slow, the brakes screeching painfully. When the train finally stopped a half-mile down the rails, all that was left of the Mustang were twin trails of debris on either side of the tracks and a burning ball of twisted steel mashed into the snout of the iron engine.

A PASSING business machine repairman called the police on his mobile phone. He then let Serling use the phone to call the MPs, and an hour later there was an assortment of official vehicles with flashing lights all along the tracks and next to the train.

State, county, and city police cars, fire trucks, ambulances, MP cars, even a couple of Amtrak vehicles, and a tow truck. Before they had begun to arrive, Serling walked over to the largest piece of twisted metal to eliminate the slim possibility that Altameyer was still alive.

It was hard to make out the body. Everything was blackened by smoke from the burning tires. Serling edged closer and closer to the still-flaming ruin, trying to wave away the black, choking smoke. Finally he could make out an arm and a hand dangling from the wreckage. He edged closer to be sure. What he saw sent him reeling into the nearby bushes to vomit.

He had seen burned men before. His mind screamed, "Boylar!"

The repairman with the car phone refused to get out of his car.

Serling spent an hour with the Georgia State Police answering questions. He told them about Altameyer being in a dark mood, nothing about the gun or the confession to killing Walden—if it was a confession. Serling's mind was still doing loops around Altameyer's rambling last words.

When the state police asked Serling why he was traveling with Altameyer, he told them that he was doing a routine inquiry into an award for action taken in Desert Storm. They nodded and it went no further than that. Serling was relieved. He didn't want to say any more until he spoke to General Hershberg.

The MPs were a little more curious, but forbearing, knowing they had access to Serling whenever they needed him. That he was on assignment from a three-star General attached to the Joint Chiefs of Staff probably helped. But it was still a half hour of answering the same questions the state police had asked.

The MPs gave Serling a ride back to the Post, where he picked up his suitcase and briefcase at the Ranger Training HQ. From there he called Hershberg to fill him in on what had happened. The General listened quietly without comment until Serling finished.

"What do you want to do now, Nat?" the General asked.

"Well, sir, I'd like you to call the Fort Sam Houston Provost Marshal and have them detain Specialist Ilario until I get there. I would very much like to talk to him."

"Detain him on what grounds?"

"Substance abuse, trafficking . . . I'm sure there will be cause."

"You are? You didn't mention this earlier in your report."

"It didn't seem . . . relevant, sir. And they were only suspicions at the time."

"These charges, will they stick? You have no hard evidence, I take it."

"None, sir. Just suspicion. I don't know if the charges will stick. I don't even care. I just want them to hold Ilario until I get there."

"Nat, can you give me one good goddamn reason why I shouldn't turn this tar ball over to CID?"

Serling had to think a moment. He knew that this was one of those moments that make or break an officer's relationship with his superior. He knew that if he asked the General to let him pursue this just as a favor it would be granted—but it would also sever any ties that he had with the General.

"Sir," he began carefully, "I have been assigned to verify the eyewitness statements in an awards submission. One of these eyewitnesses certified that his statement was true, then, under pressure of a second interview, committed suicide—in front of me. A second eyewitness retracted his original statement on the first interview. I think we should conduct a second interview and confront him with Altameyer's testimony and subsequent suicide."

"To what effect, Colonel?"

"Colonel," not "Nat." Serling was clearly on thin ice.

"Sir, Monfriez won't speak with us. Out of the service, he is more or less out of our sphere of influence. Ilario may have been lying to protect Altameyer, who may have, according to his own testimony, killed Walden. Walden may still be deserving of the medal."

"She may?"

"It may be a dirtier matter than we began with, but that should have no impact on her actions. We don't know how she conducted herself on twenty-six and twenty-seven February, and we won't know until we get the truth from Ilario—now that he doesn't have to cover up for Altameyer."

"And if she was not deserving . . . if her conduct was . . . unbecoming? What then, Nat?"

"Nat" again—and some genuine concern in Hershberg's voice.

"Then, sir, I will report back to you and you can proceed with CID or whatever the matter dictates at that time."

"Proceed, Colonel." There was not a second's hesitation.

"Thank you, sir." Serling would have felt like shouting in triumph if he hadn't been so tired. "I'll call you from Texas."

"There will be a vehicle for you at the airport. Call Banacek and leave your flight information with him."

Back on official status!

"Yes, sir. At his residence, sir?"

"I missed Letterman, he might as well get yanked out of the sack, or hopefully away from one of the D.C. secretaries he keeps calling during business hours."

"Yes, sir." Serling smiled.

The General hung up.

Serling sighed and tried to roll the knot out of his shoulders, not realizing until now how tense he had been during the phone call.

Turning to the SP/4 at the desk across from him, he said, "I need a ride to the airport."

And then, while they located a HumVee and a driver for him, Serling had the time to ponder whether he could keep his word to the General. If he did discover that Ilario was telling the truth about Walden, or at least was sticking to that version of events, would Serling be able to move on, let go of the inquiry and let CID take over?

He hoped so.

He doubted it.

Maybe it was time for him to leave the Army.

But first, Ilario. There was still a chance.

13

At the airport, once Serling had booked his flight to San Antonio, he had called Banacek's residence BOQ and gotten the answering machine. Obviously Banacek's amorous pursuits had been interrupted before and he wasn't going to allow that to happen again. Serling left his flight information anyway, not sure it would get to Banacek in time.

But when he arrived at the airport in San Antonio there was a driver, Sergeant Bettman, an MP, waiting for him. He took Serling onto the Post and straight to the barracks where Ilario had his room.

It was empty. No sign of Ilario. The MPs were still searching the room as Serling walked up the stairs and down the hall. A Lieutenant Hulcower was expecting Serling. The Lieutenant was in a good mood for such an early hour of the day.

"Good call, sir. We found a whole drugstore in his footlocker, plus morphine vials, military issue, and all sorts of drug paraphernalia. Needles and such in every little hidey place you could think of. This guy was like a pack rat with a jones."

"But no Ilario?" Serling asked.

"Not hide nor hair. But we're on the lookout. So are the San Antonio police."

Serling nodded. What should he do now? No Ilario—no answers. No answers—no reason to go on. What *could* he do? The MPs or the local police would find Ilario eventually. But the General would expect some results from him soon. Serling could push it until the afternoon, but after that . . .

Serling felt himself flailing blindly in the water again, the shore sliding farther and farther away. Where was Ilario? So much depended on this case. Because Serling had bet everything on Karen Emma Walden and her medal. He had put it all at stake—his career, his family, Meredith, the kids. . . .

The kids.

Serling turned to the Lieutenant. "I need to go downtown and stop at one of those souvenir shops by the Alamo. I have to get some T-shirts for my kids. I . . . I forgot them the last time I was here." Serling figured at least it was something for him to do, to pass the time while the MPs tried to find Ilario. "I'll find my own way back here. Your office?"

The Lieutenant looked at Serling with a slight, puzzled frown.

"At the Provost Marshal's. We can give you a lift into town, sir."

"Thanks." Serling smiled, knowing that the Lieutenant was silently cursing senior officers and wondering what was so important about a bunch of T-shirts.

But Serling had to make himself unavailable when the General called. He couldn't be sitting in the Provost Marshal's office just waiting for a report of Ilario's whereabouts. Hershberg could track him down there and Serling had to tread water for a while and become incommunicado—off the Post.

The Lieutenant took Serling back to the vehicle that had picked him up at the airport and gave him the Provost Marshal's phone number, his own card, and directions to the Provost Marshal's office.

The MP sedan with the Sergeant at the wheel took Serling back into San Antonio.

IT took no time at all for Serling to get T-shirts for his kids; there were shops for that very purpose all around the park that surrounded the Alamo. He even found something for Meredith, a little, brightly painted hand-carved frog from Mexico. It had nothing to do with the Alamo but he knew she would like it.

He sat in the little park across from the Alamo itself, a surprisingly small edifice now fighting a modern battle, this one against the towering city structures of downtown San Antonio as they crowded into the small area around the River Walk. And this assault the small mission was managing to win with new armament: history and a modest dignity.

The Alamo was constructed of the ubiquitous yellow stone indigenous to the area, and Serling, trying to pass the time, crossed the plaza and entered. Outside there was a little brass sign. QUIET.

NO SMOKING. GENTLEMEN REMOVE HATS. Serling took off his garrison cap, smiling at the quaint politeness and old-fashioned courtesy the sign was trying to preserve.

Once inside the Alamo, Serling was struck by how small the old church was, even with the domed ceiling. It was quiet, and tourists murmured to one another in hushed, reverent whispers. The names of those who had died here on March 6, 1836, were listed on brass plaques along the walls.

The personal effects, rifles, pistols, knives, wallets, razors, and Bibles of some of the men who fought that day were on display in glass cases. David Crockett, James Bowie, William Barret Travis. Legends now. Some were already legends in 1836, but on that day in March most of them were just mortal men fighting for their lives—and a cause.

This little church, once a place to worship God, was now a place to pay homage to heroes. Serling wandered out of the shrine and across the courtyard. He walked through the museum and read about Santa Anna and how he wiped out the garrison of 187 men with more than six thousand men in a siege that began on February 23 and ended on March 6.

Serling's mind wandered from February 1836 to February 1991 and then to today. Hershberg had sent him on this mission for one reason, so he could come to terms with what had happened at Al Bathra. Serling knew he had to get past what he did in the desert if he was ever to command again. Until he dealt with his actions he would be a timid combat officer, hesitant, unsure of himself. Traits not suited for battle.

The problem was that in order to get past it he had to know why it wouldn't go away. Serling walked outside and sat down in the shade of a tree in the Convent Garden.

He had failed somehow that night in the desert. Failed himself. And he needed to dig deeper than he had so far in order to find out where that failure lay.

So he did, there in the quiet of the old church garden. He went back to that cold night in the desert. *Firebringer,* his tank, his crew, Patella, the battle, the attack of the hidden T-55s, his decision—his fateful decision to fire.

And he had it.

He had been scared.

That was what he hadn't yet admitted to anyone else, or himself. He had been scared. He had issued orders to fire out of fear for his own life.

He was a coward.

Serling felt himself trembling. He got up and walked.

The weather was getting warm and the plastic bag of T-shirts was making his palms sweat as he switched it and his briefcase from one hand to the other. He needed something to drink, not necessarily alcoholic, and a cool place to sit for a while. There was a bar across the plaza, Bowzer's, that looked dark and comfortable and like a place where one could pass a lot of time.

A coward. His Army career *was* over. What kind of soldier would a coward make? The answer was simple. What kind of commander, a so-called leader of men, could he be if he was in fear for his own life? None.

Serling wasn't actually walking toward the bar, he hadn't committed himself to that, but he was ambling in that direction when an overheard snippet of conversation stopped him in his tracks.

". . . the line between the cowards and the heroes . . ."

The source of the words was a tall man wearing a straw hat with a wide, garish headband, probably from a previous vacation, Serling thought. The man, clad in a bowling shirt, had a large gut on a skinny frame. He was talking to a boy whom Serling took to be his son, a sunburned twelve-year-old in the standard-issue athletic shoes and a heavy metal T-shirt.

"Davy Crockett grew up in a log cabin, huh?"

"Probably," the father answered. "But you're thinking of Abe Lincoln."

Serling watched them stroll around the square and let his mind wander, the bar forgotten for the moment. He was trying to focus on something else, anything else but the fact that his Army career was over. Let's finish the mission at hand, then think about the next step. What? Resignation? What was his mission? Ilario. Where the hell was the medic? Serling focused on the question that fell into line so handily.

Who had called Ilario to warn him about the raid? Where would he hide? Serling went over to a plaza bench and sat down in the shade and opened his briefcase to his report describing the Ilario interview.

It took a few moments to read through the report, and when he was done, Serling's only satisfaction was that he had used up a little more time. He put the file aside, still not satisfied that he had thought of everything. Maybe there was something that wasn't in his report. . . . He thought back to the two of them sitting on the bench, watching the kids splashing noisily in the swimming pool. . . . Nothing.

A coward. Frightened for his own life. The rounds were exploding all around his tank. There were dead tanks on either side of him. The next round would have caught him dead center.

So he fired. Because he was afraid.

Serling put the file away and walked with no destination in mind, just walked to take his mind off Al Bathra.

He found himself standing over a brass plaque embedded in the stone at his feet.

"Legend states that in 1836 Lieutenant Colonel William Barret Travis unsheathed his sword and drew a line on this ground before his battle-weary men, stating, 'Those prepared to give their lives in freedom's cause, come over to me.' "

There was a brass strip an inch wide and maybe four feet long embedded in the adjacent flagstone.

The line between the cowards and the heroes. Now Serling knew what the tourist was referring to: Travis. A Lieutenant Colonel who never made it to full-bird Colonel. Neither would Serling. The only difference was that Colonel Travis was buried somewhere underfoot, just bones and dust, not feeling anything anymore.

And Colonel Travis was a hero.

Serling was a coward.

Bones and dust . . .

What had Ilario said?

Something about a cabin, on a lake . . .

Serling stood up straight in a second of realization. He looked around and spotted an Alamo Ranger, a Latina woman, across the square. He got up and walked over to her.

She wore the short-sleeved khaki uniform and a big white straw cowboy hat on her head. Her name tag identified her as Guerrero.

"Excuse me, but is there a lake around here?"

"Yes, sir. At least three of them," she replied. "Canyon, Medina, and Calaveras."

"Three . . ." Serling couldn't hide the disappointment in his voice. "Do any of them have cabins or cottages around them?"

He knew he was grasping at straws.

"All of them, I'm sure."

Serling sighed. So much for that brilliant idea.

"But there's no Skull Lake?" He asked the question, ready to walk away. To where, he didn't know. Maybe the bar across the square.

"Calaveras means 'skull,' sir," the Ranger said to Serling, and went on, clicking into part of her tourist spiel. "There are a number of Spanish place-names in Texas . . ."

But Serling was already gone.

It took too long to rent a car. The bored-looking redhead behind the car rental counter took her sweet time and the map she gave him turned out to be close to useless, so Serling had to stop at three service stations to try and buy another map. The first two stations didn't have any local maps, but the third one did.

Serling finally headed south on the 281, mumbling curses and questions, such as, When did gas stations become 7-Elevens without bathrooms, service, or any goddamn maps?

The twenty-minute drive that the car rental clerk told Serling would get him to Lake Calaveras became an easy forty minutes, what with the lack of road signs and the absence of anyone who could give accurate directions. Nobody knew road names, north, south, east, or west, and distance estimates were so far off that Serling figured those people never wandered more than six feet from where they already were. It was time they taught map reading in school, he decided.

Finally he found the lake. On the map it was a huge meandering body of water, and Serling wondered how long it would take him to reconnoiter all of the cabins. Luckily he didn't have to wander around for long.

There were no cabins. There was a gatehouse at the lake entrance where boaters and fishermen paid three dollars to enter. The uniformed man at the gate, with a badge and patch reading San Antonio River Authority, confirmed what Serling could see with his own eyes. No houses, no dwellings at all. Just a huge, ugly power plant across the lake.

Serling drove into the parking lot and parked across from some open-air wooden structures. He got out and sat on the hood of the rental car.

It must have been another Skull Lake. At another Post maybe, in another state, who knows where. It was obviously not here.

A man was gutting and cleaning a large fish on a table inside the wooden structure. He did it with the ease and efficiency of someone who had performed the task many times. A dozen buzzards—big, turkey-size black birds with mottled, naked red heads and necks—sat watching the fisherman. One was sunning itself, wings fanned out.

Serling got off the car and walked into the shade of the structure. It was hot in the sun and the hood of the car was even warmer. The fisherman looked at Serling's uniform.

"I was in the service, '66 to '69," the man said. He looked around fifty. "Hundred Seventy-third Airborne. Vietnam. Highlands."

The fish was a largemouth bass at least two feet long.

"I was in the First Cav, Desert Storm," Serling replied.

"Saw the patch. Know what we used to say about that patch?"

Serling looked at the patch on his shoulder: a big, bright yellow shield with a diagonal black stripe dividing it, and on one yellow field a chess piece, the knight. It was the symbol for the horse from the old horse-mounted days of the unit. Serling decided to play along with the fisherman.

"What did you used to say?"

"That there was the horse you never rode, the black band was the road you never crossed, and the yellow was the reason why."

The fisherman laughed. Serling laughed with him. Why the hell not? What else was there left to do?

"What you all doin' out here?" the fisherman asked, and tossed a fistful of fish guts to the buzzards. They swooped down and fought over the mess.

"Picking at the leftovers of a mystery," Serling answered. "Like those buzzards there."

"What kind of mystery?"

"Looking for a house on Skull Lake. Here I am. No houses."

"Wrong lake."

"I thought Calaveras meant skull."

"Does. In Spanish. There's a little offshoot southwest of this one. Called Skull Lake. In English . . . American."

"Could you tell me how to get there?"

The fisherman's directions were exact. Road names, distances traveled, and compass readings. The man had been an LRRP, Long-Range Reconnaissance Patrol leader in the Infantry.

Serling tried to hold back his excitement and he got back into the rental car, thanking the fisherman a dozen times.

Serling stopped at a pay phone in front of one of those ubiquitous antique stores that lined the Texas roads. He called the Fort Sam Houston MPs and asked if they had found Ilario. The answer was negative, and a few questions later Serling asked for and got a description of Ilario's car, a red '92 BMW 325i. With that and the license plate number, Serling cruised around the lake.

Skull Lake was small, a nice area, even pretty, and the weather was particularly nice and balmy, the humidity not unbearable. A nice wind off the lake sent an occasional breeze full of lake smells wafting into the rental car. At first Serling thought he would find himself sneaking up and peering through windows into people's garages, looking for Ilario's car, but it appeared that most people didn't bother with a garage. A carport was as good as it got for most residents, except for the few big mansions with four- and six-car garages. He figured those places were beyond Ilario's salary, even inflated with his drug sales. And Serling didn't relish getting caught skulking around some rich man's property.

Looking for Ilario's car almost made him miss the place. The car, as it turned out, was parked on the lawn around a corner of the small dark brown log cabin, out of sight of the road. What stopped Serling was the mailbox, there in big letters: ILARIO, WILLIAM.

Serling almost broke out laughing.

He pulled into the driveway and parked and walked toward the cabin. Then he saw the red BMW.

The house seemed vacant.

Serling looked around. There was a short dock made of pipe-and-steel decking that jutted out into the water. A small aluminum rowboat was hoisted up out of the water against the pylons.

The lake and the cabin reminded Serling of another lake someplace else. He wondered if Patella had finished painting that house. If old man Patella had his guns in a safe place.

Serling didn't know what else to do, so he stepped onto the tiny porch that fronted the water and knocked.

To his surprise Ilario answered. Ilario opened the inner door, but not the screen. The two men looked at each other through the gray mesh.

"This residence isn't listed on Post, soldier," Serling said, and immediately regretted his words. It was the surprise of Ilario answering at all, let alone so quickly, that had taken him aback. And the plain fact was that, after finding Ilario, Serling had no plan of action.

"When I go on a weekend pass I don't want anyone bothering me. I want some peace."

"I don't think that applies here, soldier. To be precise, you're AWOL."

Damn, Serling cursed himself. This is what happens when you go into a situation without a plan. You fall back on that stupid military officialese. He should know better, a lot better.

"Don't call me 'soldier.' "

"Can I come in?" Serling needed to sit down and reassess the situation, then do something right.

"Why not?" Ilario opened the screen door and Serling walked inside. The curtains were drawn and it was dark inside. The only illumination was yellow-filtered sunlight. The furniture was cheap but in good shape and the smells of dampness and cigarette smoke permeated everything. There was a TV, not on, and some prints of horses on the walls—all very bucolic, except for the drug paraphernalia spread out on the coffee table. A syringe and a couple of glass vials.

Ilario sat down on the sofa in front of the coffee table. Serling took the chair across from him and tried to look Ilario in the eye to see if he was high. The man just looked tired.

"Altameyer is dead," Serling said. "Suicide."

"Couldn't take it, huh? He should have tried drugs." Ilario nodded and smiled ruefully. "I was never much of a head—dope or anything else—before. Before . . . Now there doesn't seem to be enough of it to do the job."

"Have you tried going straight?"

"Yeah. I know what this shit does to your body. Can't live without it, though."

Ilario leaned over and played with the syringe. Serling hoped that Ilario wasn't going to shoot up in front of him.

"You turned me in. How'd you know?"

"The sad fact is that if you command in today's Army you have to keep an eye out for all kinds of substance abuse. And dealing. I saw that in the Sick Call line. Too many soldiers left for them to all be just goldbricks. What are you using? Morphine?"

"Anything." Ilario put down the syringe and picked up one of the vials and looked at it. "Anything to kill the pain. I have enough here for an overdose."

Serling was startled. He hadn't thought of that possibility. Another suicide?

"Don't worry, Colonel. I thought about it but I'm too much of a coward. That's my problem. I'm a coward."

Serling winced at the word.

Ilario tossed the vial to Serling.

"You know I was trained to save lives." Ilario lit a fresh cigarette. "I volunteered for that job. I thought it was the greatest thing. Not to do harm, but to . . . do good, only good. Now I . . . I killed. I took a life. And I'm not counting the enemy lives. But my own people."

Ilario said the last with a twisted grimace of self-disgust.

"So have I . . ." Serling said it quietly.

"What?" Ilario was obviously startled.

"I killed some of my own people. In the Gulf War. Fratricide. The investigation cleared me of all blame. We didn't know that the target signature of a tank being hit was the same as one firing . . . whatever . . . that was the official explanation—excuse. I killed some of my own men. I see them. I'm stuck in time. Twenty-two hundred hours, twenty-six February 1991. The same night you spent on the ground surrounded by the enemy. I can't get past that night."

"You poor son of a bitch." Ilario shook his head sadly. "You're as bad off as me."

"That's why I need you to talk to me . . . about Walden. I need to know . . . I'm not sure what I need to know. Talk, Ilario, I'll listen."

Ilario jumped up and paced, glaring angrily at Serling.

"You think I give a shit about bandaging your little psyche

'cause you fucked up in the desert? Fuck you, Colonel. I got my own problems. And I don't give a flying fuck about anyone but me."

"Not even Karen Emma Walden?"

That stopped Ilario in his tracks and drained him of all energy. He fell back onto the sofa.

"I want to read you something." Serling pulled out Walden's letter. Ilario's shock was evident on his face. He recognized the stationery. Serling took a moment to settle, prepare himself. He took a breath and began to read.

" 'Dear Mom and Dad. Well, this is it, the big push. Looks like it's really going to happen. And I'm afraid. Not of being hurt or killed. Well, kind of—but not much. What I am really afraid of is that I might let my people down, my crew.' "

Serling looked up. Ilario had tears in his eyes. Serling felt himself choking up, so he cleared his throat and steeled himself to go on.

" 'The wounded soldiers whose lives we try to save, these people depend on me, they put their lives in my hands. I know I have the best equipment. This beat-up old Huey has become like a person to me. And I have the training—but I'm still scared of failing these people. I love them all, I do.' "

Ilario was crying, a steady stream of tears.

" 'I love you guys, too, but I have never experienced such a closeness to people who I have nothing in common with. It's hard to explain.' "

Serling had to take another deep breath before he could go on. He had read the letter a half dozen times, and each time it affected him with the same intensity.

" 'If you get this letter, it means that I am dead. My only regret will be to never see you two again, and that I will never see Ann Marie grow up. But I know she is in good hands—the best. If anything does happen, my last thoughts will be of you three.' "

Serling didn't have to look at Ilario, he could hear the other man sobbing.

" 'I only hope that I have made you proud, that I did my job and didn't let down my country, my crew, or my fellow soldiers. I love you. Your daughter, Karen.' "

Serling looked at Ilario, eye-to-eye.

"Did she let you down, soldier?"

Ilario sniffed back his tears, wiped the tears off his nose—and he began to talk.

✳

Ilario liked their little roving tribe. Every time the front lines moved, then their Medevac company—two Hueys, two Blackhawks, and their respective crews—would literally pull up stakes on their command tent and hop to the next station. There, a water truck, a small contingent of MPs for security and traffic control, and an odd assortment of support personnel would join them. Tents would be erected, latrines dug, home could be created, and a few days or sometimes hours later, the whole cycle of moving would be repeated.

Right now their station was not a happy place. Every man and woman in the Medevac company was scanning the sky, looking for Fowler's bird. Ilario was playing poker on the Huey's deck with Rady, Monfriez, and Altameyer, who was, as usual, winning. Not big wins, but little by little slowly draining the funds from the other three. Altameyer always won. That was why Ilario had decided not to play anymore, but he was nervous right now. He didn't have anything to read and he needed something to do with his hands and mind, so he let them deal him in.

Ilario could see Walden a few yards from the Huey. She was staring out at the desert. She looked at her watch, then back at the desert again.

She finally gave up and walked back to the poker game. "I'm going to check with Teegarden again."

Rady watched her go and waited until she was out of earshot. "Leave

237

it alone, will ya? It's not our mission. She's going to put us in a world of hurt with that gung-ho shit."

"You're in a world of hurt unless you start paying attention to your cards." Monfriez scowled at Ilario. "Captain W's okay, takes care of her ship."

"And her crew," Ilario added.

"And her crew," Monfriez agreed. "Our job is to help people, remember?"

Monfriez was all right, Ilario thought. He came in to replace a well-liked man, a part of a team that had been together for years, and as the new Crew Chief he had fit himself in very comfortably with everyone. He didn't get along great with Rady, but then no one ever did.

"They call and say Fowler needs a Medevac, I'm there," Rady stated. "But it's not our mission to wander around no-man's-land looking for trouble. Raise."

"You got trouble right in your hands there." Altameyer threw it back to Rady. "Raise you five."

"If it was you out there you'd want every aircraft in the Northern fucking Hemisphere out looking for your ass." Ilario looked at his cards again. "Pass."

Walden came back to the Huey, her eyes bright with excitement.

"We're on. Let's get in the air. Altameyer, Major Teegarden wants to see you."

Altameyer gathered up his cards, a worried expression on his face. Rady tossed his cards into the pile with a lot more force than necessary. Ilario knew Rady was pissed but, as was the habit of the man, Rady wouldn't say anything to Walden. Rady was a coward around Captain Walden.

FIFTEEN *minutes later they were in the air, after Monfriez had rigged the auxiliary fuel pods and topped off. Altameyer had bungied an M-60 machine gun in the side door. Teegarden stood outside the command tent and*

Ilario watched the CO until the swirling dust kicked up by the chopper blades obliterated his view of anything on the ground. The next thing Ilario knew, they had altitude and all he saw was the desert, horizon to horizon.

Then, an hour into the flight, they ran into the sandstorm. It was like hitting a dark, solid wall and they became part of it. Finally, before getting too lost or maybe flying right over Fowler, Walden put down to wait out what Monfriez called a "beach blizzard."

The doors of the Huey remained shut, but sand found its way inside anyway. The noise of the sandstorm was a steady, monstrous drone. Rady began whining.

"I say we go back. This beer can with a rotor can't take much more of this sandblasting." Rady was always putting down the old Vietnam-era Hueys. He wanted one of the slick but overdesigned Blackhawks.

"Maybe this isn't one of your precious Blackhawks, but she'll do the job." And Monfriez was always defending the simple but reliable UH-1. "When the last Blackhawk is towed to the junkyard, the crew will fly home in a Huey."

"We'll wait for it to blow over," Walden said calmly. She never let Rady's bitching get to her. Usually it was like static on the radio, irritating at first but after a while you didn't hear it anymore. "Then we'll try a few klicks up the river."

"But all this sand in the intake . . ." Rady as usual wouldn't let it go.

Walden just turned to Monfriez. "Monfriez, your opinion, sir."

"She's fine, Captain." Monfriez stated it flatly. "It ain't healthy but it ain't going to kill her."

"What about the rotor blades? This sand is wearing the edges. We didn't get that special coating yet like all the others. . . ."

"Rady, shut up," Walden said, not as an order, just as a weary request. Ilario didn't think Rady was scared. He was simply one of those people who went around seeing a cloud in front of every silver lining.

But he had taken offense at being told to shut up in front of the rest of the crew. After all, he was an officer, only a warrant officer, but an officer still. He turned to Walden, peeved.

"Captain, you know you don't have to prove you've got more balls than a man to make Major."

Ilario looked at Monfriez, who wisely stayed out of these things, then back at Walden to see her reaction to Rady's words.

"Rady, can it, goddamn it."

But he couldn't let it go. "I'm asking for a transfer out as soon as we get back."

"What, Christmas comes early this year?" Walden looked out the window, dismissing Rady. "Looks like it's clearing. Let's get. I've got sand in places I didn't know I had places."

The crew quickly wrapped themselves in the business of getting back into the air.

The sandstorm did clear quickly and the rest of the flight was uneventful, giving Rady the time to continue his griping.

"What's that? The main rotor sounds funny."

The former Crew Chief had once described Rady as an old lady with a dick. Ilario thought it fit perfectly but he had his own doubts about the dick part.

Walden, though, had had enough.

"Now you're the Crew Chief, Rady? The Crew Chief says we are airworthy. The Crew Chief is the final word on that. I asked you before, not so fucking politely, to shut up. Now I'm telling you. If you do not keep your conversation limited to the requirements of keeping this craft in the air, I will haul your ass up for a court-martial and you won't need a damn transfer."

It was the angriest Ilario had ever seen Walden. He figured she must really be worried about Fowler. But it worked. From that point on, Rady kept his thoughts to himself.

Ilario passed the time talking to Altameyer. He told him how he had been with Fowler's chopper at Hood when Captain W came aboard as co-pilot. When Walden got her own bird she took Ilario with her.

"Ilario's the only one who can treat my sinus allergies." Walden tossed that into the narrative.

"Local bee honey," Ilario explained.

"I hate honey," Altameyer said. "Bee shit."

"Bee shit?" Ilario asked.

"Bees eat pollen, shit honey. Bee shit."

Ilario was preparing his defense of honey when they rounded the bend and came upon Fowler's crash site. Ilario took it in, the wreck of the Black-hawk, the enemy attacking it from the ridgeline, tracers, gunfire, and then—BOOM! The tank as it fired.

The tail of the Blackhawk was chopped apart and sent tumbling off into the rocks.

"Altameyer!" Walden called out. "There's your target!"

She banked the Huey so Altameyer could get a clear shot and fire. He stood on the skids and let loose a stream of bullets at the tank. Ilario could see the shots bounce off the hardened steel.

They passed over the enemy tank but Altameyer, fueled by adrenaline, kept shooting.

"Cease fire! Cease fire!" Walden called out. "I'll try another run!"

"We should go for altitude!" Rady yelled. "Call Air Rescue! Get the fuck outta here!"

Walden ignored him and banked the Huey for another run. Ilario braced himself and felt pain in his palm. His hand had pressed down upon a ragged hole in the fuselage. A bullet hole. The edges were peeled away into sharp pieces of aluminum skin.

That scared him. Up until now he hadn't had the time to be afraid. Now he was. His hand bled. He sucked on the wound.

"We'll make another try," Walden announced. "Rady, try to get on the horn to the AWACS, give 'em our coordinates! Here we go, Altameyer."

They passed over the Iraqi tank again. Altameyer fired. Ilario hung on, growing more fearful as bullet holes popped through the hull and deck of the chopper.

Rady watched the tank pass by below them.

"That didn't do shit!" he shouted. "You might as well piss on a rock! Let's go for altitude, for Chrissake!"

Rady was panicked. There was a big starburst in the windshield only inches from his head. The bullet was still embedded in the plastic. He couldn't take his eyes off it.

"Rady, get on the phone!" Walden was totally focused on flying the Huey. "Monfriez, status!"

"Stable," Monfriez reported. "Nothing prime. Rady's right, Cap, we'd need a jet with a two-ton bomb to take out that tank."

"We're not a jet, but we've got a couple of bombs," Walden called back. "Monfriez, unstrap the spare fuel pods! Altameyer, get out the flare gun!"

"What?!" Rady's voice seemed to leap two octaves. "What do you think you are, Walden, a jet jockey? Go get a fucking Cobra. This is not our mission!"

BOOM! The Huey was buffeted by the concussion of the tank cannon firing.

"Rady, just try to get on the phone to the AWACS." Walden's voice was calm. "If we don't stop that tank right now there won't be anything left to rescue. Let me know, Monfriez."

"Ready, Cap!" Monfriez shouted.

Ilario looked. Monfriez wasn't quite ready, he was still fumbling with the fuel pod straps. Altameyer had the emergency kit out and he was fumbling with the flare gun and trying to load it. The rest of the kit was bouncing on the deck and scattering itself. A small compress skipped across the floor and leapt out the door.

Ilario, braced in his seat, was frozen in fear.

"One more time, gentlemen." Walden's voice was even calmer, her tone almost soothing. "I know you can do it."

"We need that fuel to get back!" Rady pleaded.

"We've got more than enough to return, Rady." She spoke to Rady as if he were a child, softly, simply, directly. "Get on the radio. Call in our position. That's an order. Here we go."

She banked the Huey over the tank.

Monfriez dropped the fuel pod.

It missed the target.

Walden was even calmer on the second run. Ilario took confidence from her, picked up the extra flare gun rounds from the jouncing deck and helped a fumbling Altameyer steady himself.

This time Walden flew even lower to make it easier for Monfriez. The gunfire hitting the Huey was terrifying in its rapidity, a fusillade of knocks. Holes appeared everywhere before Ilario's eyes.

Monfriez dropped the second auxiliary fuel pod.

It hit the enemy tank and splashed onto it like a giant water balloon.

Altameyer fired the flare gun.

At first the flames were hard to see from their vantage point in the sky above the desert, but as the Huey banked farther, Ilario could see the fire reaching into the air.

He joined the others in a cheer as Altameyer and Monfriez slapped each other on the shoulder.

Then the chopper went bad. Ilario felt it first through his feet, the deck going through perambulations that had nothing to do with steady, normal flight.

Then suddenly they were spinning like some amusement park ride.

Ilario was overcome with nausea, not from the spiraling descent toward the ground, but from stark fear.

They were going down.

Rady screamed. There was a red splash against the cockpit windshield. Ilario grabbed the seat back.

Walden was fighting the controls and yelling into her helmet mouthpiece. "Mayday! Mayday! Mayday!"

HE didn't remember much about the crash itself, how he survived it, what he did.

The next thing he knew Rady had been pulled into the rear cabin deck and Ilario was trying to take care of him. This is what he knew how to do, to give medical aid, and he took comfort in that. The familiar procedures calmed him down.

Ilario replaced the flap of scalp that had peeled away from Rady's shiny, dented skull, wiped the blood from the unconscious man's face, and bandaged the head wound. It was no longer Rady, the co-pilot, it was just a patient.

A patient who was in a very bad way.

Rady had taken one round through the chest cavity. Frothing, bright red blood bubbled up from the wound with each breath he took and the same came out of his mouth. Lung shot. The entrance hole was neat and clean, and Ilario taped a Vaseline gauze bandage over it, taping only three sides, leaving the fourth side free and loose. That way it would breathe with the lung action. He needed the excess air in the lungs to go out with each exhalation and the suction of each inhalation to close the bandage over the hole so no air would enter the chest cavity. Ilario did the same with the exit wound, a larger, messier hole where the round, mutilated on impact, had torn its way out.

That done, Ilario hooked up a saline IV, hung the bag from the cabin wall, and checked Rady's vital signs once more. They were slow but steady.

There wasn't much else he could do for Rady. Unless they got to a hospital soon, Rady's lungs would fill with blood and he would drown.

Finished with Rady, Ilario looked around, finally becoming aware.

Walden was on the radio, clicking through the channels, trying to find a live one, continuing to call in her Mayday.

Altameyer was firing the M-60 out one door. Next to him, Monfriez was supporting him with the M-16.

"We gotta get outta here!" Monfriez was in a frenzied state. "There's hundreds of them! We can't fight this many!"

"How's Rady?" Walden asked Ilario. She was dead calm.

"One lung, through and through." Ilario tried to match her calm tone. "Filling with blood, fast."

"Call for help!" Altameyer yelled between machine gun bursts. "Call for help!"

"Radio's dead," she told him, and she climbed out of the cockpit and looked over his shoulder at the advancing enemy.

"The Blackhawk." Altameyer looked across the river at the wreckage of their sister helicopter. "They have more men! More firepower! We'll be safe there."

Walden looked at Rady, turned to Ilario.

"The head wound?"

"Bad scalp wound. Skull's creased. Concussion at least."

"Yeah, the Blackhawk," Monfriez chimed in. "We'll be safe there! Let's go!"

Ilario realized that Altameyer and Monfriez were as frightened as he was. He just wasn't giving voice to his fear as he hung on to Walden's calm as if clinging to a rock in rough water.

"Ilario," she asked him in that same firmly controlled voice. "Can we move him?"

"I wouldn't," Ilario reported. "I don't know if there's any rib damage. He's barely maintaining as it is."

"Monfriez!" She spoke louder, but still without fear. "Go to the other door! We're taking fire there."

Monfriez obeyed. Ilario hadn't even noticed the enemy movement or the gunfire on that side of the ship. He was too busy cleaning up the plastic and paper debris left over from bandaging Rady. He didn't know where to put the wrappings so he stuffed the litter into his pocket, fully aware of how inane it was to be worrying about litter when he might die at any second.

"I'll lay covering fire!" Altameyer was still shouting. "Then you do the same for me!"

"We're not leaving Rady." Walden said it simply.

"What?!" Monfriez looked at her in shock.

"He wouldn't make it," Walden told him. "I'm not sure we would, carrying him. Altameyer, conserve ammo. You, too, Monfriez. We might be here awhile."

"We gotta get out of here!" Monfriez screamed, not believing her words.

"We're not going anywhere."

"We can't fight . . . ," Altameyer opined. "We don't have . . ."

Both of them had turned away from the enemy to argue with Walden.

"Take your positions!" Walden yelled the order.

Ilario thought it was the first time he had ever seen her yell, except for the time some finance officer didn't strap in and he almost fell out of the Huey.

THROUGHOUT the night, Ilario's composure was slowly stripped away. Monfriez and Altameyer kept badgering Captain Walden about running to the Blackhawk to take refuge. She explained that there was no reason to think that the men on the Blackhawk were in a better situation than they were in the Huey, but the two men were beyond hearing any opinion other than their own.

By midnight Ilario was crouched in the back of the Huey, jumping at every noise. Rady was unconscious, his condition unchanged. He was still breathing, but there was nothing more for Ilario to do, nothing to keep him occupied but his own thoughts, and they were getting scarier and scarier.

Altameyer was at the door facing the ridgeline, M-60 in his lap. Mon-

friez was at the other door, M-16 at the ready. Walden sat between them, her Beretta pistol out.

"You know at dawn we're dead," Monfriez muttered, his panic having settled into a muted dread. "They'll have reinforcements. You know they're moving in now, under cover of the dark. We have to get to the Blackhawk before first light."

"It's so dark you can't see your hand in front of your face," Altameyer added. It was true. With the overcast of clouds and the pall of black smoke from Kuwait, there were no visible stars, no ambient light, no moon, nothing but blackness. Altameyer went on. "Now's the time to do it. Slip right by them."

"I've told you before and I won't say it again." Walden was tired of arguing with them. "Rady can't be moved."

"Rady's dead," Monfriez sneered. "He'll never make it. You know that, I know that."

"You don't even like him," Altameyer declared. "All he did was give you grief. Now you're going to die for the prick. I say we go."

"So do I," Monfriez chimed in. "Ilario?"

Ilario looked at Walden and hated Monfriez for putting him on the spot. He couldn't meet Walden's eyes.

"I just want to get out of here," he mumbled.

"That's a majority." Monfriez declared the discussion over.

"That would be great if this was a democracy," Walden said. "But it isn't. We stay with Rady. I don't like him but he's one of mine. I wouldn't leave one of you behind. I won't leave him."

"Maybe . . . maybe . . . ," Altameyer began, talking out to the night, not to anyone in particular. "Maybe if we surrendered, the ragheads would doctor him up."

Everyone looked at Altameyer. Ilario was surprised that the man could express the thought he himself had been harboring under his fear.

Walden looked at Altameyer with a hard expression.

"No surrender."

It was quiet for hours after that, making the waiting worse for Ilario. His fear was taking over his body. Once he checked Rady's vital signs and his hands trembled. Walden reached over and took his shaking hands in hers and smiled at him. That one action soothed him, calmed him for quite a while.

Until Altameyer got spooked.

"I hear something out there, goddamn it." He kept whispering that every few minutes. "I can't see 'em, but I hear 'em. They're closing in."

"Of course they are," Monfriez whispered back. "What would you do? I say we make for the Blackhawk now."

"And I say we've heard enough of that shit." Walden was getting pissed. "Now can it."

Monfriez glared at her and fingered the trigger guard of the M-16 nervously.

"Maybe we should surrender." Ilario blurted it out without thinking. The idea was just there on his mind and he said it. Thankfully nobody paid any attention to him.

"You don't have to go with us, Captain," Monfriez suggested. "We don't even need your permission. We could just go."

That got everyone's attention.

"Give me the M-16, Monfriez," Walden said.

Monfriez was looking at Altameyer for support, so when he turned back to Walden he was surprised to see that she had raised her Beretta and pointed it at him.

"You can run," she told him, "but I'm not letting you take our firepower with you."

She took the M-16 from Monfriez's startled hands. He was too surprised, too dumbfounded to resist her.

"Are you going to take my gun away from me, too?" Altameyer asked in a belligerent tone.

"If I have to." Walden met his gaze evenly.

"You just might," Altameyer returned.

"Maybe they'll treat us okay," Ilario mumbled. "I can make a white flag." He saw what was coming and he was trying to think of a way to stop it all. Surrender could work.

"Give it back."

Walden turned and looked at Monfriez. He had his own Beretta out and aimed at her. He clicked off the safety. The sound seemed to be loud and harsh. It jerked Ilario back to reality.

"Guys . . . ," Ilario moaned.

"She's trying to get us killed!" Monfriez was angry. "It's us or her. Who you with, Ilario?"

"Cap . . . ," Ilario said, turning to Walden and begging. "Rady's finished."

"Is that your expert opinion, Ilario?" Her contempt was evident on her face. "He'll never recover? If he was out in a field somewhere and we came to Medevac Rady, you'd body-bag him? You'd leave him behind?"

"Yes," Ilario replied. He was filled with shame and the lie forced him to turn away from Walden's steady gaze.

"At least he's ashamed to say it," Walden said, and turned to look at Altameyer, who glared back at her. Then she looked at Ilario again—he just stared at the deck. Finally she returned her attention to Monfriez and the gun he still had aimed at her.

She suddenly raised her own pistol and fired.

Monfriez fired back!

Walden took the bullet in her stomach.

A ragged Iraqi soldier fell out of the darkness and on top of Monfriez, a bullet in his face.

Walden hadn't fired at Monfriez! She had killed the enemy soldier sneaking up behind him!

The three men had but a second to register that fact before they found themselves in the midst of a firefight.

Ilario fumbled for his own pistol, still in the holster, but the whine of bullets zipping past his head and the thunderous cacophony of the gunfire drove him into a fetal position, and he whimpered in fear.

Brilliant flashes from the muzzles of the various weapons lit up the night. Ilario could see the faces of the enemy as they fired. Brilliant bursts of recognition, then nothing but blackness.

And just as suddenly, the firefight was over. It was quiet except for the ringing in Ilario's ears from the percussion.

Everyone stared out at the night. Nothing moved. The sound of soldiers scrambling over rocks, Arab voices, and the moans of wounded men were all they heard for a moment.

Altameyer fired off a couple of bursts, but no gunfire was returned, just a harsh shout or two in Arabic. They could have been yelling "Cease fire" or "Fuck you" for all Ilario knew or cared.

Ilario was alive—and unharmed.

Looking at the others, Ilario suddenly felt guilty. Walden was bleeding from her stomach. She was in obvious pain as she jerkily grabbed a clip from the floor and tried to reload the M-16. She managed to get the clip into the weapon, then tried to shove a new clip into her Beretta.

Monfriez and Altameyer were also reloading.

"We gotta get outta here," Monfriez said. "They'll try it again. Give me the sixteen, Cap."

Walden looked at Monfriez blankly. Ilario wondered if she was going into shock. He looked for his aid kit. It had somehow gotten kicked aside during the firefight.

"You're wounded, ma'am," Altameyer reasoned with her. "Give him the sixteen. We gotta go. We'll carry you."

Her answer was to level the M-16 at Altameyer.

"Give me the M-60," she ordered.

"You won't shoot me," Altameyer replied.

"The mood I'm in right now, Altameyer, I'd empty a magazine into your hide and reload and do it all over again just to shut you up."

Altameyer looked at Walden, at the muzzle of the M-16 pointed at his chest, then at Walden again. He tried to judge the seriousness of her threat.

He handed over the M-60.

"Pistols, too," Walden ordered, turning the M-16 onto Monfriez.

They both handed over their nine-millimeters. Ilario, getting his aid kit together, slid himself across the deck toward her.

She pointed her Beretta at Ilario.

He froze.

"You're wounded, Captain," he pleaded.

"You're with them," she stated.

"What are you going to do, keep watch on us all night?" Monfriez asked. "You're hurt, losing blood. You're tired. You won't last 'til first light."

She didn't answer him, she just shifted her position, the better to cover all of them with her guns. The movement sent an obvious blast of pain through her and she gasped.

Monfriez made a move toward her, though whether it was to help or to reclaim his gun wasn't clear. She pointed the Beretta at his forehead.

"What if they attack again?" Altameyer asked her. "How are we going to fight without guns?"

"You'll get your weapons back then," she replied.

"By the time you give 'em back it might be too late," Altameyer tried to explain it to her.

"It's already too late," she said.

"You can't stay awake," Monfriez argued. "You won't last to first light."

Walden just stared at Monfriez, grimly determined. Ilario began to cry. He didn't know what started the tears or even who or what he was crying for—for himself, Walden . . . He just didn't know.

THAT was how it went during the night. No more argument, no more talk, just the three men watching the weakening Walden and waiting for her to nod off or pass out from the loss of blood so they could grab back their weapons.

What was going to happen after that, Ilario didn't want to think about.

A couple of times Walden's eyelids slowly slid down and closed for a brief second, but then her head would jerk up and she would take a deep breath and be alert again. The moments of alertness grew shorter and shorter. It was only a matter of time. Which would last the longer, Captain Walden or the night?

When the first rays of dawn began to wash out the darkness surrounding the Huey, Ilario saw for the first time the pool of blood that had leaked from Walden's wound. A dark red puddle that had edged slowly across the deck.

She had one hand pressed into her side and Ilario suspected she dug her fingers into the wound occasionally to cause herself pain in order to keep herself awake. She looked haggard and pale. Deadly pale.

The muzzle of the M-16 was drifting downward. Monfriez watched it as well as Walden. Altameyer, tired of the game, was watching the sun come up. The ridgeline was silhouetted, the enemy tank a stark black patch that still had a curl of smoke trailing upward from the carcass.

"Aw, fuck me," Altameyer moaned. "Here they come."

Ilario looked. Figures of enemy soldiers were scrambling over the ridgeline.

"I've got movement over here, too," Monfriez called to the others. A half dozen enemy soldiers were scurrying from cover to cover along the rocky finger of land in the middle of the river.

Ilario could see the bodies now, several on the port side of the Huey, four on the starboard. Dead Iraqi soldiers sprawled across the rocks and sand, some only a few feet from the Huey.

"What now, Captain?" Monfriez asked Walden.

"Give me my gun, for God's sake," Altameyer begged her. "Christ . . ."

"Ilario." Walden's voice was a harsh croak. "How's Rady?"

Ilario checked. No change.

"Still breathing," he reported.

"What are you going to do, Captain?" Monfriez persisted.

Ilario couldn't take it anymore. He was scared, yes, but he didn't want to be on the side of these two men and their persecution of Walden for one more minute. He moved over toward her.

"Cap, let me look at that wound. I won't do anything, I promise. I swear. Please . . . ?"

She must have seen something in his eyes that caused her to believe him because she was thinking about it.

"They're getting close," Altameyer warned them.

"What are you going to do, Captain?" Monfriez spit the words out like a curse.

"Please . . . ," Ilario begged.

He had to help her. He was desperate to help her, to tell her he cared. That he remembered how she had always taken care of him and now he could take care of her in return. To show her that, yes, he was scared, but he wasn't a coward.

"What's that?" She cocked an ear to the sky.

It took him a moment to hear it.

Helicopters.

That distinctive wocking of choppers. Rescue!

All four of them looked at the sky.

Then the rhythmic churning of helicopter blades was interrupted by the staccato popping of gunfire.

The enemy, too, had heard the rescue team coming.

Everybody aboard the crashed Huey hugged the deck as bullets perforated the fuselage.

Ilario crawled over to Walden and looked up to see the sky filled with four helicopters and the F-14 Tomcat.

The Cobras strafed the enemy with the miniguns, a horrific noise that Ilario welcomed hearing.

A Huey landed on the dry spit of land between the two crashed choppers. It was Teegarden at the controls. Ilario recognized the Crew Chief, Byers, and the medic, Neville, then they were gone from sight as the chopper settled behind the rocks of the little river peninsula.

"Go!" Walden shouted to the men. "I'll cover for you!" She began firing the M-60 at the advancing Iraqis.

Altameyer and Monfriez hit the ground crouching, ready to run to the rescue Huey.

They waited for the enemy fire to abate.

Then they ran. They were hit!

It looked to Ilario as if Monfriez had taken a bullet in the leg and Altameyer one in the chest. They each got up on their own, though, and continued running toward the chopper.

Walden looked at Ilario.

"Go! Go!" she screamed. The M-60 ammo belt ran out and she grabbed the M-16.

"I'll send back a stretcher," he told her.

Walden smiled at him.

"Bring two. Don't forget Rady. Now go!"

And Ilario ran. He stumbled across the smooth, rounded rocks, breakneck running, blind panic propelling his body, bullets kicking up shards of rock and dirt all around him.

And he made it.

Byers hauled Ilario aboard Teegarden's Huey.

As he clambered aboard the helicopter he saw Monfriez lean over to Teegarden in the pilot seat.

"Walden and Rady are dead!"

Ilario looked back at the Huey. He couldn't see the interior because of the rocks in the way.

But he could hear the M-16. Short bursts of two and three rounds, just as they had been taught in Basic Training.

"Both dead?!" Teegarden asked, shouting above the sound of gunfire and the engine noise.

"Dead!" Altameyer backed up Monfriez.

Byers and Neville were poised in the doorway, ready to sprint over to the Huey. They looked at Teegarden for the "go" sign.

"Let's get out of here!" he yelled.

And the Huey lifted off the sand.

Ilario looked at Monfriez and Altameyer. Both of them stared him down. He turned back to look at the Huey, still unable to see inside as Teegarden banked away.

Teegarden was on the radio.

Ilario strained to hear him, not taking his eyes off his own Huey.

The F-14 Tomcat zoomed down across the river bottom.

The white phosphorus exploded. Brilliant blossoms of fire bloomed over the downed Huey and Fowler's Blackhawk.

White smoke surged toward the sky.

The white fire was so bright, too bright to look at, but Ilario wouldn't take his eyes away from the burning Huey. The fire hurt his eyes but he wouldn't look away—he couldn't. Maybe it would make him blind. He wanted to be blind—and deaf.

And dead.

✳

The sun had just set and Ilario's cabin at Skull Lake was almost totally dark. Ilario stared off into the distance. Serling might as well not have been there.

Serling stood and stretched to uncramp his legs, slowly so as not to startle or distract Ilario from his narrative.

"We talked . . . when we got to the hospital. Monfriez said she would have court-martialed all of us. Put us in prison. Altameyer agreed. Who knows. She was probably killed by enemy fire before the jets came. Who knows . . ."

"Do you really believe that?"

"No." And Ilario began to cry.

Serling waited.

"I figured out what all those veterans have in common," Ilario said. "Fear. They've all been as scared as they will ever get in their entire lives. They've plumbed the depths of fear. Petrified scared. Scared until your heart stops, your lungs can't get any air. Scared sick. And nothing can ever scare you like that again. You've seen yourself at your worst and . . ."

"You've been tested . . ." Serling filled it in for him. "And failed."

Ilario looked at him.

"What I did in Desert Storm," Serling began. "Everybody said I made the best decision I could at the moment. They thought that it was a bad tactical decision, but only I know that I made the call out of fear. Sheer, stark-naked fear for my own life.

"Some men died. They, the investigators and the higher echelons, can justify it all they want, but deep down inside I know I did what I did because I was just . . . plain and simple scared. Panicked. It's okay to be scared in combat, it makes sense. But when it overrides your duty, you've crossed the line—into cowardice.

"We both crossed the same line."

"What do we do now?"

"I don't know. I really don't know," Serling admitted. "I just want to finish this last assignment, clear the name of Captain Walden. Karen. She *was* a hero."

Ilario looked around the living room and reached over and turned a lamp on. The room lit up.

"This isn't going to look very good in my 201, is it?" Ilario smiled as he asked the question. He looked at Serling and lost his smile.

"I have to make out a report on all of this," Serling said.

"What about Monfriez?" Ilario asked him.

"What about him?"

"Can we let him know this is all going down?"

"I don't think so. I've met him. He didn't seem to be the type to . . . help us."

"You have him wrong. This has been eating at all of us . . . like . . . acid. Give him some slack, Colonel."

Serling thought about it. He had given Ilario a chance. The General had given a chance to Serling, he could see that now.

"All right." Serling nodded. "We'll call him."

"No, face-to-face, like a man. I need to do something like a man."

Serling waited a moment before answering. He understood what Ilario needed.

"Okay. We'll drive up."

14

Serling decided to drive to Illinois. It was a long drive but he was afraid of losing Ilario again, at an airport terminal, or in the hectic logistics of turning in the rental car, or in getting another car at yet another airport. Ilario seemed resigned to his confession and its consequences, but Serling didn't want to take the chance that the medic might change his mind.

So Serling drove through the night, purposely ignoring the

cruise control, wanting to focus on the drive, trying not to let other thoughts intrude.

But they did.

Walden wasn't a coward. She *was* a hero. And from Ilario's account she had been frightened, truly scared, but she had somehow surmounted that fear to perform her duties, to honor her responsibilities.

It made Serling's own cowardice seem that much more a damnable act.

And his future was still a big question mark.

He would leave the Army, that was for sure. To do what, he didn't know. But he couldn't serve any longer, knowing what he knew about himself.

Ilario spent most of the trip staring out of the window. Serling stopped once to fill the gas tank and to empty his bladder, but Ilario never got out of the car. He'd even stopped smoking.

At one point during the trip he spoke.

"What's going to happen to me, Colonel?"

"I honestly don't know."

"Don't feel bad. Whatever happens, I'm glad. I can get it over with—find my life again. Or maybe that's over, too."

"No. You have to move on, get past what happened in the desert that night."

"It's easy for you to say."

Serling took that remark hard. Ilario saw the look on his face.

"Sorry."

It was a long drive. Ten hours just to St. Louis. They were quiet most of the time.

Serling thought about how the Army had provided so much to him, his life. The discipline a Chicago street kid so desperately needed. The pride at first in the uniform, then the man inside of it.

The self-worth he felt as he found himself capable of leading men, of doing a good job, of completing his mission. The security . . .

Now it was all gone. What would he do? What would Meredith say? Could he go back to his family now, face his children, his wife, knowing how weak he was inside?

It was a very long drive.

Once they crossed the river into Illinois, Serling stopped at a gas station and searched the phone book for Monfriez's name. The sun was just coming up and it would be too early for the gun store to be open. He found the address he was looking for, got directions from the service station clerk, and in fifteen minutes they were on the street where Monfriez lived.

It was a nice, quiet suburban neighborhood, quite like Serling's own. Monfriez's house was a one-story ranch; there was a ten-year-old Chrysler van in the driveway. The kind with fake wood paneling on the sides.

The sun was up now. People were trickling out of their houses and driving off to work or to drop off the kids at school.

Serling hadn't slept in a long time but he wasn't tired.

He pulled into the driveway and parked behind the van.

In response to Serling's knock, the front door was opened by a fourteen- or fifteen-year-old boy. Despite his light brown hair, he looked slightly Asian around the eyes.

"Hello. I'm Lieutenant Colonel Serling. Is Del Monfriez home?"

"In the garden. This way."

The boy, Loren, opened the screen door for them to enter and took them through the house toward the back. He glanced suspiciously at Serling's unshaven face and wrinkled uniform but kept walking. A woman was sitting at the dining room table gluing seashells to a lamp base. She looked up and smiled at the two men.

"Hello," she said. She was Asian. To Serling, she looked as if she might be Korean.

"They're here to see Dad," Loren explained.

"Something to drink, Colonel, sir?" she offered to Serling and Ilario.

"No, thank you, ma'am," Serling replied. They followed the boy on through the house and into the backyard.

It was an immaculate yard, with a stone waterfall and a concrete stream coursing through the flower beds. A miniature windmill turned and there were flowers everywhere with a small greenhouse in one corner of the lot next to the fence. The landscaping was very elaborate and clearly took a lot of time and effort to maintain.

Monfriez was bent over a raised flower bed built out of railroad ties. He was weeding furiously.

He looked up at the two men walking toward him with his son. Monfriez's face slowly became sad, grim even.

He had been expecting this.

"Loren, could you restring the Weed Eater and hit the west fence?"

The boy nodded and went over to the fence opposite the greenhouse where the tool had been left.

Ilario walked over to Monfriez and stood next to him while he continued to weed.

"Altameyer's dead . . . ," Ilario whispered. "Suicide."

"I know, I know," Monfriez replied, not looking at them. "I called his barracks. Yours, too. All I got was MPs."

"You told him to kill me, didn't you?" Serling said.

Monfriez looked up at Serling, then looked over at his son.

"Can we take this to the greenhouse?"

Monfriez didn't wait for an answer. He just got up and walked over to the glass-covered building. Serling and Ilario followed.

Monfriez opened the door to the greenhouse and held it for them, gesturing for the two men to enter ahead of him.

Serling followed Ilario inside and turned around and faced Monfriez.

Just in time to see him open a drawer in a cabinet stacked with red clay pots. Out of the drawer he pulled a pistol. It looked like a Browning automatic, .32 caliber.

The Weed Eater could be heard whining outside.

"That's not the way, Monfriez." Serling tried to stay calm.

"Don't, don't, Del, that stuff's all over." Ilario's voice was tired.

"I'm not going to spend the rest of my life in Leavenworth." Monfriez was scared, his gun hand trembling. He didn't appear to be in control of himself, his panicked eyes flitting from Ilario to Serling, then to the house.

"What are you going to do, kill us?" Serling asked, trying to soothe Monfriez with the soft voice of reason. "In front of your son and wife? Pack the family into the van and hide for the rest of your life? Things don't work that way. Put the gun down and let's talk this out."

Serling took a cautious step toward Monfriez, who was on the edge, barely in control.

"Don't try to move in on me, Colonel." He raised the gun to the level of Serling's chest. "I'll kill you. I will."

Monfriez sounded as if he were trying to convince himself that he could do it.

"No, you don't want to do that," Serling continued. "The killing is over."

Serling took another step. Monfriez flicked the safety off, warning Serling.

Ilario jumped between them.

The gun went off!

Ilario took the bullet in the chest. It spun him around and he spiraled to the ground.

The sound of the edge trimmer stopped.

Serling bent over Ilario. He was alive, his eyes blinking rapidly from the surprise.

"Look what you made me do." Monfriez said it in a small voice, very much like a child's.

"Dad? Dad!" Loren was running toward the greenhouse. That jerked Monfriez out of his shock.

"Everything's okay, Loren!" he shouted, trying to make his voice sound normal. "Just go back to trimming."

"I need a new string reel. What was that sound?"

Over Monfriez's shoulder and through the whitewash-spattered glass Serling could see Monfriez's wife standing next to her son, a bottle of Elmer's Glue in one hand.

"I was showing a gun to my friends and it went off." Monfriez's voice was strained. "There's a spare reel in the garage."

The boy waited a moment and then walked toward the garage. Mrs. Monfriez hesitated, then walked back into the house, glancing once at the greenhouse.

Serling stood and took a step toward the door.

Monfriez pointed the gun at his head.

"Don't." It was an order.

Ilario moaned. Serling bent over him. The wounded man grabbed Serling's hand. His grip was weak, childlike.

"Put your hand here." He whispered to Serling. "Press down."

Serling pressed his hand over the wound, over the wet, sticky blood on Ilario's chest.

"The pressure stops the bleeding." He smiled at Serling. "Not so hard."

263

"I didn't want any of this to happen, really . . . ," Monfriez said. He was sweating now and his body was shaking.

"I know how to do this," Ilario said, "but I think I need a doctor. I'm good at this, you know."

Ilario's voice was getting softer, his eyes losing focus and rolling. Serling could feel Ilario's heartbeat begin to slow.

Serling stood up. The barrel of the gun followed his upward movement.

"We need to get Ilario to a hospital." Serling looked Monfriez in the eye, trying to give the man his best command presence. "I'm going into the house and calling 911."

Serling took a step toward the greenhouse door.

"Don't." It wasn't an order this time, it was a plea.

Serling stopped.

"I didn't want to hurt him," Monfriez tried to explain. "I didn't want to hurt . . . her."

"I know." Serling nodded. "You were scared. We all get scared. We're only human. Sometimes we're frightened. Sometimes we're heroes—like Ilario just now. One day he's scared—on another day he's a hero."

"I'm not a coward," Monfriez said, desperation heavy in his voice.

"It's a fine line." Serling spoke as calmly as he could, keeping an eye on the gun and Monfriez's trigger finger. "We all live astride it. The secret is . . ."

Serling took another step. Monfriez adjusted his aim from Serling's chest to his face.

"The secret is what? What?" he demanded to know.

"The secret is to admit to the weakest part of ourselves and accept it and . . ."

Serling took one more step. The gun was inches from his face.

The barrel looked huge to his eyes. And it wavered in front of him as Monfriez trembled.

Serling continued. ". . . and ask for help when we're too weak to help ourselves. You need help, Monfriez. Ilario needs help. We all do."

"Nothing can help me," Monfriez said.

And he pointed the gun at his own head.

Serling leapt toward Monfriez and grabbed the pistol. Monfriez fought him. They fell to the floor of the greenhouse.

They rolled across the floor, fighting for the gun; Serling and Monfriez both had their hands on it. Monfriez kicked at Serling, catching him in the stomach with a knee. Serling felt the air go out of him but clung stubbornly to the gun. Monfriez bit at Serling's hands.

The barrel passed across Serling's eyes.

The gun went off.

Deafening shots, inches from Serling's ears. BAM! BAM! BAM! BAM! BAM! BAM!

The glass roof of the greenhouse exploded above them. Shards of glass fell in on all three men.

Serling felt a harsh, deep pain in his shoulder.

Monfriez stopped struggling and Serling rolled away from him. He heard a snap and felt the chunk of glass embedded in his back snap off. He cried out from the pain. Serling looked over at Monfriez.

A jagged piece of glass was embedded in the other man's throat.

Serling heard running feet and looked at the doorway. Loren was frozen there, dumbfounded.

"Call 911! Call 911!" Serling shouted.

It took a moment for the boy to respond, but then he turned and ran toward the house, almost colliding with his mother.

Serling got up and bent over Monfriez and removed the dagger of glass. He tried to apply pressure to the wound, but could not stop the great gushes of arterial blood that were being pumped out onto the dirt floor.

"I was just . . ." Monfriez tried to speak, but blood filled his broken throat and choked him. He coughed bloody spittle and tried to speak again.

"I was just . . . scared. That's all. That's all." Monfriez's eyes pleaded with Serling for understanding. His wife knelt by his side and took his hand.

And Monfriez died.

Serling turned to Ilario to see what he could do for him.

15

The presentation took place at the White House. The President presided over the Medal of Honor ceremony. Ed Bruno had set up a regal tableau of the Senator and Representative from Captain Karen Emma Walden's home state and stood behind the cameras himself, looking for choice bits of eye candy.

General Hershberg was there, as were Major Teegarden, an Army Honor Guard, looking formal in their dress blues, and the Blackhawk survivors. Most of the survivors looked solemn and a bit uncomfortable. Lieutenant Chelli had met General Hershberg in the Rose Garden before the ceremony and had made an appointment with him at the Pentagon for the next day. He was so nervous that his face had broken out with the first pimples he had experienced since his college days.

But the center of attention were the Waldens: Joel, Geraldine, and little Ann Marie, all dressed in their Sunday best. Ann Marie had refused the offer of a new dress and she insisted on wearing a pinafore that had been her mother's favorite. Captain Walden had purchased the dress for her daughter at the mall to wear to a fancy dinner the week before she left for Desert Storm. The dress no longer fit, of course, and Geraldine had driven all the way to Fort Worth to find a fabric store that had matching cloth. She had labored on her old Singer to patch together a semblance of something presentable.

The resulting dress was somewhat untraditional, but Ann Marie wore it proudly, standing tall and almost noble. She promised her grandfather that she wasn't going to cry and she was going to make her mother proud of her.

Captain Banacek read the citation. Ann Marie didn't understand a lot of the words.

". . . Captain Walden's courage under fire, conspicuous gallantry, intrepidity, and supreme dedication to her comrades, her extraordinary valor and inspirational sacrifice were in keeping with the highest traditions of the military service and reflected utmost credit on herself, her unit, and the U.S. Army."

The Medal of Honor was presented to Ann Marie in a velvet box. The medal was glorious, beautiful. The President gave it to her himself and mumbled something about rather having this than being the President of the United States. She didn't believe him.

There were a lot of flashing lights from across the room, where there seemed to be hundreds of TV cameras and photographers. The President stood with the Waldens, Ann Marie holding the box with the medal.

Ed Bruno kept jumping forward to angle the medal just right for the cameras. Ann Marie didn't like him. He reminded her of Ed Grimley, a character on an old "Saturday Night Live" rerun that had scared her when she was little.

Then the ceremony and the picture taking were over, and everybody began talking at once. Joel tapped the President's arm.

"Mr. President, could I have a word with you?" And Joel started the little speech he had been rehearsing on the plane from Abilene.

The Blackhawk survivors surrounded Geraldine to thank her. She began to cry—for the third time that day.

Ann Marie looked at the medal. It was pretty, the metal shining, the ribbon brilliant. The kids at school were going to be so jealous. And her grandfather had told her that she was probably going to be on TV, at least on CNN. Wait 'til her friends saw that.

Using one finger, she tentatively touched the gold and silver. It was so beautiful. She had promised not to cry, but she began to sniffle and tears ran down her cheeks.

She wanted her mother back.

SERLING's body was stiff. The stitches had been removed from his back, but he still felt twinges of pain when he moved his arm. He stumbled once and Patella caught him.

Serling had skipped the ceremony. He preferred to go out to Arlington and pay his respects to Captain Walden in his own way.

The cemetery always put him in awe. So many dead, so many wars. Was it all worth it? That was the obvious question raised by seeing so many graves. But answering that question wasn't his job. His job was to go and fight to the best of his ability. Still, he hoped Joel Walden did go ahead and give the President a piece of his mind.

Serling hadn't left the Army.

He had fully intended to, but when the paramedics were carting Ilario away, before they hoisted the wounded man into the ambulance, Ilario had gestured Serling over and had whispered to him.

"You're a hero, sir."

Serling's bafflement was obviously evident on his face, so Ilario continued.

"You saved my life. And you tried to save his." Ilario smiled. "You're a hero."

"I guess we both are, soldier," Serling replied.

Then the paramedics shut the ambulance doors and Serling was led to his own ambulance. He never saw Ilario again, not even at the hospital.

But he had time to think about what the medic had said. Hero. Coward one minute, hero the next.

Maybe we all have both in us. That was what Serling said that had been baffling Monfriez. Serling himself hadn't even been conscious of his own words, he'd just been vamping to get past Monfriez's gun.

We're both—hero and coward—and we don't know which way we will react from one crisis to the next.

And Serling could live with that, both as a soldier and as a man. A man who knew what his weaknesses were, who was strong enough to be aware of the worst parts of himself. Accepting the worst, he was prepared; a better man, a better soldier.

I get scared. I can deal with that.

So he stayed in the Army. It hadn't come to him all at once. Some of it came during recuperation at Fort Sam, at the very hospital where he had met Ilario. More of it was revealed to Serling when General Hershberg visited him on the second day of his stay.

Serling was completely surprised and pleased to see Hershberg. Banacek came in first, shook his hand, and promised him a "big-ass" party when Serling got back to D.C.

Then General Hershberg sat down next to Serling's bed. The General was as casual as Serling had ever seen him, even at Hershberg's house. The General popped off a couple of the current D.C. insider jokes and went over and shook the hand of the patient in the next bed.

Then he sat down again and looked at Serling and asked how he was.

"Great, sir, just great," Serling said, meaning every word of it. "Will Walden get her medal, sir?"

Serling had insisted, despite the doctor's and nurses' protests, to dictate his report to Hershberg about Ilario's testimony. He reported only what Ilario had said. The actions at Monfriez's house were recorded by the MPs and CID from Ilario's testimony.

"She'll get her medal, Nat. Come hell or high water, I guarantee it. Your mission is accomplished, soldier. Now heal up so I can give you another."

"Another . . . Tell me, sir, that the Walden assignment was one of your devious plans. To fix a broken piece of military equipment, to be specific myself."

"Well, I'm not a man who likes to see anything go to waste, Nat, especially a piece of equipment that performed so well in the past." The General paused and cleared his throat. "Let's pass over all this metaphorical bullshit, Nat. You were hurting. You needed something. You weren't . . ."

". . . a good soldier anymore." Serling finished the thought for him.

"Oh, you were a good soldier, Nat, a damn good soldier. But you were hesitant, you had lost confidence in yourself, in your decision making. There's no room for that on the battlefield, especially if you're in a leadership position."

"I see, sir." And Serling did.

"I can't take credit for the results, though. I'll revert to the military metaphor." The General smiled to himself. "You send out recon patrols to scout an area, hoping they come back with the piece of intelligence that wins the battle. Most come back with nothing of value. But you send out the patrols anyway, with high expectations."

Hershberg leaned over to Serling.

"I had the highest expectations with you, Nat, and they were met."

"Thank you, sir."

The General took Serling's hand and shook it and then was gone, in a hurry as usual.

Serling had returned to D.C. the morning of the ceremony and reported to Hershberg's office, where Banacek, slipping out of his military decorum for a moment, told Serling that it was likely that the next field assignment coming through the pipeline would have Serling's name on it.

Then Serling had driven his own dusty, dirty Buick to the train station and picked up Patella. The two men had talked on the phone for hours while Serling was waiting for the doctors to complete their microsurgery of his shoulder muscles. He and Patella hadn't come up with any easy solutions, but they had a plan.

Right now Serling had one last task to perform for Captain Karen Emma Walden. He and Patella followed the map and directions the Arlington staff had given them.

Then they were standing in front of the proper grave.

Serling watched two cemetery workers drive up on a small fork-lift. The old stone was removed from Captain Walden's grave and a new one put in its place. The name was the same—Captain Karen Emma Walden—and so were the dates. But the new marker had one addition: a gilded engraving of the country's highest military honor—the Medal of Honor.

Serling, in his dress blues, saluted. To his surprise, Patella, looking small and too thin in his civilian suit, saluted, too. They stood there a moment not wanting to leave, but not knowing what to do next.

"Is CID going to get involved?" Patella asked.

"No. They're going to let it die of its own accord. She's still a hero. The rest of it only muddies the water. And makes Ed Bruno and the White House uncomfortable. So they'll let it rest. Two of the eyewitnesses died tragically, suicides, and the third is in rehab, more testament to the hardships of that mission over Al Kufan. And Karen Emma Walden is a hero by any definition of the term."

That seemed to be as good an epitaph as any other, and they walked away.

THE first thing Serling noticed as he pulled into the driveway was that the lawn needed mowing. He and Patella got out of the car and walked up the driveway and onto the porch. It felt funny to be ringing his own doorbell, but Serling did it.

Meredith opened the door. She had wanted to come to him at Fort Sam, but Serling had asked her not to, that he had some things to work out. And he had done that.

She looked at him with concern.

"You're home." It was half question, half hope.

"I'm home."

She hugged him. There were tears and kisses, but it was the hug that Serling cherished. He let himself sink into the well of comfort that her embrace meant to him.

Finally they pulled away from each other and laughed at how silly they were acting. Meredith looked at Patella then, and straightened her hair and wiped her eyes.

"This is Patella."

"I've heard about you." Meredith extended her hand.

"He's going to stay with us for a little while if it's okay. We've joined this . . . program together. Is it all right?"

Meredith was so happy that Serling was home that he could have adopted a herd of rhinos and marched them through the living room and she would say it was great.

"Welcome to the house of chaos, Mr. Patella."

Then she turned back to Serling.

"But . . . you're home . . . for good."

"For good."

She took Serling by the arm and led him inside.

"C'mon in, Mr. Patella. Know anything about refrigerators?"

Serling closed the door behind him and braced himself for the children, who were running into his arms.

COLIN FALCONER

DANGEROUS

Vietnam. El Salvador. Bosnia. Three of the hottest combat zones of the last three decades.

For Australian combat photographer Sean Ryan and British war correspondent Hugh Webb, they are not only the platform for their soaring careers, but also for their enduringly complex rivalry.

The flamboyant and charismatic Ryan loves the excitement of the battle zone. But for him the dividing line between observer and protagonist becomes more blurred with each new conflict.

Webb is Ryan's conscience. Haunted by the moral dilemmas of his profession, Webb chooses to pick up the human flotsam that Ryan leaves in his wake: his Vietnamese mistress, his American wife, the warbaby daughter he believes to be dead.

Shot through with turbulent passions, betrayed ideals, and lives forever lived on the edge, *Dangerous* is the story of an extraordinary love affair and an extraordinary friendship.

HODDER AND STOUGHTON PAPERBACKS

BOB MAYER

ETERNITY BASE

While rifling through some inactive government files, Sammy Pintella, determined to discover the fate of her MIA father, stumbles upon a few faded black and white photographs. They prove the existence of a secret US military base built in Antarctica during the height of the Vietnam War.

With her sister Conner, a reporter looking for a big story, Sammy sets out to find out more. What was a Special Forces MACV-SOG unit, supposedly operating in Vietnam, doing in Antarctica? Why has the existence of this base remained top secret for more than 25 years? Is there a link between the secret base and the disappearance of their father?

Aided by ex-Special Forces officer Dave Riley, Sammy and Conner head for Antarctica to the place where all their clues seem to lead. The mysterious military installation known as Eternity Base.

'Mayer's portrayal of Green Beret operations and techniques takes you deep into the covert world of special operations'

W E B Griffin

'Bob Mayer has stretched the limits of the military action novel'

Assembly

HODDER AND STOUGHTON PAPERBACKS